"I said you are beautiful." A smile every bit as soft as his eyes played over his attractive, masculine lips. "Do you, I wonder, realize that your gown is clinging to you, outlining every alluring curve of your body?"

"Oh!" Darcy's hands flew to her gown, pulling the damp material away from her form—now shivering in response to an intense awareness, of herself as a woman, of him as a man.

"Darcy, Darcy." Murmuring her name, Jonathan raised his hand to her flushed cheek.

Darcy gasped. As had happened before, she could feel the same sensation of warmth, excitement, arousal streaking through her with more effect and fury than the lightning streaking through the massive storm clouds darkening the evening sky.

"Am I frightening you?"

Darcy shook her head in quick denial. "No, Jonathan. I'm not frightened," she said, unconsciously lifting her hand to cover his. . . .

Books by Joan Hohl

COMPROMISES

ANOTHER SPRING

EVER AFTER

MAYBE TOMORROW

SILVER THUNDER

NEVER SAY NEVER

SOMETHING SPECIAL

MY OWN

SHADOW'S KISS

Published by Zebra Books

SHADOW'S KISS

Joan Hohl

ZEBRA BOOKS
Kensington Publishing Corp.
http://www.zebrabooks.com

ZEBRA BOOKS are published by

Kensington Publishing Corp.
850 Third Avenue
New York, NY 10022

All Kensington titles, imprints, and distributed lines are available at special quantity discounts for bulk purchases for sales
promotion, premiums, fund-raising, educational or institu-
tional use.

Special book excerpts or customized printings can also be
created to fit specific needs. For details, write or phone the
office of the Kensington Special Sales Manager: Kensington
Publishing Corp., 850 Third Avenue, New York, NY 10022,
Attn. Special Sales Department, Phone: 1-800-221-2647.

Zebra and the Z logo Reg. U.S. Pat. & TM Off.

First Printing: September 2001
10 9 8 7 6 5 4 3 2 1

Printed in the United States of America

For the spirited companions Lori, Karen, and Jerry.

Prologue

Philadelphia, Pennsylvania
June 1871

Darcy Flynn sat at her dressing table, staring into the sad hazel eyes reflected in the oval mirror. The fingers of one hand resting in her lap curled around a sheet of paper. The letter had been delivered to her less than twenty-four hours before, disrupting the even, uneventful routine of her life. The missive had been sent to her from a solicitor in Denver, Colorado, tactfully informing Darcy of her mother's serious illness and probable demise. In closing, the solicitor had implored her to travel to Denver with all due haste.

Her carpetbags were packed and sitting on the floor next to the door; the rest of her belongings would be sent to her later if the necessity arose. Her travel arrangements were made. The hired carriage would be arriving shortly to take Darcy to the train station.

Colleen Flynn was dying.

It was nearly impossible for Darcy to imagine the life fading from the beautiful, vivacious woman she had never been afforded the opportunity to get to know. Colleen had always been so vibrant, so very vital and alive during the infrequent visits she had made to her daughter.

Darcy watched as a mirrored tear trickled down her cheek. With her mind's eye, she could see the small, dainty, flame-haired beauty who had captivated every staff member of the Reinholt Boarding School for Young Ladies. With her senses, Darcy could smell the light, intoxicating fragrance of her mother's special perfume.

A second then a third tear followed in the path of the first. Pensive and saddened, Darcy could not help but wonder if her tears were for the beautiful Colleen or for the child who had grown into womanhood indulged with an exorbitant quarterly allowance, an extensive wardrobe, the very finest of everything, yet denied the closeness of her mother's love.

A genteel tap sounded on the bedroom door, disrupting the flow of Darcy's memories.

"Darcy?" Miss Reinholt, the headmistress as well as the daughter of the founder of the private girls' school, called in a cultured voice. "The carriage is here to convey you to the station. Are you ready to depart?"

"Yes." Darcy dashed the tears from her cheeks as she rose and hurried to open the door. "I . . . I am ready," she said, smiling at the austere-looking woman. Miss Reinholt had played the roles of surrogate mother, headmistress, employer, and friend to Darcy for nineteen years.

Now, at age twenty-five, Darcy could smile in gentle remembrance at her own initial youthful fear on her first sight of the stern-looking woman.

She had been only six, after all, a hurt and confused six-year-old, feeling rejected by the mother who had uprooted her from her home in New Orleans and delivered her to the school in Philadelphia.

And now she was being uprooted once again, Darcy reflected, uprooted from the only home she had known for nineteen years. Bending, she gripped the handles of her carpetbags. She had been summoned to this place called Denver, where her mother had relocated in 1859, when Darcy was thirteen.

"There is no cause for trepidation, Darcy," the older woman said in her strongest instructional tone.

Lifting the bags as she straightened, Darcy offered her friend and mentor another bright, false smile, and an equally false assurance. "I know. Colorado Territory is a part of the country, isn't it?"

Miss Reinholt was not deceived by Darcy's show of calm nor her too bright smile. "You have absolutely nothing to fear, my dear," she said kindly, bracingly. "You have been properly educated as well as trained to conduct yourself to advantage in any place or circumstances. I have full and complete confidence in you."

"Thank you," Darcy murmured, trying but failing to maintain her facade of calm. "I wish I did as well."

A tiny smile softened the severity of the older woman's thin lip line. "Although I may know that you are awash with uncertainty and doubt concerning your journey, please see to it that I am the only person who knows."

"Yes, ma'am," Darcy promised, her gratitude for the other woman's unfailing understanding and moral support for nineteen years revealed by a genuine smile. "I will endeavor to be an exemplary representative of the school."

"I am convinced you will be, my child." Miss Reinholt's eyes grew misty for an instant, then she took a brisk backward step, turning away from the door. "Come along now. You do not want to miss your train."

Darcy felt tears sting her eyes once more as she followed the ramrod-straight back of the headmistress along the third-floor corridor to the circular staircase.

She felt intuitively that she would never return to her teaching position at the school. Darcy would miss it, the friends she had made with the other teachers, the children, but most of all she would miss the austere, correct, sometimes stern but always fair and completely wonderful Miss Reinholt.

Darcy had her composure intact by the time she boarded the railroad car located a short distance behind the loud, smoke-belching engine. To any and all observers, she appeared cool, contained, confident, withdrawn. Inside, she felt rippling tremors along her spine, and slightly as if she were going to be sick to her stomach.

She was scared. She didn't know what to expect to find at the end of her journey, not only concerning her mother but also in regard to her destination itself.

Darcy had never in her twenty-five years been farther west than Lancaster, Pennsylvania.

Denver, Colorado Territory
June 1871

Jonathan Stuart sat at his ease at the table in the elegant but subdued gaming/barroom adjacent to the plush parlor of the house of pleasure known as La Rouge.

The night was mild; a soft breeze fluttered the lacy curtains at the long, narrow side windows. The combined scents of good whiskey, musky sweat, and tantalizing perfume clung to the gray cloud of cigar smoke permeating the air. At odd moments an occasional feminine giggle or deeper rumble of male laughter intruded on the low voices of men at play.

But in the main, the atmosphere inside the house was somber and subdued, for upstairs, in the private quarters belonging to the proprietress of the house, the vivacious woman also known to all as "La Rouge" lay hovering at death's door. Even so, the establishment was, on the express orders of La Rouge, open for business as usual.

Although Jonathan felt sympathy for the woman, he did not really know her, in any sense of the term, since his only contact with the beautiful Colleen Flynn had been of the most casual and impersonal kind.

The woman was dying and that was sad, but for Jonathan, the sadness was overridden by a growing excitement inside him, an excitement generated by a renewed sense of purpose. That renewal had been a long time coming.

For six long years, Jonathan had suffered, a victim of a most debilitating attack of massive ennui.

The condition had been growing steadily inside him since before Appomattox, and the historic surrender of Lee to Grant, which ended the conflict between the North and the South.

With that terrible war at last over, Jonathan had found himself at frayed loose ends. He could not go home. There was nothing left of his home to return to. And even if there had been something left, Jonathan was too well aware that he would not be welcome there.

He was a Southerner, a Virginian, yet along with his father, Luke Stuart, the gentle Virginia schoolmaster, Jonathan had chosen to follow the dictates of his conscience by aligning himself with the North.

The war had not lasted long for Luke Stuart; he was just one of the more than sixteen thousand Union casualties at the battle of Manassas. Over a year would pass before Jonathan learned of his father's death, and that blow had been doubled by the delayed news of the death of his mother, who had succumbed to a severe bout of pneumonia less than a month after being informed of her husband's fall at Bull Run.

Though Jonathan had continued to fight on, he did so with a lack of the zeal and conviction he had felt at the beginning, when he had abandoned his small church's congregation to fight alongside, and minister to, his fellow defenders of equality and the Union.

By the time hostilities ended at Appomattox, after too many years, too many battles, too many soul-destroying moments of witnessing the depths of brutality humans were capable of, Jonathan had lost all hope of man's salvation, and all belief in God.

Empty, disenfranchised, a stranger to the South, alien to the North, Jonathan had drifted along with the swelling tide of new hope seekers headed West. He had turned his hand, and occasionally his considerable intellect, to whatever work presented itself in any given place and situation, and had arrived in Denver with the Kansas Pacific Railroad the previous August.

Jonathan wasn't sure himself why he had tarried in the city, beyond the fact of the approach of winter. Yet even with the onset of spring, he remained, biding his time, primarily within the ornate house of pleasure.

And it was in this very house, this very early evening, that Jonathan had experienced a stirring, a freshening renewal of purpose. The spark had been generated by, of all people, one of La Rouge's "girls," a sixteen-year-old discard with cornflower blue eyes, a heart-wrenching smile, and a hesitant entreaty.

"Mr. Stuart, do you think I could be taught to read and write my name?"

The tremulous, half-hopeful, half-fearful sound of the girl's voice had echoed inside Jonathan's head through the evening and into the night, defeating the ennui, imbuing a gathering interest and excitement.

This was something he could do; this was something to look forward to, a reason for going on, for living. He could teach her to read and write . . . and in so doing, free her to pursue a more productive existence.

Yes, and a reason for his own continued existence, Jonathan mused, frowning as the growing altercation penetrated his introspection. What was this racket? he railed in sudden annoyance. Didn't the fools know La Rouge lay upstairs dy—

"Look out! He's got a knife!"

Jonathan pushed back his chair at the sound of the warning cry, and stood as the blade flashed across the room. It had not been intended for him but, nevertheless, found its mark to the left of center in his chest.

Eyes wide with confusion and disbelief, Jonathan stared down at the billowing red stain smearing his white shirt.

Well, goddamn! he thought in amazed protest, feeling himself growing fuzzy around the edges of his mind. Goddamn, this was not fair! Had he survived the horrors of that dreadful war and the wandering emptiness of the years since then, to die by sheer happenstance in a whorehouse, just when he was feeling a resurgence of life?

Goddamnit, no! Not now that I have a purpose, a reason to live! I will not die!

The vehement denial was Jonathan's last living thought.

Arizona Territory
June 1871

Wade Dunstan sat hunched over the campfire, his broad-brimmed hat tucked low over his forehead, the collar of his jacket flipped up, his back turned to the chill mountain night air. The flickering firelight reflected a muted red on the drawn lines of weariness around his mouth and narrowed eyes, in the hollows beneath his jutting cheekbones, and in the desultory movements of his broad hands as he idly fed twigs and small sticks into the hungry blaze.

The pungent scent of juniper and sagebrush mingled with the tantalizing aroma of coffee rising on the steam puffing from the spout of a battered tin coffeepot set on a flat stone stuck into the center of the fire.

From a distance behind Wade, the stamp of a shod hoof and a snort from his tired horse were the only sounds intruding on the natural nocturnal noises of the mountain terrain.

Dunstan could empathize with the animal; they had both been on the trail for a long time.

Eyes bleak, he stared into the blaze, cringing as, yet again, the leaping flames conjured an image of his wife, Mary, alive, her soft brown eyes alight with laughter, her lips parted, her arms open to embrace him, welcome him home.

"Mary."

Wade was unaware of murmuring her name aloud. The pain, the never-ending agony of her loss, clawed at his gut, his mind, his soul, like a sickness, a death wish.

Wade wasn't merely physically weary; with Mary gone, he was weary of living.

One purpose, one emotion, kept Wade going, searching, hunting for the men who had raped then killed his Mary.

Hate. It was a cold, sustaining purpose.

Bile rose in Wade's throat. Coughing, he spat

into the fire, causing the flames to flash and change the flickering image.

"Oh God, no," he groaned as a new image formed, the picture piercing his heart.

He closed his eyes, willing the picture gone with all his great strength. The grisly scene remained, imprinted on his memory, burned into his mind the day he'd come home, tired but relieved to have another job done, and time off to spend with his Mary.

"Goddamn." Unconscious of the muttered curse, which had more the sound of a desperate prayer, Wade stared in ever-renewing horror at the searing mental scene.

He had found Mary in the middle of the floor in the neatly kept parlor of their small house. She was naked, lying in a pool of her own blood.

Wade shuddered and made a low, growling noise deep in his throat. Those men had used Mary's body, in turn, in every way a sick, animalistic mind could devise to use a woman's body before—Wade bit down on his lip, drawing blood—before shoving the barrel of a pistol into her soft mouth and then pulling the trigger.

Hate. It was an icy, warming emotion.

Since that terrible day, Dunstan had breathed, eaten, slept, lived to unleash his hate on the four bastards who had attacked his wife while he was away from home, performing his duty as a U.S. Marshal.

No, there were not four men, there was a fifth. Yet Wade could not, would not allow himself the luxury of destroying the fifth, if unconnected, perpetrator of that most atrocious of crimes.

Dunstan still retained just enough of his conscience to allow Sheriff Will Banks to live, even though Will Banks had vowed to protect Mary during Wade's absence from his home in that dusty, desolate, nowhere town in the southernmost corner of New Mexico.

In truth, there were no longer four men, there were three. Dunstan had caught up with one of the men the week before. The sniveling coward had holed up in an abandoned adobe hut on the fringes of the Sonora desert. Before Wade had condescended to let that man die, he'd chattered like a town gossip. It was from that man that Dunstan had learned that there were four men involved, and that they had split up after the deed was done, going their separate ways in hopes of getting lost and getting away with the murder.

If Wade could believe what the killer confessed to him—and with the form of persuasion Wade had employed, he did believe him—one of the men had headed for the vicinity of Promontory, Utah Territory, one for a ranch located near Laramie, Wyoming, and the third for the gold fields close to Denver, Colorado Territory.

Wade had been on the trail for more than a week, heading for the first of his destinations—Promontory. If he met with success there, he'd move on to Laramie, then on to Denver.

To Dunstan's way of thinking, Denver was as good as any other place to die . . . for the killer . . . for himself.

Mary would be avenged, if it took him fifty years, and from one end of the country to the other. He would mete out justice without mercy for what they did to her. Then and only then would he escape this unbearable burden, this living hell that had become his life.

But first things first, Wade told himself, sipping without tasting the bitter black coffee he poured from the battered pot into an equally battered tin cup.

Promontory.

Laramie.

Denver.

Blessed death.

1

A house of ill repute. What could she do with it? Darcy Flynn stood before a long, narrow, lace-curtained window in her mother's bedroom, listening to the questions revolving inside her whirling mind. There were no answers; it was too soon. The shocking discoveries were still too recent, too incredible, to fully comprehend. Everything had happened so swiftly.

Darcy had arrived in Denver that very morning, and had been swept away from the train station by her mother's solicitor, a short, middle-aged man who introduced himself as Paul Mansford, Esquire.

"Thank God the train wasn't yet another hour late," the bespectacled, harried-looking man said in between labored gasps for breath. Grasping her by the elbow, he rushed her to a waiting buggy.

"My bags!" Darcy exclaimed, trying to resist his efforts to hand her into the conveyance.

"I'll have them collected later," Mr. Mansford promised, appearing frazzled as he settled on the seat beside her. "As it is, we'll just make it."

"Make it?" Darcy repeated, jolting back against

the leather seat as the driver cracked the whip over the head of the horse, setting the buggy jerking forward with the sudden and abrupt motion. "Make what, sir?"

"Oh, indeed, I am sorry, Miss Flynn. But of course, you cannot know," Mr. Mansford said, removing his hat as he turned on the seat to face her. "I regret that it is my unhappy duty to inform you of your mother's demise. The funeral procession is on its way to the cemetery at this very moment."

The effect on Darcy of the blurted, unsoftened news was not unlike a physical blow. Deep sorrow doubled the weariness instilled by the long journey, clouding her eyes, dimming the brightness of the early summer day.

She was too late, too late. Now she would never have the chance to get to know her mother.

"When did . . ." Darcy began, but had to pause, unable to force the words past the tight lump in her throat.

"Yesterday," Mr. Mansford replied, shaking his head. "She seemed to be clinging to life for such a long time, as if waiting, and then . . ." He sighed and spread his stubby-fingered hands. "I am sorry, Miss Flynn."

"I . . . ah, thank you." Tears filled Darcy's eyes and she turned away to stare sightlessly at her surroundings. "I came as quickly as possible."

"Yes, of course. Transportation cross-country is unreliable, at best." He cleared his throat. "We . . . er, please understand that we could not wait."

Oh, God! Realization of his meaning struck another blow. Darcy clenched her teeth against a rising flood of stinging sickness.

Mother.

Call me Colleen, darling. It's so much friendlier.

Darcy could hear the memory echo of her mother's lilting voice, could see her lovely, animated face, the quick, enchanting movements of her delicate features and hands.

They had never been friends. There had never been time enough together for them to get to know each other, let alone develop a friendly relationship.

Darcy had always hoped, prayed that someday, someday . . . Now that someday would never come.

She was a mess. Sniffing, blinking, Darcy brushed her palms down the lapels of her short jacket, grimacing at the residue of coal dust smearing her gloves. She felt unkempt. Being jostled about for days on end while confined within a lurching railroad car was not conducive to neatness, she fretted, blunting the shock of utter finality with muting thoughts of the mundane. She was being conveyed to her mother's funeral, and she was a disheveled mess.

After ineffectually trying to smooth the wrinkles from her skirt, Darcy raised her hands to her hair. She had settled her small hat into place and was moving her fingers to reposition the pins anchoring the twist-knot of hair at the back of her head when she caught sight of the procession.

It was small. Two buggies and three horsemen trailed along behind the glass-sided black hearse, which was drawn by one black-plumed black horse.

But what was this? Darcy jolted as the procession turned onto a narrow pathway bordering a barren sweep of land. She glanced at Mr. Mansford in confusion on hearing him direct the driver to pull the buggy up behind the hearse, which had come to a stop parallel to what appeared to be an open grave a few yards off to the side of the rutted path.

Shock and consternation filled Darcy as she watched the other vehicles and the horsemen come to a stop.

What was this? The thought repeated inside Darcy's baffled mind. She had expected, anticipated a quiet, well-tended graveyard next to an imposing church. Her mother was, had been, a devout Roman Catholic! Surely Colleen would not be laid to rest here, in this treeless, desolate place, in a shallow hole dug in unconsecrated ground?

"Mr. Mansford, there must be some mistake," she said, shuddering at the mere idea of the site as a final resting place for her mother. "I'm sorry, sir, but I must protest your choice of location."

Mr. Mansford sighed and shook his head. "I had no choice, Miss Flynn," he muttered, heaving himself from the buggy before turning to offer his hand to assist her. "Come along, please. I will explain later."

"But . . ." Darcy's voice failed her as she caught her first real look at the assembled mourners.

Women! Other than the three horsemen, the mourners were all women. Darcy counted seven, ranging in age from their teens to late twenties.

And every one of the women had a look about her, a flamboyant appearance of . . .

Harlots! Darcy's eyes widened at the thought. But that was preposterous! Impossible. Denying the evidence of her sight, she glanced at the three men and felt a sick, sinking sensation deep inside her. The men were burly, tough-looking, their clothing neat and clean but rough, precisely as Darcy would imagine the peacekeepers of a house of ill repute would look.

Why were these people here? Why were they the *only* people here? Shaken by the questions hammering inside her head, Darcy stumbled over the uneven ground after Mr. Mansford, her stark gaze fixed on the casket being borne to the open grave site by the three horsemen, followed by another man attired in a white collar and black frock coat.

Who was this . . . Darcy's thoughts fractured as the man, obviously of the cloth, began to speak.

"Dear Lord, we are gathered here to bid farewell to one of Your lost lambs."

Lost lambs? Standing exposed to the unrelenting rays of the summer sunlight, Darcy felt a chill permeate her being. A lost lamb? Her mother? A sense of unreality invaded her tired mind, shielding her from the man's droning voice.

There was a mistake, Darcy assured herself. That self-assurance sustained her throughout the shockingly brief graveside service, the bumpy ride away from the cemetery, and the short journey along a rutted road to where the driver drew the vehicle to a stop in the curved driveway before an isolated, tree-shaded, large and imposing house some distance outside the sprawling city of Denver.

Yes, a mistake, Darcy silently reiterated, as she gazed at the subdued grandeur of the structure. Victorian in design, the house was decorated with lacy gingerbread trim. A deep, roofed porch supported by six solid-looking pillars ran the length of the front of the house. The breeze fluttered the black draping above the entranceway in silent testimony to the bereavement within.

But there had been no mistake. The awful truth crashed through Darcy the instant she stepped into the house—and *house* was the definitive word.

No one, not even the most naive of women, could possibly have mistaken the house for a home. The large painting of a reclining nude hanging in full view on a side wall left little to the imagination and no doubt at all as to the function of the residents of the establishment. And if there had been any lingering doubt in Darcy's mind, the arrival of one of the horsemen and all the women who had been at the cemetery, banished it from her mind.

"Why have you brought me here, Mr. Mansford?" Darcy demanded in an appalled whisper, averting her eyes from the painting as she took an unsteady step backward. Her retreat was halted by a hand placed firmly against her spine.

"I can imagine what you're thinking, Miss Flynn." Mr. Mansford paused to heave a sigh before continuing. "This was your mother's house." He winced at the stark look Darcy gave him. "If you will come with me, please." Moving his hand from her back to her elbow, he urged her into the house and toward a broad, open staircase set against the wall opposite the painting.

"Where are you taking me?" Darcy asked, struggling to maintain a semblance of her composure.

"To your mother's office."

"But . . ." Darcy broke off, turning to him with a questioning look when the man and the seven women clattered up the stairs behind them.

"There's the matter of your mother's last will and testament," Mr. Mansford said, his expression one of abject apology. "And by necessity, Mr. Dugan and the, er . . . ladies must be present at the reading."

"So soon after . . ." Darcy's voice broke, and she was forced to bite her lip to suppress a sob.

Mr. Mansford glanced at her in sharp concern. "I am following your mother's instructions," he explained.

The shock of learning about her mother's death, following on the heels of her arduous journey, instilled a feeling of utter exhaustion within Darcy. She was bereft, not only from her loss, but of arguments or protests. Numbed by the swiftness of events since her arrival, she moved to the direction of Mr. Mansford's hand at her elbow.

Having attained the landing at the top of the stairs, he turned to the right and guided Darcy to the first door set in a narrow corridor. Removing a key from his vest pocket, he unlocked the door and ushered her inside.

The small room was comforting, inasmuch as it was sparsely decorated, businesslike, devoid of the obvious plushness Darcy could not help noticing on the lower floor. She sank with relief and a murmured "Thank you" onto the straight-backed wooden chair the solicitor drew forth for her.

"Come inside, ladies, Mr. Dugan," he said to the group hovering in the doorway. Circling around the rolltop desk facing Darcy, he seated himself on the desk chair, removed a document from his inside coat pocket, and cleared his throat. Then, in a monotone, he began to read.

Though Darcy kept her gaze fixed on Mr. Mansford's expressionless face, she could feel the presence of the women and man standing in complete silence behind her chair. As if from a distance, she heard the solicitor's droning voice read aloud the small sum of money her mother had bequeathed to two bartenders and a handyman and a more generous sum allotted to each of her "girls," the cook, and her bouncer, Mr. Dugan.

The very words *girls* and *bouncer* bruised her mind and senses, causing a shudder to quake through Darcy.

"And to my beloved daughter, Darcy," Mr. Mansford finally read, capturing Darcy's full attention, "I leave my house, the balance of my fortune, my holdings, and all my worldly possessions." He coughed, then raised his eyes from the will to stare at Darcy. "All of which are of considerable value. I have an inventory for you to look over at your convenience, and will, of course, answer any questions."

"Ah . . . thank you." Try as she would, that was all Darcy could manage to say.

"And are we to finally meet the lass, then?" The query came in a booming voice from behind Darcy.

She stiffened.

Mr. Mansford frowned.

"Yes," a confident-sounding female voice stated. "We want to meet Colleen's daughter."

The solicitor quirked an eyebrow at Darcy in silent question of her approval.

A chill invaded Darcy's spine. For nineteen years, she had enjoyed a sheltered existence, surrounded by genteel companions, protected from the seamier side of life. Although she knew of them, to Darcy's knowledge she had never actually seen a prostitute. The idea of meeting not one but seven ladies of the evening unnerved her in the extreme. And yet how could she refuse? Apparently, these women were, after all, her mother's employees.

Darcy's throat was too parched to allow speech; she nodded her head in silent consent.

Rising, Mr. Mansford immediately began tossing out names; Darcy caught a Katie, a Molly, a Jane, a June, a Sally, a Daisy, and a Sarah—whom Darcy judged to be about sixteen and who had bright blue eyes and an even brighter smile.

Darcy's mind was whirling, trying to match up names with faces, when the solicitor tossed another name at her.

"And last but not least, let me introduce Mr. Dugan, the man who keeps the peace in the house."

Mr. Dugan was huge, tall, wide, a mountain of a man, with an unruly shock of jet black hair, a crooked nose, and an amazingly gentle-looking smile. His grip was as gentle when she extended her hand to him.

"H-how do you do, Mr. Dugan," Darcy mur-

mured, her voice growing faint from strain and
sheer weariness.

"Can't complain, Miss Flynn," the bouncer replied, frowning as he peered at her. "But you now,
you look like you could do with a bit of a rest."

"I am a little tired," Darcy admitted, forcing a
smile to her stiff lips.

"Yes, yes, of course you're tired, what with your
long journey, and then . . . er, everything." Mr.
Mansford gave another discreet cough. "Ladies,
there will be ample time later to get to know the
new owner," he went on, flicking one hand in a
shooing motion. "Mr. Dugan, if you will be so kind
as to show Miss Flynn to her suite?"

"Yes, sir." Mr. Dugan took a step back, opened
the door, and made a sweeping movement with
his massive right arm. "Right this way, Miss Flynn."

Feeling a desperate need to be by herself, to
absorb the shock of events of this incredible day,
Darcy had to impose every ounce of training and
composure she possessed to tarry long enough to
thank Mr. Mansford for his assistance and bid a
polite good afternoon to the assembled women.
But finally she was free of the small office, rigidly
erect as she trailed the huge bouncer to a door at
the end of the corridor.

"These were your mother's private quarters,"
the big man said in a surprisingly soft and compassionate voice. "You won't be bothered here,"
he went on in harder tones. "I'll be seeing to
that."

"Thank you, Mr. Dugan, I appreciate your . . ."
Darcy's voice faltered at the intensity of the man's

narrow-eyed, probing stare. "Is there something wrong, Mr. Dugan?"

"Wrong?" He blinked. "Why would you be thinking there was something wrong?"

"You were staring at me with such a strange expression," she hastened to explain.

Mr. Dugan's face was transformed once more by his gentle smile. "Ah, lass, I do ask your forgiveness," he said in a crooning voice. "It's just that, damned if you're not the image of herself."

"My mother?" Darcy's eyes flew wide to stare at him in utter disbelief.

"Who else, then?" Mr. Dugan frowned. "Surely you knew you were cast from the same mold?"

"I . . . I . . . no." Darcy shook her head, too flustered by the compliment of being compared in looks to her mother's stunning beauty to say anything else.

"Well, then, you can take my word for it, for you are herself all over again, if a mite taller." He grinned and pushed the door open. "Now I'll be leavin' you to get some rest, but if you need anything, you just yell for Dugan."

Some hours had elapsed since Mr. Dugan had taken his leave. Other than to remove her hat and jacket, Darcy had not relaxed one whit during the ensuing hours.

Upon entering the room, Darcy had come to an abrupt, awed halt, and was barely aware of the bouncer quietly closing the door. The distinctive scent of her mother's French perfume lingered on the breeze wafting into the room through an

open window, robbing her mind of all but one
thought.

*Had her mother drawn her last breath in this very
room?*

Feeling closer to her than she had ever felt while
her mother lived, Darcy glanced around, seeking
a deeper understanding of Colleen in the examination of her personal material possessions.

Colleen's bedroom was exquisite, exceeding
Darcy's most vivid imaginings of elegant decor. Located at the right corner of the house, the cham-
ber was aglow with late afternoon sunlight
streaming through the lacy curtains on the room's
four long, narrow windows, two of which faced
onto a side garden, the other two onto the tree-
shaded yard at the front of the house. The light
enhanced the vibrant colors in the Oriental carpet
on the floor and sparkled off the gold threads
woven through the pale rose coverlet on the big
four-poster bed and matching upholstery on the
chaise lounge placed between the side windows,
opposite the bed.

Pink for a redhead? Darcy mused, trailing a
hand along the satiny material covering the chaise.
Bemused, she drifted into a small attached dressing room and was delighted with the amenities
she found there. A long wardrobe was packed with
day dresses and gowns suitable for any occasion.
A gilded oval mirror hung on the opposite wall
above a pedestal table, upon which sat a beautiful
porcelain wash basin and pitcher. A footed metal
bathing tub was placed against the wall a few feet
from the table, and set in the corner of the
room—to Darcy's heartfelt sense of relief—was an

elaborately carved wooden chair, with a lidded seat.

After using the chair for its intended purpose, Darcy continued her examination of the apartment. A connecting door in the bedroom led into a spacious sitting room, where the decorating colors of pale rose and green highlighted with threads of gold had been carried through.

Growing ever more tired and confused, Darcy returned to the bedroom, intending finally to rest. Instead, she spent an inordinate amount of time alternately studying a large portrait of her mother, which hung above the fireplace mantelpiece, and her own reflection in a large gilded mirror hanging on the opposite wall.

Although Darcy could see a resemblance between her own reflection and the woman in the portrait, she was unable to discern what Mr. Dugan had termed an "image" of her mother. Indeed, Darcy had been blessed with the same pale, flawless complexion, and there were the similarities of hair and eye coloring. But whereas Colleen had had flame red locks, complemented by clear green eyes, Darcy possessed a mass of darker auburn hair and amber-flecked hazel eyes. And though it was true her figure was as slender as her mother's had been, Darcy's form was a good six inches taller and lacked the appearance of Colleen's fragile daintiness.

Having given up her fruitless search for signs of herself in her mother's portrait, Darcy had still not sought the comfort of the bed or the chaise lounge, but had turned with drooping shoulders to stare blankly through the lacy curtains of one of the side windows, seeking answers to the myriad questions taxing her tired mind. One question in particular kept rising to the fore, and without conscious thought, Darcy repeated the fatiguing query aloud.

"What in heaven's name can I do with a whorehouse?"

2

"Run it."

The answering voice was male, soft, and attractive.

Darcy went stiff with shocked surprise. She believed herself alone in the room. There had been no knock upon the bedroom door, no request for entrance. Was the man yet another employee . . . or a former client of her mother's?

Darcy was upset and outraged by both the intrusion and the speculative consideration. The house was closed. Wasn't the front door draped in mourning black? Who dared to invade the privacy of her bereavement? she silently railed, whirling to confront the rude intruder.

"Who are you?" Darcy demanded angrily of the tall, darkly garbed man standing near the foot of the large bed. "The house is permanently closed." She glared at him. "How did you get in here?"

"Good question." The man frowned. His expression conveyed bafflement as he glanced around the room.

His answer and his puzzled look were startling to Darcy, to say the least. Didn't the man know who he was? Where he was? Who she was?

Beginning to feel a decided sense of unease, Darcy took a step back, only to be brought up short when the back of her legs made contact with the windowsill.

Trapped!

The uneasiness expanded inside Darcy to dance along her spine. Her gaze flashed to the door. Could she make it? Darcy strongly suspected that she could not. He was standing too close, and the door was too distant, all the way over on the other side of the bed. A chill of fear shot up her spine to clutch at her throat.

"Who . . . who *are* you?" Darcy repeated in a choked whisper. "How did you get in here?"

His roving glance came to rest on her face, making her aware of the confusion in his soft gray eyes. Pinned by his intent stare, unable to look away, Darcy was also suddenly made aware of how very handsome he was.

Against her will, Darcy noted the sculpted symmetry of his clean-shaven, strongly masculine features, the sheen of his wavy jet black hair and the curious, unfathomable depths of his soul-stirring eyes.

"My name is Jonathan Stuart," he said, inclining his head in an absentminded gesture of respect. "And I'm not sure exactly how I got here," he went on, his baffled expression changing to one of consternation.

"Not sure?" Darcy stared at him in stunned amazement. Was the man a blithering idiot—or a cunning thief? Exerting her will over the fear growing inside her, she drew herself up to her full height, stiffened her spine, and instilled her sternest schoolteacher tone into her voice. "Your claim is ridiculous, sir! You most certainly did not fly in through the window." A flick of her hand indicated the raised side window.

"No, of course not. I . . ." Jonathan Stuart's voice faded. His eyes grew wide, as if from a sudden flash of inner knowledge. "I simply materialized here." His frown darkened, drawing his winged black brows together. "I don't know why."

The expanding fear exploded full-blown inside Darcy. The man wasn't an idiot, she thought wildly. He was a raving lunatic! The light of madness disguised as astonishment now blazed from his deceptively soft eyes.

Growing really frightened, yet determined to maintain her composure, Darcy squarely met his gaze, attempting to stare him down. "I have heard more than enough of your nonsense," she said repressively. "I must insist that you leave at once," she ordered, "or I shall be forced to summon Mr. Dugan to remove you from the property."

"Clancy?" He raised his eyebrows and smiled with infuriating amusement.

His use of the brawny man's Christian name put Darcy at a disadvantage; she knew the bouncer only as Mr. Dugan. "I beg your pardon?" she said icily.

"Clancy Dugan," he explained, his smile taking on a hint of condescension. "The house bouncer. Of course, by all means, call him if you like." He moved his shoulders in a negligent shrug. "He can't harm me."

"Oh? Really?" Darcy arched her brows as she ran a skeptical glance over his tall form, measuring his lean, tightly knit body against her memory of the bouncer's massive brawniness. Her lips curved into a mocking smile. "And why not?"

"Because I'm dead," Jonathan Stuart answered in calm tones of acceptance.

There ensued an instant of utter silence, an instant during which every one of Darcy's nerves seemed to writhe beneath her skin, and then the silence was shattered by her frightened scream peeling throughout the house.

"Mr. Dugan, come at once!"

The intruder who called himself Jonathan Stuart didn't move, but stood as before, seemingly relaxed and at his ease, smiling with noticeable understanding and compassion into Darcy's terror-filled eyes.

Within mere minutes of her fearful outcry, the door burst open to frame the huge figure of the house peacekeeper, the former bare-knuckle prize fighter, Clancy Dugan.

"What is it, Miss Flynn?" Clancy demanded in a respectful tone, flushed and panting from his headlong race up the stairs. "What's wrong, lass?"

"There's an intruder in my room," Darcy snapped, impatient with the man's obvious lack of comprehension. "Remove him, please," she ordered, gesturing at her uninvited guest.

"My pleasure!" Grinning with gleeful anticipation, Clancy charged into the room—and right through the solid-looking form of Jonathan Stuart. "But . . . where is he?" His ruddy face blank with confusion, the bouncer swung his large head back and forth, peering into corners and behind chairs.

Her eyes wide with stark disbelief, Darcy stared

into the gentle expression of the image before her. Had he spoken the truth? Good God! Could it be possible? Was her exhausted mind hallucinating? Or was he . . .

Darcy swallowed the brackish taste of fear.

"He . . . he was here just a moment ago," she said in a strangled whisper, staring, staring into those so soft and so real-looking gray eyes.

Clancy's fierce, combative expression changed to one of pity. "Ah, lassie, no one's been here," he said in a gentle, crooning voice. "You've had a rough go of it, losin' your mother and all. You need to rest," he advised, turning to retrace his steps to the door. "And don't you be worryin' now, no one will be gettin' into this house." His lips tightened into a hard line of determination. "I'll be seein' to that."

Darcy stood, her mind and body frozen, for long moments after the door softly closed behind Clancy. When, at last, she found her voice, it was thin and reedy, as lacking in substance as the shadow facing her.

"You . . . you are a . . . a . . ." Darcy paused, unable to force the word through her stiff, parched lips.

"A ghost?" He spoke the dreaded word for her, smiling in understanding. "Yes, I'm afraid so."

Darcy experienced an uncanny sensation of everything inside her compressing. Her breath stopped, then sped up to an alarming rate. A dark mist rimmed the outer edges of her vision. Her heart fluttered inside her constricted chest. Her mind went blank.

The floorboards seeming to drop away beneath

her feet, Darcy crumpled to the carpet in a dead faint.

"Miss Flynn!"

In an instant, Jonathan was kneeling beside her. She was so still, so pale . . . so very beautiful.

"Darcy?" Jonathan softly called, reaching out to lift her up, off the floor. His arms went through her, not around her.

Damn! Without substance, he was useless, he railed in silent frustration. Then he went still, startled by a light, feathery feeling quivering through his arms.

Feeling? Yes, slight, but definite feeling!

Jonathan's bemused thoughts scattered as a bellowing Clancy burst into the room, followed by every one of Colleen's girls and the house cook.

"We heard a thump against the flo—Miss Flynn!" The bouncer charged across the room and dropped to his knees beside Darcy. His left knee slid through Jonathan's bent leg.

"Get your brawny body off my foot, you great oaf!" Jonathan ordered, drifting up and away like a whisper of smoke from the man and the converging females.

Of course, neither Clancy nor any of the women heard his terse command, but only because Jonathan didn't *want* them to hear him. Just a modicum of experimentation since the time of his demise had ascertained that useful bit of knowledge. Anxious, he hovered over the bouncer, nodding approval as the man gently gathered Darcy into his arms, effortlessly got to his feet, and as if his burden weighed no more than thistledown, carried her to the bed.

"What's wrong with the lass?" Clancy asked of the women, shaking his head in bewilderment.

"She fainted, you fool!" Jonathan snapped.

"I'd guess that she fainted." The observation came from Katie, the oldest of the girls. Bending over the bed, she began to undo the buttons on the high stiff collar of Darcy's shirt. "Dora, fetch a cup of tea for Miss Flynn," she instructed the cook. "Sarah, you go wet a washcloth."

The buxom middle-aged cook and the young girl scurried to do her bidding. Then she raised her head to look at the bouncer. "Clancy, you'd better go—"

"But—" he interrupted in protest, only to be in turn interrupted.

"Miss Flynn will be all right," Katie said. "In fact, she's starting to stir now. But you can't stay, because we are going to make her more comfortable by undressing her."

"Oh!" His ruddy cheeks going beet red, Clancy made a beeline for the door.

Giving a moment's thought to the dictates of convention and propriety, Jonathan considered following the big man from the room. Then, reminding himself that convention and propriety were worldly concerns, he shrugged and perched on the end of the bed to observe the disrobing procedure.

The women were remarkably efficient, which should not have been surprising to him, in light of their occupation. In short order, they whisked off Darcy's shoes, skirt, and hose. Working together in silence, Katie and one of the other women—was it Jane or June?—gently removed the stiff, vertical-pleated, very proper-looking shirt.

The shirt had intrigued Jonathan ever since she had spun away from the window to confront him. The garment was almost masculine in appearance, somewhat uniform, and one such as he had never before seen worn by a woman.

The latest in fashion from Paris or London? Jonathan recalled wondering, noting her jacket draped over the chaise lounge. At the time, with more pressing questions nagging at his mind, the uppermost concerned with how he had suddenly found himself in La Rouge's bedchamber, he had dismissed the query, while eyeing the garment with appreciation; conversely, though the shirt was masculine in appearance, Darcy had looked enticingly feminine clothed by it.

Now that the shirt was gone, Jonathan lounged at the foot of the bed, riveted by the senses-stirring sight of Darcy stripped down to corset, chemise, drawers, and petticoats.

"Hmmm?" Darcy murmured, lashes fluttering.

Jonathan reluctantly raised his gaze from her chest to her face, gratified to see a tinge of color returning to her ashen cheeks. In that instant, he revised his earlier opinion; Darcy was not merely beautiful, she was exquisite.

"She's coming around," Katie said, reaching for the dampened cloth clutched in the hand of an anxious-looking, nervously hovering Sarah.

"What?" Darcy started when the damp cloth was drawn across her forehead. "What are you doing?" she demanded, if tremulously, skimming wide-open, confusion-filled eyes over the faces surrounding her before settling on Katie. "How did I get onto the bed?" A frown drew her delicate brows together.

"Here's Miss Flynn's tea," the cook announced as she entered the room bearing a serving tray.

"Tea?" Darcy blinked. "I did not request tea!" She struggled to sit up. "And how did I get into bed?"

Relieved at her apparent recovery, and not wishing to upset her again, at least not this soon after her swoon, Jonathan smiled . . . and faded.

"Clancy lifted you onto the bed, and I asked Dora to get the tea," Katie answered in a soothing voice.

"But why? What happened to me?" Darcy asked, still feeling fuzzy around the edges of her consciousness.

"You fainted, Miss Flynn."

Katie's answer brought memory surging into Darcy's mind. There had been an intruder in her room, a man. A man without substance! Her eyes wide, frightened, Darcy quickly looked around, searching for shadows in the bedchamber.

"Where is he?" she asked in a whispery, quavery voice.

"Clancy?" Katie smiled. "Don't be alarmed, Miss Flynn, he bolted out of here before me and the girls undressed you to make you more comfortable."

Clancy? No, not Clancy, Darcy thought, shaking her head. She opened her mouth, but caught herself just in time. Clancy had dashed right through the man who had called himself Jonathan Stuart. These women would think she was mad, and rightly so, if she asked about the whereabouts of a disembodied spirit. Her shoulders drooped, and she heard the murmurings of the women circling the bed as if from a distance.

"Are you all right, Miss Flynn?" Katie asked sharply, leaning forward to peer into Darcy's face. "You look kinda funny, and you've gone pale as a ghost again."

"I . . . I, yes." Darcy choked on an incipient burst of hysterical laughter. "I am just so very tired."

"Well a'course you're tired!" Dora exclaimed, pushing through the gathered females to the side of the bed. "What with losin' your mother and all, it's been a trying day for you." The buxom older woman shot a stern look at Katie. "I think you'd better herd these girls out of here so that Miss Flynn can get some rest," she said, bending to place the tea tray on the small bedside table.

"You're right." Katie nodded. "Come on, girls." Offering Darcy a smile, she turned and headed for the door.

"Miss . . . ah, Katie," Darcy called, halting the woman as she stepped into the corridor. "Thank you." She glanced in turn at each of the women crowding the doorway. "All of you."

There came a chorus of "You're welcome" from the girls, then the door was quietly shut behind them.

"Now, then," Dora said, planting her work-roughened hands on her well-padded hips. "I brought a cup of custard along with the tea. You look like you could do with some nourishment," she went on, fussing with a napkin she placed over Darcy's knees. "When you've finished, you have a good long nap."

"Thank you . . . er . . ." Darcy gave her a helpless look.

"Dora," the woman supplied her name, smiling kindly. "And you're welcome. And don't you worry about the tray," she went on, heading for the door. "I'll get it later."

"You're very kind." Darcy blinked rapidly to stem a warning sting of tears in her eyes.

"Turn about," Dora said in a soft, sad tone of voice. "Your mother was kind to me."

"Yes, my mother was always kind to everyone," Darcy replied, managing a faint smile for Dora.

Dora nodded emphatically. "Now you drink your tea and eat the custard, then have a nice little nap." With that final directive, the woman bustled out of the room.

Alone and pensive, Darcy ignored the custard and sipped at the cooling tea. Yes, she reiterated in dejected silence, her mother had been kind and generous as well as beautiful. Finishing off the tea, she sighed, set the cup on the tray, then slid down on the bed. With all her good qualities, it was a shame that Colleen had not been a particularly good mother.

Settling her tired body into a comfortable position, she yawned and gave in to the weight of weariness tugging on her eyelids.

Where was he? Darcy wondered sleepily, sinking into the plump pillow, the soft mattress, and the gray mist of encroaching nothingness. Had she imagined him, conjured him from the depths of her shock-numbed mind? No. Darcy moved her head back and forth on the pillow. No, she was not at all fanciful. She would never have imagined something so . . . so unnatural.

So then, where was the specter?

It was Darcy's last coherent thought before sleep came to fully claim her, rescuing her from the chain of shocks she had endured throughout the day.

She was asleep.

Jonathan stood beside the bed, a tender smile curving his lips as he gazed upon the slumbering woman. She was so very lovely, every bit as beautiful as her mother, but in a different, more elegant and refined way.

The rigid control Darcy imposed on her features while conscious was softened by slumber into beguiling lines of innocent vulnerability.

A stray lock of auburn hair lay curled against her satin-smooth cheek. Without thinking, Jonathan bent over the bed and reached out to brush the lock off her face. A groan rose in his throat as his hand began passing through her soft flesh.

Damn. For a moment, he'd forgotten that he couldn't touch her, Jonathan thought. He couldn't lift her from the floor, or brush the errant lock from her cheek, or feel the softness of her creamy skin.

But wait! What was this? Jonathan frowned, then he jerked his hand away from her face. His brows shot up in startled surprise. The groan in his throat was expelled from his lips on a murmur of wonder.

He had felt something again! Jonathan marveled. And this time the feeling was stronger, deeper. At the moment his hand slid through her flesh, Jonathan had experienced a warm tingling sensation, a feeling quite similar to physical contact, but at the same time more, a sense of contact with her spirit, the very essence of Darcy.

Stunned by the discovery of the tingling sensation, Jonathan stood by the bed, staring at the sleeping woman in bemused delight. The bouncer, Clancy, had charged right through him, not once but twice, and Jonathan had felt nothing.

And yet . . . he had felt a responsive physical sensation from contact with Darcy.

Gazing down into Darcy's sleep-softened face, Jonathan felt a very human, very physical inner pang, not unlike the remembered emotion of tenderness.

He cared for her! Shock jolted through Jonathan. Cared? He examined the word. He cared for the child-woman Sarah, all the women of the house, for that matter, and he had on one or two occasions since his death unwittingly drifted through several of them—before he had gotten the hang of his new, unencumbered state. He had felt nothing. Nothing.

On consideration, Jonathan had never deeply cared for any woman, if one discounted the callow, confused yearnings for something he had felt for a few young girls while he was still a youth. And Jonathan did discount those feelings, recognizing them for what they were—simple growing pains.

But this caring for Darcy . . . this feeling was entirely new and, because it sprang from the depths of his being, could not be discounted or ignored. He cared. Deeply.

Yet how could this be? Jonathan asked himself. Surely it was impossible; he was a ghost, and ghosts couldn't experience the feelings and emotions of living beings . . . could they?

Well, apparently they could, Jonathan mused, trying to come to grips with the amazing concept. The sound of the door being opened carefully brought him out of his stupefied reverie. The sight of the young woman who tiptoed into the room reminded him of why he had resisted the light, rejected the offer of guidance out of the darkness.

"Just set the bags inside the door," Sarah said in a whisper to someone in the corridor. "I'll slide them off to the side, out of the way."

"Is she sleeping, then?" Clancy muttered, setting two carpetbags down just inside the door.

"Yes." Sarah shoved the two cases against the wall, and smiled at Darcy as she backed out of the room.

Young Sarah wanted to learn how to read and write. Jonathan had determined to teach her. His determination had given him purpose, a renewed will to live.

And Jonathan's will had rejected the light.

3

Dunstan sighed as he slid his long body down into the tub of steaming water. After three weeks on the trail, he wasn't sure which he was more of, tired or dirty.

A wry smile quirked his lips as he considered the two possibilities. Must be more dirty than tired, Wade decided, luxuriating in the deep wooden tub. On hitting this dingy town with the lofty if misplaced name of Paradise, Utah, he had walked his horse right by the building with the hotel sign nailed above the door, and made straight for the smaller building a little way down the street with a red and white pole standing next to the open door in front and a wallboard sign advertising shaves, haircuts, and baths.

The trail dust and sweat caking Wade's skin turned the hot water a dirty brown before he ever applied the bar of homemade soap to his weary limbs.

Shrugging, Wade lowered his head between his bent and parted knees and plunged it into the water. The dust-clouded liquid streamed from his long, shaggy mane as he raised his head. Rubbing the soap between his palms, he worked up a meager lather and vigorously applied it to his scalp, washing weeks of accumulated grime from his hair. When he figured the hair was as good as it was going to get, he worked the harsh soap down the length of his tall frame, scouring the dirt from his skin.

A few minutes later, his eyes squeezed shut against the sting of soapsuds dripping from his hair, Wade groped with one hand for the bucket of clear water set on the floor beside the wooden tub. Grasping the handle, he hefted the bucket and dashed the steamy water over his head and shoulders.

God, it felt good to be clean again.

Sending a shower of droplets around the tub with a shake of his head, Wade sluiced the water from his face with his hands, then leaned back against the tub to savor the soothing effect of the hot water on his saddle-weary muscles.

"I hear that new girl over to the Last Ditch is more'n happy to please."

Floating in a half-sleep, Wade heard the voice as if from a distance. The comment penetrated the thin wall separating the tiny bathing room from the barber shop in front.

"That so?"

A faint smile touched Wade's lips at the non-committal response from the barber, one Harry Kelly.

"Yeah, I heard the same," another voice piped in. "Fella told me she's not only good but willing and eager to oblige . . ." Then his tone took on a lascivious note. "Even with her mouth."

Wade shivered, but not from the rapidly cooling

water. Beneath the waterline, his body had grown, becoming rigid in response to the conversation.

"It must be true, then, 'cause that's what I heard too." The voice of the first man now had the definite choking sound of sexual excitement. "God Awmighty, I ain't never poked a woman in the mouth."

"Then you ain't never lived, boy," the second man said in a tone of pitying condescension.

Damn. Wade swallowed a groan. His body was fully aroused, painfully hard. He hadn't been with a woman in more than six months, not since he had left home that last time. Now the men's talk had reminded Wade's body that it was still alive, still capable of feeling lust, as well as hatred.

"Well, what I heard was that she had one customer week or so back who lived a couple ways," Harry said in a low, confidential tone.

Wade suddenly felt cold as stone.

"Now what in all git-out is that supposed to mean?" the first man, obviously the youngest of the three, groused.

Mary. Her name pierced Wade's mind, deflating the heat and fullness in his loins.

"How old are you, boy?" the other man demanded scathingly, making a snorting sound of muffled laughter.

"It means the girl's customer used her in all the ways there are," Harry explained, apparently taking pity on the younger man. "And that means front and rear."

"Holy shit!" the first man exclaimed.

"Nothin' holy 'bout it," Harry said. "And the

way I heard it was that she wasn't either happy or eager to oblige."

Wade shut his eyes and clenched his teeth to keep from crying out against an engulfing wave of pain and fury. Mary had been used in all the ways there are.

Could there be a connection between this girl's customer and the rapist-murderer he sought?

Water sloshed over the rim of the tub as Wade surged to his feet and stepped onto the wet floor.

Coincidence?

Possibly, Wade conceded, drying off with a rough towel. He had been trailing his man for weeks. Wade knew he was closing the gap between them. Coincidence? Wade grimaced. Possibly . . . maybe, but unlikely.

Tossing the sodden towel aside, Wade dug in his saddlebags for the one clean shirt, set of underwear, and socks he had packed. After donning the clean clothes, he reached for the denim pants he had purchased less than an hour before at the mercantile store down the street from the barber shop. After pulling on the close-fitting pants, he pocketed the coins he had removed earlier from his dirty pants.

The denims were stiff, and Wade did several knee bends before perching on the solitary chair in the room to pull on his well-worn and scarred boots. Standing, he stomped fully into the boots, then lifted his gun belt from where he had looped it over the back of the chair. He buckled the single-holster belt around his waist and settled it into place. Grunting at the stiffness of the pants, he bent and scooped up his dirty clothing, his wide-brimmed, rather battered hat, and saddlebags off the floor. From habit, Wade checked to make sure his money was still securely tucked into an inside pocket of one of the saddlebags before strolling into the front room.

Except for the barber, the shop was now empty. Caught up in his thoughts, Wade hadn't taken note of the two customers exiting the shop.

"Feel better?" Ensconced in his own barber chair, Harry peered at Wade over the top of the finger-smudged, ragged newspaper he'd been reading.

"Yeah." Wade nodded. "Now I need a trim," he said, lifting his hand to spear his fingers into the still damp, wildly tangled hair curling over his shoulders.

"Sure thing." Harry leapt out of the chair and grinned, revealing crooked, tobacco-stained teeth. "Looks like you could do with a shave too."

"How much?" Wade raised his eyebrows as he settled into the chair.

"Five bucks."

Wade scowled. "Hell, I can get laid for that."

"Sure can. Laid good." Harry agreed with another grin. "But the fun of the screwin' will only last a little while, the shave and haircut'll last a couple days." His grin broadened. "Besides, the five includes the bath." He inclined his own neatly barbered head to indicate the soiled clothes clutched in Wade's arms. "And for my wife to do your laundry."

Wade recognized a bargain when he was offered one. "You got a deal." Leaning over the arm of the chair, he dumped the clothing, hat, and bags onto the floor. "I was planning to drop these off at the Irish Lady's Laundry down the street."

"Saved you a trip." Harry laughed aloud as he swung a long barber's cape around Wade's shoulder. "My wife *is* the Irish lady down the street."

Harry proved to be inclined to chat while he worked. Long before he removed the now hair-sprinkled cape, Wade had learned more than he really wanted to know about the town and most of the residents in it. The only things Harry didn't talk about were the two subjects of interest to him.

"Anything else I can do for you, sir?" Harry asked, briskly applying the barber's brush to the back of Wade's neck.

"Yes, there is," Wade drawled. "You can tell me where to find a hot meal and a hotter whore."

"Need your stomach stoked and your ashes hauled, do you?" Harry laughed suggestively.

"Yeah." Wade nodded and managed a convincing leer. "I couldn't help but overhear the talk while I was in back." He indicated the bathing room with a head jerk. "What's the name of the obliging girl over to the Last Ditch?"

"Name's Maybell." Harry supplied the name with a final flourish of the brush. "And you can have both your needs taken care of in the Last Ditch."

"They serve meals?" Wade asked, digging in the tight denim pants pocket for a five-dollar piece.

"Best steak in town," Harry promised, pocketing the coin with a nod of thanks. "Can't miss the place, it's right fancy. It's at the corner on the other side of the street."

Wade was pulling the door open before Harry

had finished speaking. "Much obliged," he said, settling his hat low on his forehead and the saddlebags over one shoulder as he stepped onto the raised boardwalk. "Oh, by the way," he said, glancing back at the barber, "when can I pick up my laundry?"

Harry frowned and scratched his head. "By sometime soon after noon tomorrow, I expect."

"Good enough," Wade said, pulling the door shut—he had planned to sleep until noon anyway.

Outside, Wade stood in the long rays of late-afternoon sunlight, uncertain which way to turn, right to the hotel to secure a room for the night or left to the saloon.

Eyes narrowed against the glare, he observed the traffic of local residents, on foot along the sidewalk as well as those mounted on horses and on buckboards, in wagons, and in buggies in the rutted, dusty street. For all the dingy look of it, the town appeared to be thriving.

Wade didn't care one way or the other. He had no plans to sink roots there. All he wanted was some information, some food, and some twelve hours of uninterrupted sleep.

But in what order? Half afraid that if he went to the hotel first, he'd hit the bed and be dead to the world in a flash, Wade nevertheless turned right. The weight of the saddlebags decided the issue. He'd stash his stuff, then see to his other two requirements.

Leading his horse, Wade ambled along the board sidewalk to the hotel a short distance down the street. After tying the horse's reins to the rail in front, he untied his bedroll behind the saddle, hefted it to his other shoulder, then made his way through the open door into the hotel.

"Good afternoon, sir." The desk clerk wore wire-rimmed glasses on his pinched nose and had a prissy look about him, as if he would collapse in upon himself should someone stare him straight in the eyes and say boo.

"Afternoon. I need a room, private, and a place to stable my horse."

"Certainly, sir." The clerk indicated a large registration book on the desk. "If you will sign your name, or make your mark, I will get someone to take care of your horse."

"I appreciate it," Wade drawled, picking up the pen lying beside the book. Out of sheer perversity, he signed his name with a flourish, then added *U.S. Marshal* alongside it for good measure . . . and effect.

"You looking for someone here in Paradise, Marshal?" the clerk asked on taking note of the registration, eyeing Wade nervously.

Wade exhaled and shook his head. "Just passing through."

The rabbity clerk was visibly relieved. "Oh, good. I mean, I hope you enjoy your stay with us." Snatching a room key from one of the hooks on a board mounted on the wall behind him, the man scurried around the desk. "If you will follow me, Marshal, I'll show you to your room."

Wade felt forced to compress his lips to contain a smile, knowing the usual practice was to hand the key over to a customer and let him find his room for himself.

The room had little to recommend it, other

than its location at the far side of the building, away from the noise of the street and the stink of the stable. It had one small window, uncurtained but affording privacy with a fly-specked tan rolled paper shade. Even with the shade drawn and the window open, the room was stifling.

The furniture was old and scarred and sparse. Besides the bed, the room boasted a narrow chest of drawers, a rickety washstand, sagging beneath the weight of a washbowl and pitcher, and one uncushioned ladderbacked wooden chair. But the room looked tidy and the bedding appeared freshly washed. Wade had expected nothing more. In fact, the clean bedding was a pleasant surprise.

After stashing his saddlebags and bedroll under the bed, Wade left the room, locked the door, and retraced his steps to the board sidewalk. Twilight softened the stark, unattractive look of the town. Touching his fingers to his hat brim, he nodded respectfully to two ladies passing by, then strolled along toward his destination at the corner of the street.

Though it was larger than all the other buildings he had seen, except the hotel, in Wade's opinion it was a long way from fancy. To him, the place looked exactly like what it was—a combination saloon and bordello. The only thing distinguishing the place from most other saloons was the solid entrance door instead of the usual swinging doors.

The inside wasn't a whole lot fancier, except for the gaudy nude painting hanging behind the bar and the red globed lamps hanging from the ceiling beams. But the steak and potatoes Wade was served lived up to Harry's promise.

Polishing off his meal, Wade lounged back in his chair, took a generous swallow of tepid beer from the thick mug, and sent a casual look around the dimly lighted room. When he'd entered the place, there had been only a few customers in the saloon, but the room had begun to fill with the onset of evening.

While eating, Wade had observed several women escort men up the narrow staircase to the second floor. Now, as he nursed his beer, he watched two of the couples returning to the bar. Catching the attention of one of the women, he inclined his head at the chair opposite him in silent invitation for her to join him. She gave a brief nod, murmured something to her "customer," then sashayed across the room to his table.

"Looking for company, cowboy?"

"Sure," Wade replied, not bothering to correct her. "Can I buy you a drink?"

"Sure," she echoed in a whiskey-roughened, tired-sounding voice. "I'll get it." She raised artificially darkened eyebrows questioningly. "You ready for another beer?"

"Among other things."

She smirked but didn't respond. With a swish of her bright green skirt, she turned to walk to the bar.

Still lounging, Wade studied the woman as she made her way back to his table, a foam-topped mug of beer in one hand and a squat whiskey tumbler in the other. He judged her to be no more than nineteen or twenty but even in the dim light, he could see she had not been young in a long time.

The realization caused a twinge of sadness inside Wade. He had been around for a spell, a lot of those years spent hunting the lawless. A man got to know people. He knew the kind of life most "soiled doves" endured on the frontier, and the desperation that drove them into it. Without family or men of their own, they faced hardships their more secure, respected contemporaries could never comprehend.

"You gotta name?" she asked, setting the glasses on the table before settling herself across from him.

"Dunston, Wade," he said, lifting the mug to her in a mute salute. "You?"

"Smith." She gave him a bright, false smile loaded with cynicism. "Maybell."

Pay dirt. Wade returned her smile, set his empty mug down, and lifted the full one. "Here's to better days."

"And nights to come in?"

Wade stifled a sigh. Hell, for all he knew, she might enjoy being ridden by strangers. "Depends on what the nights to come in cost a man."

"Five dollars." Maybell's voice had the hard sound of finality; there would be no bargaining.

Wade made no attempt to conceal a wry smile; appeared five was the going rate in Paradise. "Whenever you're ready," he drawled, giving a mental shrug.

"In coin," she cautioned. "I won't take no paper."

Wade's smile slipped into a grin. "Don't blame you for that. Coin it is."

"Well, then, Wade Dunston, drink up." She

tossed back the whiskey neat and got to her feet. "Time's money, and the night and I ain't getting any younger."

Unconcerned with the beer, Wade set the nearly full glass on the table. "After you," he said, making a sweeping motion with his arm as he heaved himself up from the chair.

A feeling of conspicuousness caused a creepy sensation at the back of Wade's neck as he followed Maybell up the narrow staircase. The world had turned too many times to count since he had panted up the stairs after a whore.

Maybell's room was no bigger than the one Wade had recently paid for at the hotel—no bigger and not halfway as tidy. There were few signs of femininity, other than the assortment of paints and powders littering a small dressing table.

She had been dead serious about time and money. Maybell's fingers went to work on the fastenings at the back of her dress before he had pulled the door shut behind him.

"Don't bother," Wade said, reaching out with one hand to halt the action of her fingers. "You don't have to undress."

She sighed and shot him a sharp, suspicious look. "What did you have in mind, cowboy?"

Wade returned her look with a tired smile. "Nothing," he assured her. "All I want from you is some information."

"You let me waste my time bringing you up here only to talk?" Maybell demanded angrily. But before he could reply, she snapped, "Look, fella, I ain't your mother. If you need someone to talk to, go see the parson." Giving him a disgusted look, she moved to go around him to the door.

Wade barred her way by backing up to block the doorway with his body. Dipping his fingers into his shirt pocket, he produced his badge and held it in front of her.

Maybell's look of disgust deepened. "So you're a United States Marshal . . . so what?"

"So, the man I'm looking for wouldn't have spent time with the parson," he retorted. "But I have reason to believe he did spend some time with you."

Maybell glared at him.

Wade endured her stare with silent and immovable stoicism, letting her know he wasn't going anywhere until he got the answers he had come for.

She was the first to give ground. "Does this man you're hunting have a name?"

"Most likely," he said. "I just don't know it." Though the one man he had caught up with in Arizona had babbled like an idiot before Wade mercifully put him out of his misery, he had told Wade the names of the other three killers he sought were all aliases, and that he didn't know their real names.

"That's a helluva lot of help." She grimaced. "Can you tell me what he looks like?"

Wade shrugged. "Average . . . height, appearance, build. I do know he's got brown eyes and brown hair and—"

"Jesus Christ!" Maybell exclaimed in exasperation. "You're describing over half the men I see."

"I've also been told that he's got a long scar on

the back of his right hand," he went on calmly as if she hadn't interrupted him. "Seems he favors a knife."

She became alert at the mention of a scar. "Well, why in hell didn't you say so in the first place?" she asked in surprised exclamation. "I was with a man with a scarred hand a week ago yesterday." Her lips curled in a sneer. "The son of a bitch used me like a dog . . . rode me long and hard, payin' no never mind while his belly slapped my ass." Her eyes glittered with outrage and fury. "He tore me up some, the bastard. I couldn't work for a couple days for the bleeding and the soreness."

Everything inside Wade seemed to clench and freeze. "Sounds like my man," he murmured in a deadly cold voice. "Did he tell you his name, or where he was headed?"

"Said his name was Jack Pritchart and that he was making his way up toward Promontory."

"That *is* my man." His voice was even colder, icy with renewed determination. The first of the four men who had abused then killed Wade's wife had told him that the name one of the men was using was John Price, and that he had said he was making for Promontory.

Wade had been a lawman for more years than he cared to recall; he knew how often men living on the wrong side of the law used aliases with the same first initial . . . most likely because they usually weren't too bright, and using the same first initial made it easier to remember the current alias.

Maybell's smile held pure vindictiveness. "What do you want him for, Marshal? What did he do?"

"He's one of four men who raped and murdered a woman," he answered grittily.

"I'm not surprised to hear it. That cruel bastard seemed capable of anything." Now her eyes blazed with hatred. "What are you gonna do when you catch up to him?"

Wade's smile was not pleasant. "I'm going to kill him."

"Good." Her voice was as hard as railroad spikes. "I only regret that I won't be there to see it."

Wrong woman to rile, Wade reflected, shoving a hand into the tight pocket to dig out two coins.

"You don't have to pay me," Maybell said, discerning his intent. "This time the pleasure was mine. Fact is, I feel I ought to pay you for taking care of that belly-crawler."

Yes indeed, she was definitely the wrong woman to rile. Smiling inwardly at the thought, Wade held out his hand, palm up, to reveal two coins. "Like you said, time's money, and I took up some of yours. Now I want you to take this."

Maybell eyed the two five-dollar coins. "That's too much. I told you the price was five."

"I know." Wade nodded. "But I also know you must give a percentage of that five to the owner of the place." He moved his hand closer to her. "The other five's for you."

Maybell ran a speculative and flattering look over his tall, muscularly fit body. Apparently she liked what she saw. "Are you sure you don't want a quick roll for that extra five?" she asked with obvious interest. "I'd be happy to oblige."

So he'd heard. Wade kept the observation to himself. He shook his head, and wondered why, after the physical reaction he'd experienced while in the tub, he *wasn't* interested. The answer lay in the weight of bitterness, hate, and deep weariness pressing down on him. Wade knew that, more than a woman, he needed rest, sleep, and vengeance. Besides, she was the wrong woman.

"I appreciate the offer," he said, meaning it. "But no, thanks. I've got to be going."

Less than an hour later, Wade lay naked and sprawled on the bed in the hotel room. The over-tired muscles in his body jumped and jerked in the throes of relaxing, then grew tense as an image seeped into his mind to torment him.

"Mary." The whispered sound of her name brought a warm sting to the backs of his eyelids.

Desperate to chase the soul-destroying memory, Wade cast about for something less painful to ponder.

Money. Wade pounced on the thought. Not knowing how long his hunt would last or how far he'd have to journey, he had brought with him all the money he possessed. In addition to the five he had handed Harry, he would have to shell out more money at the mercantile tomorrow to replenish his dwindling supplies, and he had just needlessly handed over a portion of his hoard of funds to a whore.

Yawning widely, Wade turned onto his side, his expression one of utter unconcern. He had enough dinero to see him through the job he had to do, he reasoned, yawning again. And after that it wouldn't matter.

There were no pockets in a shroud.

4

Darcy awoke to the soft pink glow of dawn stealing in through the windows. She felt rested and refreshed from her long hours of sleep, despite a hollow feeling of hunger yawning inside her. Stretching, she sat up in bed and let out a sharp gasp at the sight that met her startled eyes.

The specter hovered in a lounging position at the foot of her bed, smiling at her and looking for all the world as if he belonged there.

"Sleep well?" he inquired, sitting up in a floating movement that appeared effortless and fluid.

Darcy had to swallow several times to moisten her throat before she could manage a simple one-word answer. "Yes," she croaked, sounding strained. "Thank you."

"You're welcome." His smile took on a teasing slant. "Still having trouble with the fact of me, aren't you?"

"You are real," she said tremulously. "You are not, as I had hoped, a figment of my imagination."

"Real?" Jonathan repeated, shrugging. "I certainly feel real, in a nonphysical sense." He smiled. "It's all rather interesting, learning the boundaries, so to speak."

"Boundaries?" Darcy repeated in a faint whisper.

"Hmmm." His smile took on a curve of inner delight. "Learning exactly what I can and cannot do. For example: I cannot eat food, but that's of no matter because I experience no physical appetite. I can speak directly into another's mind, and I can read . . . mentally."

"Oh!"

"Do not be concerned," he hastened to assure her. "I said I can, but I will not invade any human's thoughts without permission." His eyes glowed from an inner, gentle light. "All the history and information of the physical plane is as an open book to me; I have simply to glance at the pages of life." He gave a mock sigh, while his lips quirked in amusement. "Alas, I still do not have all the answers, or know all the rules. But one thing I do know is that, yes, I am really a ghost and I am really here. If that's what you are asking."

"Uh . . ." Darcy wet her lips with a glide of the tip of her tongue. "Yes."

His smile tilted, conveying compassion and comprehension. "I won't hurt you, you know." He chuckled. "Come to that, I can't hurt you. In case you haven't noticed, I have no substance. I can't hurt anyone."

Darcy had a flashing memory of Clancy rushing into the room, and right through her uninvited guest. "I'm afraid I must disagree, sir. I fear you could do a great amount of harm," she corrected him, recalling her heart-stopping reaction at the time. "In my experienced opinion, you could very easily frighten someone to death."

He laughed, and it was a delightful sound, deep and rich, utterly masculine and charming. "If I had frightened you to death, you might now be here, without substance, beside me," he rejoined, his gentle gray eyes gleaming with deviltry. "Instead, you are there, in solid . . . enchanting flesh."

Jonathan's remark drew Darcy's attention to her state of dishabille, causing a blush of embarrassment, and in truth, pleasure to flare scarlet on her naturally pale cheeks.

"Oh!" she exclaimed, snatching at the coverlet to draw it around her scantily clad form. "Oh, my goodness!" Never before had any man seen her less than fully clothed. "You must leave me at once, sir, so that I can get dressed!"

"Pity." Jonathan sighed and gave her a sorrowful look. "If you insist," he said, beginning to fade. "But," he went on, in a distant-sounding warning, "I will be back as soon as you are properly attired."

And with that he simply disappeared.

Wide-eyed, uncertain, Darcy glanced around the room, searching for she knew not what—perhaps a wisp of smoke to denote his passage. Of course, there was nothing; she really had not expected anything. Still . . .

A light, tentative knock sounded on the door, causing Darcy to start. "Yes, who is it?" she called out in a nervous, quavery voice.

"It's me, Dora," the cook replied. "I was just checking to see if you were up, and to tell you that breakfast is ready . . . whenever you are."

Tossing the coverlet aside, Darcy slid from the

bed and went to open the door. "Good morning, Dora," she said politely, then rushed on, "I am ready now. In fact, I am famished."

"Figured you might be." Dora offered her a smile as bright as the rising sun. "And good morning to you, Miss Darcy. Did you sleep well?"

"Yes, thank you." Since the woman's question reminded her too vividly of Jonathan's earlier query, Darcy quickly continued, "I will come down directly, just as soon as I have bathed and dressed."

Dora frowned and shook her head. "Well, land sakes, you don't have to wait that long to eat."

Darcy went stiff all over with a sense of impropriety. "Well, I certainly cannot come to the breakfast table as I am, dressed in my undergarments," she admonished.

"You could if you put a robe on," Dora said, looking perplexed. "The other girls do."

"Please remember, Dora, that I am not one of the 'girls' in this house," Darcy said in icy reproval.

"I ain't about to forget it, miss. It only takes one look for a body to know that you're a real lady."

Darcy had always been susceptible to the mildest of compliments; becoming the owner of a house of ill repute had not altered her susceptibility. The ice coating her voice noticeably thawed. "Thank you, Dora."

"You're welcome." The cook gave her another sunny smile. "Anyway, I wasn't thinking of you coming downstairs to eat in your underwear, robe or not. What I had in mind was bringing a tray up here to you."

"Why, thank you, Dora." Darcy felt positively pampered; she had never been served a meal in her bedroom. "That is very thoughtful of you."

"It's no more than I did for your dear mother, God rest her kind soul." Dora blinked rapidly, then hurried on. "Clancy can use the other door into your dressing room to fill the tub for you while you eat."

Other door? Darcy frowned; she couldn't recall noticing another door leading into the dressing room. "There is another door into that room?" she asked, mentally reviewing what she remembered of the room, and coming up blank.

Dora's smile revealed understanding. "It's kinda hidden," she confided. "Your mother liked her privacy."

"You will have to show me where it is," Darcy said, feeling grateful to her mother for the trait of desired privacy she had passed on to her only child.

"Be happy to, but later," Dora promised, turning away. "First I'll go down for your breakfast, and roust Clancy to fill your tub."

The breakfast tray Dora subsequently set before Darcy could be described in two words: abundant and delicious. Darcy ate every morsel of the meal and drained every drop of rich, aromatic coffee provided in the silver pot included on the tray. Of course, Darcy might have thought any food delicious after not having eaten for nearly twenty-four hours. Nevertheless, being a woman of some discernment, Darcy heaped lavish praise upon Dora for her cooking skill when the woman returned to the bedroom to remove the tray.

Flushed and flustered, obviously pleased and flattered by her new mistress's accolade, Dora bustled about the room, unpacking the two carpetbags while Darcy luxuriated in the tub of hot water, liberally sprinkled with flower-scented salts she had chosen from the varied selection arrayed atop a shelf positioned on the wall near the bathtub.

"Most of these clothes need pressing," Dora grumbled to Darcy as she reentered the bedroom, bringing with her the scent of attar of roses and blooming all over with a rose-colored blush from the invigorating bath.

"Hmm," Darcy answered absently, mellowed by the warm soak.

"I laid out the things that didn't seem as wrinkled as the others." She indicated the undergarments and day dress spread out on the neatly made bed.

"Thank you, Dora." Darcy smiled at the woman in appreciation and gratitude. "Is there a laundress in the vicinity who can press the clothing?"

"Laundress!" Dora appeared shocked. "I wouldn't trust anyone else with your pretty things. I'll press them myself, same as I did your mother's."

"You will spoil me," Darcy warned, quite seriously. "As I suspect you spoiled my mother." Her lips curved into a teasing smile. "And I, I'm afraid, will quite honestly and outrageously adore being spoiled."

Laughing softly, Dora scooped up the neatly piled clothing and headed for the door. "You deserve some spoiling, after what you've been through lately," she stated. "Now, don't you worry none about anything. Whenever you're ready, either me or one of the girls will show you around the house."

The *house*. The word, and all its connotations, echoed in Darcy's mind as she stood staring at the door long after Dora had quietly shut it behind her.

"You look lovely in that gown, even with the wrinkles Dora couldn't smooth from the material. That pale green color becomes you, but . . ." He raised one brow. "No bustle?"

Darcy gave a muffled yelp and spun in the direction of his voice. "Good heavens!" she exclaimed, frowning in disapproval at the specter, now appearing to sit at his ease in the very same chair she had occupied while eating her breakfast. "I'm beginning to suspect that you are trying to frighten me to death, Mr. . . . did you tell me yesterday that your name was Stuart?"

"Correct." He grinned at her. "Come to that, it still is Stuart; my dying hasn't changed it."

"I . . . ah . . . see." Darcy drew a deep, hopefully calming breath; being in the presence of a disembodied spirit certainly upset one's nerves and equilibrium. "Then, Mr. Stuart, *are* you trying to frighten me to death with your abrupt and unexpected appearances and disappearances?"

"Not at all." Though his voice was solemn, his lips twitched suspiciously. "If you will recall, I did warn you that I'd be back as soon as you were properly attired." His soft gray eyes swept her rigid form. "And, permit me to repeat, you are not only properly but prettily attired."

The unexpected compliment rendered Darcy every bit as flustered and flattered as Dora had so recently been. "Why . . . uh, th-thank you."

"You're welcome," he responded, gazing at her speculatively. "From your reactions, I must conclude that you are unaccustomed to receiving compliments." He arched one dark brow quizzically. "Am I right?"

"Well, yes, I haven't . . ." Darcy's voice faded as her wits came together, and the realization struck her, not only of his observation of her, but of her own earlier question to him concerning his sudden appearances and disappearances. "How did you know about my reactions?" she demanded, beginning to feel uncomfortably warm. "Were you here all the time, in an invisible state, while I bathed and dressed?"

"No, I was not." His tone held affronted decisiveness. "I could have been, but I was not."

Darcy exhaled a sigh of relief; she didn't know exactly why she believed him, but she did. "I do thank you for your consideration, Mr.—"

"Call me Jonathan, please," he interrupted her to make the request. "And may I call you Darcy?"

"But I hardly know you!" Even to her own ears, Darcy's protest sounded incongruous.

Jonathan erupted in a bark of good-natured laughter aimed at her prissiness.

And he had every right to laugh, Darcy chided herself. From habit, she had protested his request for familiarity out of a sense of shocked propriety, foolishly forgetting she was speaking to a ghost, a specter with the ability to come and go at will, anywhere he chose.

"Don't look so upset, Darcy." Jonathan smiled at her with tender understanding. "You will get used to me, and our unusual situation, in time."

"Situation?" Darcy pounced on the term, made uneasy by the sound of it. "What situation?"

Jonathan appeared surprised by the query. "Why, you and I, naturally. Together . . . here." He gave a wave of one hand to indicate the room or entire house; Darcy knew not which, but she intended to find out.

"You are planning to stay . . . here?"

"Of course," his answering tone implying that the answer should have been obvious. "That is why I refused to go when I was summoned."

Rather than clarifying, his response deepened her confusion about the issue. "Refused to go? Summoned?" Darcy stared blankly at him. "Refused to go where? And summoned by whom? I don't understand what you're saying."

"No, of course you don't." Jonathan smiled. "Come, sit down." He flicked a hand in the direction of the dainty satin-striped chair at the opposite side of the small table set close to one partially open window facing onto the front of the house. "I'll explain, as best I can."

Darcy hesitated for just a moment, unsure, indecisive, and then she slowly crossed to the table. Following the dictates of years of training, she sat as she had been taught a lady should sit, spine straight, knees and slender ankles primly together, hands folded in her lap.

"So formal and so proper." Jonathan revealed signs of wanting to laugh again. Then, out of the blue, he repeated his earlier observation. "No bustle." His eyebrows arched. "I can't help but wonder why."

"Miss Reinholt did not approve," Darcy said primly.

"Miss Reinholt?"

Darcy nodded. "Miss Reinholt is the headmistress of the private school I attended in Philadelphia, first as a live-in student, and then as an instructress."

"Ahhh . . . you're a teacher." Jonathan's voice held the purring sound of satisfaction.

"Yes." Puzzled, Darcy frowned. "At least I was a teacher until I received a letter from my mother's solicitor, urging me to come here, to Denver."

"I'll wager you never expected to find this . . . er, house upon your arrival," he drawled.

"Certainly not!" Darcy exclaimed, going stiff.

"Upon my arrival, all I expected was to find my mother ill. Beyond that, I . . ." Her voice drowned in a flood of memories.

"Why don't you tell me about it?" Jonathan suggested in tones of commiseration. "Sometimes talking helps."

Until that moment, Darcy had been unaware of needing a confidant, someone to listen to and sympathize with her trials and travails. Still, being reticent by nature, she held back, uncertain.

"Who better to talk to about it?" Jonathan's voice was soft, insidiously alluring. "I'm a ghost, remember, a mere shadow of the man I once was. All things considered, I am very likely the best confidant you could ever hope for."

He had a point, Darcy conceded. Who better to

talk to, indeed, other than her uninvited guest? Were Miss Reinholt in residence, Darcy knew she wouldn't hesitate for an instant in taking the older woman into her confidence. But Miss Reinholt was halfway across the country. Darcy was on her own, alone and feeling rather lost. And she most definitely would never dream of confiding in one of her mother's girls.

"Darcy?"

Jonathan's cajoling voice nudged Darcy out of her depressing reverie, and into speech. Her tone austere, she gave him a brief account of the circumstances surrounding her life up to the day she received the upsetting letter from Mr. Mansford. It was only when she reached the part in her story concerning the events following her subsequent arrival in Denver that emotion began coloring Darcy's voice, revealing the series of shocks she had suffered, culminating with the final confidence-crushing and traumatic realization that her mother had owned and managed a house of ill repute.

"What was your life like before you were installed in that school in Philadelphia?" Jonathan asked, doggedly persisting with his quietly voiced inquisition.

"Happy." Darcy's features softened and her eyes took on a dreamy expression. "I was so young, and my recollections are hazy, more impressions than actual memories."

"You lived in New Orleans?"

"Yes." Darcy murmured, her voice now gentle. "I recall a small, delightful house, adorned with lacy trimwork. I have vivid memories of my mother at that time, so young, beautiful, and vivacious. She attracted people to her quite like a flame attracts moths."

"She had many friends."

"Oh, yes." Darcy nodded vigorously, caught within the silken threads of flashing glimpses of yesteryear. "The house was always filled with pretty ladies, chattering and laughing over endless cups of pungent . . ." She paused to frown, and executed a delicate shrug. "I suppose the amber-colored liquid in the dainty, hand-painted cups must have been tea."

"Umm." Enmeshed in her childhood memories, Darcy missed the wry, knowing expression that swept across Jonathan's features; the look was gone almost as swiftly as it appeared. "Tea. Yes, well. And your father?" he probed.

Darcy blinked. "My father? Why, I barely knew him." Her soft mouth curved in sorrow for an instant, then reversed itself into a sweet, reminiscent smile. "His name was Charles, and he was wonderful, handsome, and charming." Her eyes and smile grew misty; it didn't matter, Darcy was no longer gazing at Jonathan, but inward, at the father she had adored, and the loving child she had once been. "When he was there, the house seemed brighter, even more vibrant and alive. He loved to laugh . . . and derived great pleasure from teasing mother and me, making us laugh along with him." A longing sigh shuddered through her now sadness-curved lips. "After Mother delivered me to Miss Reinholt at the school, I never saw him again."

"He died?" Jonathan asked, softly, sympathetically.

Although she should not have been, Darcy was startled by his question. "Why, he must have," she answered, more to herself than to him. "Mother never mentioned him again after I was sent off to school. I wonder why."

Jonathan's expression was unreadable; his observation was all too clear. "Passing strange . . . don't you think?"

Darcy withdrew, chilled by his intruding, too insightful query. "Not necessarily," she said in a low voice, tight from inner strain. "I was only six years old when I was placed into the school, you understand," she pointed out to him, while trying desperately herself to understand. "Knowing how very much I loved him, Mother possibly thought it best not to tell me about his demise and simply let my memories of him fade," she theorized, wondering, as she had done for a very long time, if that was what had, in fact, transpired.

Blatant skepticism transformed his features for a moment. Jonathan raised one eyebrow—a trait that Darcy was quickly becoming accustomed to—then his expression changed to one of bland smoothness.

Ignoring a niggling feeling that he had cause for skepticism, and feeling a sudden need for motion, Darcy stood, only to prowl back and forth between the table and the doorway leading into the connecting sitting room.

What had happened to her father? The question nagged at Darcy, causing a sick sensation to invade her stomach . . . and her mind. In an attempt to silence the inner voice, she decided to turn the tables on Jonathan.

"What about you?" Darcy came to a halt some three or so feet away from where he continued to hover over the seat of the chair. Without conscious volition, she mirrored his expression by raising one delicate auburn eyebrow. "What about your life"—she frowned and shook her head—"and death." Not pausing long enough to allow him to respond, she rushed on, "I mean, how did you die . . . and why are you here, in this . . ."

Darcy broke off abruptly, startled by the unmistakable sounds of a raucous altercation at the front of the house, carried into the room on the warm summer breeze.

"What in the world . . ." she began, only to be cut off by a harsh masculine voice, raised in anger.

"And I said I'm comin' in!"

The man's threatening statement was followed by protests from several female voices.

"Now what *is* going on?" Darcy exclaimed, turning to stride with purposeful steps to the door.

"And where in hell is Clancy?" The deep-voiced question came from directly behind her right shoulder.

Darcy gave a muffled gasp, startled by Jonathan's silent swiftness in his move from the chair to her side. "I sincerely wish you would not do that!" she admonished him, swinging the door open with an unsteady hand.

"Do what?" Jonathan asked in feigned innocence, gliding silently behind her as she strode along the narrow corridor toward the stairs.

"You know perfectly well . . . what," Darcy

scolded, increasing her pace at the sound of shouting from below. "You are beginning to unnerve me with your here-then-gone trick."

"I'd apologize but, you see, I'm having so much fun with it." Jonathan laughed, teasing her senses in an even more intense, unnerving manner.

But Darcy didn't have time to probe the uncanny sensations thrumming through her. She had to investigate what sounded to her like a full-blown riot ensuing at the front door.

She didn't hesitate upon reaching the second-floor landing, but immediately began descending the stairs. Even as Darcy started down the stairs, Katie started up them.

"I was coming to get you," she said, casting a quick glance behind her.

"What is all this racket about?" Darcy demanded, coming to a stop midway on the staircase.

"There's a man, a miner from the gold fields, insisting that he be let inside," Katie explained, grimacing.

Darcy took in at a glance the situation in the foyer. Dora stood, her hands planted on her broad hips, in the open doorway, denying entrance to a tall, thin, scruffy-looking man, whose face was ruddy with anger.

"Where is Clancy?" Darcy asked with enforced calm, while fighting against an urge to flee back to her bedroom.

"My question, exactly," Jonathan drawled from behind her right shoulder.

Darcy cast a quick, nervous look at the woman standing to her left, one step below, to see if she had heard Jonathan's remark, and sighed with relief when it was instantly obvious that she had not.

"He left not fifteen minutes ago," Katie was saying, gazing narrowly down the stairs, not noticing the specter over Darcy's shoulder. "Had some supplies to pick up in town."

Before Katie had finished speaking, there was a loud outcry from Dora as the dirty, unkempt man roughly pushed the cook's solid figure aside and stomped into the foyer.

"Where's La Rouge?" the man bellowed. "A man gits tired of humpin' those dirty whores up there in the camps. And La Rouge promised me that I could have Sarah," he railed on, jerking his head at the girl cowering in the parlor doorway with the rest of the women of the house.

"The clod's a swine," Jonathan murmured in tones of anger and disgust.

Shocked to the core by the man's crudity, Darcy ignored Jonathan, even though she did agree with him.

"I told you the house is closed," Dora said, shaking with fury as she glared at the man.

"It ain't closed to me," he snarled, lifting a hand to brandish a bulging leather sack. "La Rouge told me I could have Sarah on the day I could show her my poke filled with gold worth a thousand dollars."

"Only because she believed he'd never see that much gold, let alone own it," Katie muttered. "Colleen wouldn't have let him anywhere near young Sarah."

"You'll have to come back later," Dora said, and everyone knew she meant when Clancy was there.

"Come back!" the loudmouth shouted. "I ain't movin' a step from here until I see La Rouge."

"La Rouge is dead."

There was an instant's silence at the slicing sound of Darcy's cold voice; then the uncouth man raised his eyes to the stairs and fixed a hard stare on her.

"Dead," he repeated, squinting up at her. "I don't believe you at all."

"You are free to believe what you wish, sir," Darcy returned in icy hauteur. "Nevertheless, this house is closed, in mourning for . . . La Rouge."

"That so?" The man took a step toward the stairs, forcing Darcy to plumb the depths of her willpower to remain motionless, back straight, chin raised in apparent fearlessness. "And just who might you be?"

"I am La Rouge's daughter," Darcy replied cuttingly. "I now own this house. And your name, sir?" she asked, not out of politeness but because she might have need of the knowledge to relay to the local law authorities.

The man's eyes shifted evasively. "Name's . . . er . . . Mason!" he announced, shifting his eyes, and a smug expression, back to her. "Robert Mason."

"Well, Mr. Mason," she said, repressing a shudder of utter revulsion for the man. "Now that you are aware of the situation, I would appreciate it if you would remove yourself from the premises."

"I could materialize in front of him," Jonathan whispered close to her ear. "I've been practicing my new abilities, and I could do it without the others seeing me. That ought to get him moving—just nod your head if that's your wish."

"Be silent," Darcy hissed beneath her breath.

Jonathan laughed, causing her to shudder again, but for an altogether different reason than her recent revulsion.

"I dunno," Robert Mason said, moving closer to the stairs, thereby capturing Darcy's full attention. "I bin waitin' all winter and spring, piling up this here gold, just to dip my wick in that sweet-smellin' Sarah."

Darcy felt suddenly sick, and panicky. Continuing to appear coolly composed was becoming more difficult with each passing moment. "Mr. Mason, I insist that you leave this house at once," she ordered in a voice even she could hear was beginning to lose its strength.

"Not 'til I get what I came for," he said, giving a sharp shake of his filthy, lanky-haired head. "But now I changed my mind." He hefted the bag in his hand and ran a hot-eyed look the length of Darcy's body. "I don't want Sarah no more," he went on, fastening his avid gaze on Darcy's breasts. "I wanna pump into you."

Darcy gagged, and grasped the stair railing to keep herself upright on her suddenly weakened knees.

"Over my . . . er, recently dead body," Jonathan snarled.

"Don't you dare to talk to Miss Flynn like that!" Quiet throughout the proceedings, Dora now shrieked like a banshee. "You get yourself out of here . . . this minute."

"Who's gonna make me go?" he sneered, not even bothering to look at the cook. "You?"

"No," Katie answered, slowly removing her right hand from the deep pocket in her night wrapper. "This," she told him, producing a long-barreled pistol and pointing it directly at him with a rock-steady hand.

5

"I knew there had to be more than the one obvious reason that I liked Katie."

It took a few moments for Jonathan's drolly delivered remark to register on Darcy's overshocked mind and jangled emotions. And then, when it did register, she could do no more than stare at him for another few moments.

Upon reentering the bedroom, Darcy had collapsed onto the elegant chaise longue, weak and shaken from the terrible scene enacted in the foyer. The excitement was over; peace had been restored to the house and its residents. The crude and foul-mouthed interloper had been ejected— thanks to Katie, and the lethal-looking weapon she had secreted within the pocket of her wrapper.

Having by now become accustomed to Jonathan's hovering presence, Darcy had not been startled and unnerved by the mere sound of his voice, but by the content of his dryly voiced statement.

"Obvious reason?" Darcy frowned with disapproval. "Are you saying that you have been . . ." She paused, forced to swallow against a sudden, inexplicable tightness in her throat. "You were *intimate* with Katie?"

"Darcy . . . think," Jonathan chided, gliding across the room to take up a languid position near the open window, and appearing as solid in substance as the wood frame encasing it. "This is, or at least was, a house maintained for the sole purpose of pleasure. Being quite normal, as well as quite alive, at the time, I did occasionally seek my pleasure here."

"With Katie." Darcy's voice was faint, little more than a disbelieving whisper.

"Yes," Jonathan replied with blunt candor. "But please understand, I do not tell you this to upset or shock you, but because I cannot be less than honest. You asked, Darcy. I must answer truthfully."

For some totally obscure and confusing reason, Darcy felt stricken, drained, and close to the point of tears by Jonathan's admission of having indulged with a prostitute. Intellectually, she knew that men, decent as well as disreputable, being men, had occasion to frequent these houses of ill repute and, intellectually, she accepted it.

But Darcy's reaction stemmed, not from an intellectual level but from an emotional source; therein lay the root cause of her confusion.

Why should she care how and with whom Jonathan had appeased his sensual appetite? Darcy asked herself. Of a certainty, she felt a sense of repugnance for his apparent lack of accepted moral concepts, she conceded. But in all reason, why should the question of morality matter now, when he no longer existed in the physical plane?

"Darcy?" Jonathan snagged her attention with his soft call. "Have I shocked your sensibilities?"

"No, of course not," she denied quickly, too quickly, lying to herself as well as to him.

"No?" He performed that now familiar exercise of arching one eyebrow. "Then why are you staring at me with that shattered expression on your beautiful face?"

Why indeed? Darcy derided herself, lost to his compliment within the maze of her mind. If she was the intelligent woman she considered herself to be, then why was she experiencing this dreadful hollow feeling?

The answer lay close to the surface of her consciousness, waiting for her to acknowledge it, if she dared.

"Darcy, are you feeling ill?" Jonathan's tone and expression revealed growing concern.

Darcy knew she had to respond to him, either by contriving some story to put him off, or confessing to her true feelings—if she could find the courage to do so, by examining the contents of her heart as well as her mind.

Miss Reinholt did not suffer cowards; she instilled strength of character and purpose into the students under her tutelage and care. Darcy had been no exception.

Gathering her resources, Darcy faced the truth of her discomfiture. The name of her truth was Katie; it was the fact of Katie that bothered Darcy, more than the self-admitted fact of Jonathan having used a prostitute.

But in addition to her sense of dismay concerning Katie, and incredible and ridiculous as it most certainly was, within the course of one short day, Darcy had begun to think of Jonathan as somehow belonging to her; her own special and private live-in spirit, as it were.

The cause of her internal dilemma at least partially resolved, Darcy opened her mouth to confess, if only regarding Katie, then as quickly shut it again when another, even more upsetting, consideration struck her.

Jonathan had admitted to occasionally seeking his pleasure in the house with Katie but . . . had he sought his pleasure in her mother's bed as well?

Without conscious volition, Darcy's body reacted in two ways: Her gaze flew to the bed, while one hand moved to cover her queasy stomach.

"My mother," she blurted out artlessly. "Did you also occasionally spend time in this room, on that bed, with my mother?"

"No."

The absolute, unequivocal sound of Jonathan's voice sent a quiver of sheer relief through Darcy. The queasiness in her stomach miraculously vanished; a conciliatory smile teased the corners of her sternly set mouth. Once again, without question, she accepted his word.

"But what difference would it make now if I had enjoyed the singular privilege of your mother's bed?" Jonathan continued, looking genuinely perplexed.

His inquiry created a quandary in Darcy, a plight so fraught with uncertainty she completely missed his use of the term *singular* in relation to her mother.

The connotations of the word *singular* were far

overshadowed by the initial part of his query. How could she explain a purely emotional reaction she herself barely understood? If her feelings had stemmed from the unsavory fact of her mother's occupation, she could then explain away her sense of repugnance. But in truth, that was not the case. Shocked as she had been, and still was, by the information about her mother's choice of lifestyle, it was not the reason for her recoil at the thought of Jonathan and her mother being together.

Jonathan waited patiently for a few minutes while Darcy plowed through the puzzle of her own feelings, then he regained the initiative.

"We are both no longer of this world, confined and controlled by its conventions and constrictions," he reminded her, his eyes aglow with inner amusement. "The moral strictures conceived and imposed by physical beings no longer apply. Colleen and I are both now free spirits."

"Spirits!" Darcy sent a wide-eyed look around the room. "She's here, in spirit?" Not waiting for a reply from him, she leapt from the chaise to dash about, into the dressing room and from there to the sitting room, and back again into the bedroom, crying out plaintively, like an abandoned but hopeful child. "Mother . . . Mother!"

"Darcy, stop." Jonathan's tone contained equal measures of command and sympathy. "She is not here."

"Not here?" Darcy asked, shoulders slumping dejectedly. "Not here?" she repeated in a wail.

"No." Jonathan frowned. "At least I have not seen her."

"But . . ." Darcy blinked against a rising flood of stinging tears. "Where is she, then?"

"I don't know," he admitted, his frown deepening in consternation. "But I must assume that Colleen is somewhere in that realm of light."

His response triggered a recent memory in Darcy, recalling to her mind his earlier mention of a light . . . and a summons of some sort. "You said something about a light before," she said, moving closer to him. "You also mentioned a summons." She stared into his so-real-looking eyes. "What light? What summons?"

Jonathan gazed into Darcy's anguish-dimmed, tear-sparkled hazel-green eyes and felt a pang of emotion he had assumed he was now beyond experiencing. The sensation was similar to the one he had previously felt when he had reached out to touch her cheek while she was sleeping.

Odd, he mused; the sensation was almost physical. How, he pondered, was this sense of feeling possible in a being no longer of the physical dimension?

Unable to find answers for himself, he directed his attention to answering Darcy's questions.

"Come," he said, drifting past her as he made for the sitting room. "Sit down," he invited, smiling as she followed him without question or protest. "I will endeavor to answer all of your questions concerning my presence here." He frowned, then qualified, "As best I can."

"Why are you here?" Darcy asked, mirroring his frown. "I mean, in this particular house?"

"Oh, that one's easy," Jonathan replied, smiling. "I died in this house."

"Died here!" Darcy exclaimed. "When? How?"

"Recently," he answered. "On the same night your mother passed over, as a matter of fact," he clarified. "While Colleen lay dying up here, in her bedroom, I was murdered downstairs, in the barroom."

"Murdered!" Darcy blanched.

"Accidentally," Jonathan said, hastening to reassure her. "The knife had been meant for another man."

"Knife," Darcy repeated in a faint, shocked whisper. Then, her wide-eyed gaze darting wildly about, she muttered, "I cannot remain here."

"But this is now all yours, your responsibility," Jonathan reminded her, giving a sweeping move of his hand to indicate the property and all it contained.

"I don't care," Darcy retorted, bolting out of the delicate chair. "Ever since I arrived in this . . . place, I have received one appalling shock after another." She visibly swallowed before going on to recount the disturbing events. "I only learned about my mother's death when Mr. Mansford literally pulled me from the train station. Telling me he would explain later, he then practically flung me into a buggy, which conveyed me not to the church cemetery I expected to see but to a barren, desolate place where my mother was interred in unconsecrated ground."

"Darcy," Jonathan said soothingly in an attempt to both comfort and calm her. But it appeared that Darcy had gone beyond the point of being comforted or calmed.

"From that dreadful place," she rushed on as

if he had not interrupted, "I was conveyed to this house, only to learn about my mother's *business*, and to be introduced to her employees. Then, as if that had not been enough, I was escorted to this apartment, only to subsequently be confronted by a man whom I believed to be an intruder, only to learn he was a ghost!"

Jonathan sighed. "I thought you had accepted it."

"Accepted! Accepted!" Darcy cried. "I may have come to accept my mother's death, that terrible burial place, the circumstances of this house, even *you*," she ranted. "But I cannot accept that horrible incident downstairs created by that despicable man, or the fact of murder . . . inside the house."

"I told you that was an accident," he said in a reasonable tone, hoping to calm the storm of her emotional outburst. "There was a flare-up of tempers, and a knife was tossed. It could happen anywhere."

"No. No." Shaking her head in sharp denial, Darcy moved around him—as if he were not ethereal but as solid as the furniture—and marched into the dressing room. "It could not happen in Miss Reinholt's school."

Jonathan was beside her in an instant, simply by desiring to be there. "What are you doing?" he demanded, scowling as she removed the two carpetbags from the armoire.

Darcy didn't bother to look at him, but began pulling clothes from the overlarge cupboard. "I am returning to Philadelphia, on the first available train."

"Darcy, wait." Jonathan reached out to grasp her shoulder, and sighed when his hand passed through her arm; sighed and jolted with surprise at the zephyr of sensation he experienced in that briefest of instants.

Jonathan went still for a moment; as it had before, when he had thought only to brush the auburn tress from her cheek, the tingling of feeling intrigued him. Then he shook his head. He had no time to pause and reflect on it. Since he could not stop her in a physical sense, he knew he had to use some convincing argument to halt her precipitous actions.

"What about the house?" he asked, moving to stand in front of her, which required blending with the armoire.

Darcy started at the sight of him with the wood grain appearing to run through his face. "Honestly, Jonathan!" she exclaimed, clutching the armful of clothing to her chest. "You are enough to give a body the fits."

"Sorry, but I needed to get your attention," he apologized. "What about this house?" he repeated.

"I cannot stay here." Turning, she marched back into the bedroom and tossed the clothes onto the bed. "I will instruct Mr. Mansford to sell the property."

"And the women with it?" Jonathan inadvertently startled her again by appearing before her.

Darcy drew a quick breath and gave him a stern, chastising look. "You cannot sell women."

"No?" He arched a brow in mockery. "Perhaps

not, but you can condemn them to a life of degradation."

"I!" she protested hotly. "I am not responsible for their situation or for their choice of occupation."

"Ah, Darcy, do you really believe that, for the most part, they had any real choice?"

"What do you mean?" She gave him a wary look, as if expecting a trap.

Jonathan couldn't contain a tiny smile since, of course, he was attempting to snare her. "Well, take Sarah, for instance. She is barely sixteen. She lost her mother a year ago; the poor woman died in self-defense against physical and mental abuse as well as overwork." He felt a thrill of satisfaction from the sympathetic, attentive expression on Darcy's lovely face. "Sarah's father is a brute and a drunk," he continued with cool deliberation. "When he had a skinful, as the saying goes, which was most of the time, his favored form of expression was beating his wife and daughter."

"Oh, no."

From the look on Darcy's face, in her eyes, Jonathan knew she was envisioning the young, timid woman. Feeling the thrill of satisfaction deepen, he pulled the snare a little tighter. "Yes, but that isn't the worst of it. Though Sarah suffered many beatings, at least while her mother lived, she had a roof over her head and the comfort of her mother's love. But within days after her mother passed over, her father brought another woman into the house to 'do' for him and, without a care or a warning, threw Sarah out, into the streets."

"Dear God," Darcy whispered, seemingly unaware of the tears trickling down her pale cheeks.

"Indeed," Jonathan agreed, while consciously tugging once more on the snare. "Since she has received no training, tell me, what was she supposed to do to earn her way?" He didn't give her time to reply before delivering what he felt sure was his most effective information. "Young Sarah is uneducated, you see. She can neither read nor write."

"What?" Darcy said, reacting precisely as Jonathan suspected she would. "Are there no schools in Denver?" she demanded, quivering with responsive outrage.

"Certainly," he answered. "But their mere presence does not guarantee attendance by every child. A parent has to be willing to send a child off to school, and in Sarah's case, as in many of the others, the parent was not willing."

"But what will happen to Sarah now?" Darcy cried, as if in actual pain.

Jonathan shrugged. He was intentionally manipulating Darcy, he knew, and from deep within his consciousness he sent out a plea to the light for forgiveness.

"My mother bequeathed a sum of money to each of the women, surely with that they can—"

"Do what?" Jonathan interrupted her to ask. "Buy a 'house' of their own, in a city already full of such 'houses'?"

"But isn't there something else they can do? Some other form of occupation?"

Darcy was beginning to look harried, and fatigued; Jonathan had to fight an urge to relent, give way, and let her rest. But he could not, not after resisting the light. "What, exactly, would you suggest?"

Darcy waved one hand in a helpless manner. "Couldn't they use their legacies to purchase some sort of shop? A ladies' emporium . . . or something?"

"Maybe Katie and one or two of the others could succeed in such a venture," he conceded. "But the other three or four? I doubt it. You see, Darcy, Sarah's story is not unique. The majority of prostitutes have little choice in profession." His smile was gentle, and sad. "To practice it, to earn a living, one does not need a formal education."

"But what can I do?" Darcy asked in a desolate whisper as she sank wearily onto the side of the bed. "I absolutely cannot operate a . . . a . . ."

"Whorehouse, bordello, brothel, crib, cathouse?" Jonathan inserted. "They are only words, Darcy. Take your pick. You can't be tainted by merely saying a word."

"You're making fun of me," she accused him in a tremulous, injured voice.

"No, dear lady, I am not," Jonathan denied, offering her a sympathetic smile. "I am attempting to assure you, help you to understand that there is really no reason for you to put yourself through this upheaval."

"But I don't see, don't under—"

"Miss Flynn?" Sarah's soft call was followed by a light tap against the door.

"Yes, Sarah, what is it?" Darcy responded, casting a worried look at him.

"May I come in, please?" the girl requested in a shy, hesitant tone of voice.

"Yes, of course," Darcy answered, staring questioningly at Jonathan.

He smiled and inclined his head in a gesture of agreement and approval.

"The door is unlocked."

In a gliding move, seemingly casual and unplanned, but in fact calculated and experimental, Jonathan positioned himself directly in the path the young woman would take upon entrance into the room.

As Clancy had the day before, Sarah opened the door and walked in—passing right through Jonathan. He felt nothing, not a tingle, not a shiver of sensation, not even so much as a breath of awareness. So far as he was concerned, the results of his experiment were conclusive; his sensory-like feelings were aroused by the essence of only one physical being. Jonathan smiled as he observed her reaction to the scene.

For her part, it was obvious that Darcy was neither amazed nor shocked this time by witnessing a solid being pass through his ethereal body.

Without so much as a flicker of one eyelash, she merely smiled at him as he glided back to her side, and at the visibly nervous young woman. "Is something wrong, Sarah?" she asked, but rushed on before the girl could reply. "I pray you have not come to tell me there is yet another insistent customer demanding entrance at the door."

"Oh, no, ma'am," Sarah said, shaking her head vigorously. "It's right quiet now. Besides, Clancy's back, and he'd make fast work of anyone who'd cause a ruckus." She picked at her skirt with nervous fingers, then blurted out breathlessly, "It's just that we, that is, the other girls and me, were wonderin' if you would like to eat dinner with us."

"Dinner?" Darcy echoed, quickly glancing at the window in disbelief, as if in astonishment that the day had slipped away so swiftly.

"The midday meal, Darcy." Jonathan enlightened her in an inner whisper.

Though he knew Darcy heard his lowered voice, he saw the confusion she felt at having it sound inside her head. A very corporeal feeling of tenderness welled up in him as he watched her search the unchanged expression on the girl's face, and sigh softly in relief that Sarah had not heard him.

"I . . . ah," Darcy began, as if she had lost track of the discussion at hand.

"Dora's heated up the beef stew from last night's supper," Sarah said, ending Darcy's dilemma. "And she made apple cobbler this morning," she added as an inducement. "And we really would like it if you sat down with us."

"Thank you, Sarah," Darcy said without hesitation. "I am a little hungry, and would be happy to join all of you for the meal. I will be down as soon as I freshen up."

"Oh, that'll be grand!" Sarah exclaimed, her smile brightening her entire face. "I'll tell the others," she said, turning and dashing from the room.

"Excellent." Jonathan praised her decision, this time speaking to her ears, not her mind. "I'm certain you won't regret it." He gave her a wry smile. "Despite what is considered their unsavory profession, I think if you give them a chance, get to know them, you will find that they are good people." He softened his smile. "And in case you didn't know, each and every one of them adored your mother."

Darcy gave a brief, negative shake of her head, loosening a shimmering strand of hair at her nape. Jonathan was so intrigued by the look of vulnerability the auburn curl lent to her otherwise composed appearance, he nearly missed her adamant, astonished reply.

"No, I did not know that. How could I have? I didn't know about them until I arrived here."

"Of course," he conceded, nodding. "But now you've been offered an opportunity to learn, and as a teacher yourself, I hope you will not waste it."

Darcy appeared affronted, as if her integrity had been impugned. "What, exactly, are you suggesting?" she demanded, drawing herself up stiffly.

"Only that you talk to them as equals." Jonathan infused a note of sternness into his voice. "And I implore you to listen and learn, and not pass judgment."

"I . . . I . . ." Darcy faltered, lowering her eyes in silent admission of having already passed judgment on the women of the house. "I will do my best," she finally murmured, raising her eyes to meet his.

"That's all I ask." He smiled at her. "I suspect your best is more than adequate."

"Will you be there?" The tremor in her voice betrayed her feelings of anxiety.

"I'll be there." His smile widened into a grin. "If only to help you over the rough spots."

* * *

It was not until Darcy stood before the wash-stand in the dressing room, splashing water into the washbowl from the matching pitcher, that the realization struck her that she not only had not heard the whole of Jonathan's own story, but had received very little actual information other than the appalling fact that he had been murdered in-side the house.

Darcy shuddered reflexively, and frowned at her reflection in the mirror above the washstand. The wide hazel green eyes staring back at her revealed the conflict churning inside her.

Gnawing on her bottom lip, Darcy acknowl-edged that, while part of her longed to remove herself from the dangers inherent in the raw and apparently often brutal conditions of the Western frontier, and flee back to the accustomed, civilized environs of Philadelphia, another part urged her to stay and experience the earthier side of life.

A sampling of that experience awaited Darcy downstairs, in the dining room. Splashing cool water onto her face, she decided to approach the coming meeting with the women of the house as an experiment, a test of her own inner fiber and strength.

If she managed the meeting with a modicum of aplomb, Darcy mused as she dried her face, then absently tucked a wayward strand of hair into place, perhaps she would remain in Denver for a while.

Her muscles clenching in preparation for her impending ordeal, Darcy smoothed her palms over her skirt, straightened her spine, and pulled her composure around her like a cloak before returning to the bedroom.

"Ready?"

Not trusting her voice to answer her spirit companion, Darcy responded with an acquiescent nod of her head.

"There is really no need for you to be nervous," he said, gliding through the door before she could open it. "I'll be right there, by your side," he finished after she had exited the room and joined him in the corridor.

"Prompting me with a voice inside my mind?"

"Yes." Jonathan chuckled.

"How do you do that?" Darcy demanded, coming to an abrupt halt at the top of the staircase.

"I'll have to explain later," he promised, inclining his head to indicate the group of women waiting at the foot of the stairs and gazing up at her.

And that's not all he will explain, Darcy promised herself, smiling as she slowly descended the stairs.

Whether her decision afterward was to go or stay, Darcy was bound and determined to hear the whole of Jonathan's story and his reasons for remaining—or, as he had stated it, resisting the light, whatever that meant.

6

Although he consumed none of the food Dora set before them, Jonathan was very much a presence at the dining room table, appearing then disappearing from one vantage point, only to reappear again somewhere else, to hover alongside or behind yet another of the unsuspecting women.

Well, perhaps not entirely unsuspecting, Darcy allowed after noticing the fourth member of the party shiver and glance uneasily over her shoulder. And even though none of them mentioned the cause of their disquietude, it early on became patently obvious to Darcy that they all were experiencing unusual sensations from his nearness.

Since she alone of the women could actually see him, Darcy had at first been distracted by Jonathan, and not unreasonably so, considering the fact that he was not only there but determinedly vocal as well.

Fortunately, for Darcy's understandably jangled nervous system, Jonathan chose to speak in the normal sense, rather than project his voice directly into her mind. Even so, beginning to feel panicked because she suddenly couldn't recall any names other than Katie and Sarah, she had started at the initial comments he had made after they reached the women waiting for them at the bottom of the stairs.

"We're glad you decided to come down."

"That's Katie," he drawled, passing through the woman to observe the proceedings from the fringes of the group. "Blunt and to the point." His smile was as dry as his tone of voice. "She *chose* the way of prostitution after her miner husband was killed in a dispute over placer mining rights. Being smart, if uneducated, Katie soon learned that the fastest way to get her point across was to get directly to the point—whatever that point might be."

Though she felt grateful for the information he provided her, Darcy had been forced to suppress a jolt of reaction to his move before responding to Katie's remark. "I . . . I am glad you invited me," she said, averting her eyes from the cause of her unsteady voice.

"Invited you!" an amply endowed, curvaceous woman exclaimed. "Why, you're the owner of the place. Colleen's daughter. You don't need no invitation."

"That's Daisy," Jonathan said, a gentle smile curving his lips as he gazed at the woman. "She was a foundling, never knew her parents. She ran away, with reason, from the orphanage when she was thirteen." His soft eyes were darkened by compassion. "She was in pretty bad condition when your mother took her in, and under her protection."

"Nevertheless, I do appreciate being asked,"

Darcy replied, unknowingly mirroring Jonathan's compassionate smile. "I consider it a kind and friendly gesture."

Jonathan drifted in the lead as they slowly made their way into the dining room. But his voice seemed to come from beside her as he continued to give the name and a brief history of each successive woman who spoke.

"It's well deserved, in a way." The coolly voiced remark came from a tall, slender, handsome woman with warm brown eyes and enviable classic and ageless bone structure. "Your mother, Colleen, was ever friendly and more than kind to each and every one of us."

"That's Jane." Jonathan projected his voice to Darcy from the dining room. "Everyone good-naturedly calls her 'Lady Jane' because of her regal bearing and air of breeding. It's a facade, copied from Colleen and assumed for self-protective purposes. In truth, Jane was born in a make-shift hovel. Her father raised hogs, when he could work up the energy to bother. The place was isolated, located some distance from the nearest neighbors and town. Jane had three older, larger brothers with equally large sexual appetites. In between their infrequent visits to town, they used Jane as a source of relief."

Darcy suddenly felt sick to her stomach, and had to force herself to keep walking toward the table. She didn't want to hear any more, but Jonathan wasn't finished.

"Jane escaped from the pigsty when she was seventeen by running away with a drifter, who was passing through the district and stopped at the hovel to beg a meal. The drifter forced Jane into selling herself in exchange for their food and lodging. But he made his mistake when he approached your mother." His voice took on a note of grim amusement. "Colleen befriended Jane, and let Clancy take care of the drifter."

Darcy and her eager entourage had entered the dining room by the time Jonathan stopped speaking. The aroma wafting on the steam rising from the bowls Dora was setting on the table increased the sick feeling in Darcy's stomach.

"You sit yourself down right here, Miss Flynn," said yet another of the women, indicating the chair at the head of the table with a wave of her arm. The woman was small, pretty, apple-cheeked, with a fresh-from-the-farm look. "It was Colleen's place, and now it's yours."

Feeling weak-kneed from the education she was receiving on the realities of life, Darcy gratefully sank onto the chair and managed a smile of thanks for the sweet-faced girl.

"That's Sally." Now Jonathan's voice held genuine amusement. "Sally's story is simple . . . she got into the business because she likes it."

Darcy nearly choked on the sip of water she had taken in hopes of washing down the taste of bile in her throat.

Positioned behind Katie's chair, Jonathan grinned across the table at Darcy. "Sally considers being paid for what she likes to do a delightful bonus."

"Oh, do stop, please," Darcy blurted out unthinkingly, gazing back at him in entreaty.

Absolute silence settled on the room for several

long moments; the women around the table stared at Darcy in stunned disbelief; Dora stopped dead midway between the kitchen and the dining room, to also stare at her.

Appalled at her lapse, Darcy sat mute, barely breathing as she stared in chagrin into Jonathan's sparkling, laughter-filled gray eyes.

"Stop?" Katie repeated, finally breaking the silence—very likely because Darcy appeared to be staring at her. "Stop what, Miss Flynn?"

Darcy's mind had gone blank for one terrifying instant. In desperation, she had looked to Jonathan for help; but obviously enjoying himself, he had chosen that moment to remain quiet, feigning innocence.

With the realization that Jonathan had no intention of helping her extricate herself from the situation she had created, Darcy raked her mind for a response to Katie, and said the first thing that flashed through her consciousness.

"Why, er, why, stop calling me Miss Flynn." She slowly exhaled her pent-up breath as she watched their expressions change from shock to pleased surprise. "I would appreciate it if all of you would call me Darcy."

"Quick thinking," Jonathan said, grinning at her quite like a proud parent or tutor.

On guard, Darcy then ignored him, turning instead to respond to the chattered comments from her suddenly animated and vocal companions.

"Well, Darcy," Katie said, with real warmth in her voice, "it seems that you don't only look like Colleen but really are like her."

"Yeah, and I'm so glad!" Sally gushed. "I was

kinda worried that you'd be stuck-up or something."

"Here, Darcy, help yourself to some stew," Daisy urged, passing one of the steaming bowls to her. "You'll like it, 'cause Dora makes the best stew in the territory."

"Get on with you," Dora said, flushing with pleasure as she continued into the room and directly over to Darcy's chair to offer her first choice from the basket of hot rolls she was bringing to the table.

"Thank you," Darcy murmured, smiling at Daisy as she served herself from the bowl, and then at Dora, as she took a roll from the basket. The combined aromas of hearty beef stew and warm, yeasty rolls banished the sick feeling in her stomach. Her hunger renewed—and her audience watchful—Darcy sampled a bite of the savory stew and followed it by tasting a small piece she broke off the roll.

"Delicious." Her enthusiastic pronouncement broke the strain of anticipatory expectation. Smiling with evident relief, Darcy's table companions dug into their food, while Dora returned to the kitchen with a lighter step.

"Wait 'til you taste Dora's cobbler—it's even better than my own mother made, and hers was wonderful." The praise came from a dark-haired woman of twenty or so, whom Darcy realized had to be either June or Molly.

"June," Jonathan said, continuing with his supply of personal histories. "June suddenly and tragically found herself on her own at the age of fourteen when her parents were killed during a raid on their small farm by a band of marauding Cheyenne Indians in the spring of '64. She escaped her parents' fate only because her mother had sent her out, into the bushes, to gather the first of the wild strawberries, and she burrowed into the thick brush, hiding until the Indians had gone. With no relatives to go to, and no one to care about her, she found work in several rough bordellos before coming here. June almost worshipped your mother, because Colleen treated her not only as a human being but as an equal as well."

"After tasting Dora's stew and rolls, I'm looking forward to the cobbler," Darcy replied, smiling warmly at the woman. "And the scent of coffee from the kitchen positively makes my mouth water."

Her response elicited laughter from the women around the table, and comment from the last one of the group, whose story Darcy had not yet heard.

"Ahh, the smell of Dora's coffee could make the mouths of angels water." The woman had chestnut hair, laughing blue eyes, and an abundance of freckles sprinkled over her fair-skinned nose and cheeks.

"Molly," Jonathan stated. "Molly was a throwaway, a child nobody wanted, including her shiftless parents. Chasing the mythical pot of gold, they abandoned her here in Denver on their way through to the fields and mines. No one cared enough to look for them. Clancy found her selling drinks, and her body, in one of the worst saloons in town. He brought her to Colleen . . . who did care. While Molly loved your mother, she was and

is *in* love with Clancy." He grinned. "The dumb
Irishman has yet to realize it."

It was as Darcy fought to contain a reciprocal
grin that she became aware of a change in her
perception of the women. Her feelings of sympathy and compassion were still there, but underly-
ing those emotions was a growing sense of
admiration for their endurance and fortitude.

If put to the test, would she measure up to the
mettle of these courageous women? Darcy mused,
looking at each one with respect as well as admiration. If she were to suddenly find herself in dire
straits similar to those faced by these women,
could she not only survive but find the inner
strength to laugh as easily? Darcy seriously
doubted it.

The conversation flowed smoothly throughout
the meal, the majority of which consisted of the
eager questions aimed at Darcy by the women, her
answers to them, and the occasional comment
tossed in for her benefit from their unseen guest.

Darcy was fascinated by the range of queries put
to her by the women. At one time or another, she
was asked her opinion on such diverse subjects as
the latest Philadelphia fashions, the stories they
had heard of the devastation of the reconstruction
of the South, speculations about the golden dream
of California and Oregon, and about advance-
ments in the field of medicine for women and children.

Darcy could not recall ever having felt quite so
stimulated by an impromptu conversation.

Now, with the remnants of the meal cleared
away, and cups of rich dark coffee before them on

the table, an atmosphere of relaxed congeniality prevailed.

"It must have been wonderful, being a teacher and living right there at that school," Sarah said in a wistful, longing tone of voice.

"Yes, it was," Darcy replied, feeling a pang inside for the girl who had never attended any kind of school.

"The school I went to for three years was cold in winter and hot in summer," Katie said, grimacing. "I hated it and the teacher. She was old and mean."

Well, Jonathan certainly was correct in his assessment of Katie, Darcy reflected. She was blunt and to the point.

"They envy you." This time, Jonathan's voice whispered through her mind.

I admire them, Darcy thought in silent response.

"I never went to school," June recalled, capturing Darcy's wandering attention. "But my mama taught me to read and write some before she . . . er, died."

"I'd like to be able to read and write my name," Sarah said in that same wistful voice. "There was a man killed here the night your mother died," she told Darcy. "He told me I could still learn to read and write." Her eyes revealed heartbreaking appeal. "Could I, do you think?"

"Of course you could," Darcy concurred at once, flicking a quick glance at the gently smiling specter. "Who was this man, Sarah?" she probed, hoping to learn something herself.

"I didn't know him too good, but his name was Jonathan Stuart, and he was a real gentleman."

She slid a sly look at Katie. "He was a regular customer during the last year or so, wasn't he?"

She shifted her glance around the table.

"Yes, he was," Katie said, answering for everyone. "But I was the only one he ever chose, and that not too often."

"Blunt and to the point," Jonathan reiterated.

"Yet he spent a lot of time here?" Darcy asked, noting that Katie had confirmed Jonathan's claim of having only occasionally appeased his needs with the woman.

"Hmm." Katie nodded. "He was here nearly every night, just sitting in the barroom, nursing one drink."

"The man kept to himself," Jane inserted. "He never bothered anybody. He was always polite, and spoke kindly to everyone. As Sarah said, a real gentleman."

"In public and private, too," Katie murmured. "He treated me like a lady, gentle and considerate." Her lips tightened. "He was never rough or brutish, like some of my customers."

"I didn't even know him, but I cried when he died," Sarah said in a soft tone of regret.

"We all did," Molly put in, shaking her head in sad remembrance. "What a night that was, all of us weeping and wailing, for our Colleen, and the nice Mr. Stuart."

"Yes," Sally murmured. "It's hard to believe it was only a coupla nights ago."

How terribly sad, Darcy thought, feeling a sting behind her eyelids. Life had been so very difficult for these women, and yet a kind word, a soft voice possessed the power to wring a deep emotional response from them.

"Regrettable, isn't it?" Jonathan whispered into her mind. "That it should require so little to gain such regard."

"Yes," Darcy answered Jonathan, unaware that she had answered Sally as well.

"We better change the subject, or we'll all start blubbering all over again," Katie said, impatiently brushing a tear from her cheek. "I think we need some more hot coffee," she decided as she pushed her chair back and stood up.

"And maybe a bit of a nip to lace it," Molly suggested, rising also. "I'll get the bottle."

At that moment, the sound of the brass knocker being struck against the front door reverberated through the house. Katie stopped dead midway around the table, her right hand slipping into her dress pocket and her eyes narrowing as she swung to face the dining room doorway.

"If that's that man again," she began, stalking to the doorway, "I'll take—"

"No, lass," Clancy interrupted her as he came charging out of the kitchen. "*I'll* be handling him."

"This should prove interesting," Jonathan observed, drifting along in Clancy's wake.

Almost as if the women had heard him, they moved as one, Darcy included, following Clancy into the foyer. With bated breath, they waited until the bouncer opened the door. A collective sigh eased from their throats at the sight of the neatly attired man standing on the porch.

"Ah, it's you, Mr. Singleton," Clancy said, smiling as he swung the door open wide. "Come right in," he invited in a deferential tone. "What can we do for you, sir?"

"I've come to pay my respects and offer my condolences to Miss Flynn," he replied, removing his jaunty-looking hat as he stepped into the foyer.

Darcy hung back for a moment, giving the man a thorough perusal before moving forward away from the others. The man was of average height, perhaps an inch or so taller than Darcy herself. He had a shock of sandy-colored hair and dark blue eyes, and was rather handsome.

"I am Darcy Flynn." Her composure intact, up to the standards insisted upon by Miss Reinholt, Darcy slowly walked toward him to extend her right hand. "Mr. Singleton?"

"Yes," he answered, taking her hand in a firm clasp. "James Singleton." His voice was pleasant, as easy on the ears as his appearance was on the eyes. "How do you do? I was your late mother's banker." His smile was charming. "She told me quite a bit about you, and it is indeed a pleasure to finally make your acquaintance."

"I'm afraid I am at a disadvantage, Mr. Singleton," Darcy confessed, removing her hand from his while returning his smile, if not quite as brightly. "My mother never mentioned your name to me."

"Of course, there would have been no reason for her to do so." Mr. Singleton did not appear chagrined; he merely inclined his head in acknowledgment. "And still, you had regular, if unknowing, contact with me."

"I did?" Darcy stared incredulously at him, startled by his claim. "I do not recall ever—"

"Your monthly allowance checks," he interrupted her gently. "I personally saw to their prompt dispatch."

"Oh!" Darcy exclaimed. "Yes, I understand." Her smile grew brighter, warmer. "And I am compelled to thank you for your dedication to duty on my behalf."

"Thank you, but I assure you it was my pleasure," James Singleton replied graciously. There was a low murmur of approval, and as if becoming aware of their avid audience for the first time, he frowned. "Soon I would like to meet with you privately, to discuss your account," he went on guardedly. "But for now, as I have already mentioned, I stopped by today to make your acquaintance and offer my condolences." He took a step back, toward the still open doorway. "I will be most happy to meet with you, either here or in my office in the bank, at your convenience, Miss Flynn."

"And I thank you for your understanding, consideration, and your kind offer of condolences, Mr. Singleton," Darcy replied, stepping closer to him to extend her hand once again. "I will contact you soon about a meeting."

"That will be fine." He took her hand and held it just a moment longer than propriety would admit. "Until then, it has been a distinct pleasure, Miss Flynn." Settling his hat on his head, Mr. Singleton nodded and stepped across the threshold, onto the porch.

Clancy quietly closed the door after him.

"Such a lovely man," Molly said on a wistful sigh.

"I always thought he was rather pompous," Jane retorted in an astringent tone of voice.

Darcy glanced at her in surprise.

Jonathan chuckled.

Katie gave Jane a knowing smile. "That's because he's never noticed the longing looks you give him."

Her remark elicited a burst of teasing laughter from the other women, as well as Clancy, who had begun making his way back to the kitchen.

"I never did!" Jane protested, flushing a dark red. She bristled a moment, then smiled deprecatingly. "All right, I admit it, I find James Singleton attractive."

"And you're sore because you've never found him in your bed," Daisy chided her raucously.

Stiffening, Darcy headed for the stairs. "If you will excuse me, I am a little tired." She paused at the base of the staircase to offer them a hard-fought-for smile. "Thank you all again for inviting me to join you for luncheon." Her smile held a hint of entreaty. "May I join you for dinner, too?"

Her request was answered by a chorus of indistinguishable voices, but all conveying a resounding "Yes."

"You handled that very well." Jonathan complimented Darcy the minute they were alone again.

"Thank you." Heaving a sigh, Darcy crossed the room to stand staring out the side window. "But which 'that' are you referring to? That initial mealtime meeting, or that period following Mr. Singleton's departure?"

Jonathan laughed, and zapped himself across the room to her side. "Both."

This time, Darcy didn't so much as blink at his sudden appearance, but merely slanted a wry glance at him instead. "I did appreciate your unsolicited information concerning the women, even though it was unnerving at first."

"Glad to be of assistance," Jonathan drawled, suppressing an inner desire to pass his hand through her hair, gleaming with enticing streaks of red in the afternoon sunlight.

She turned to him with a puzzled look. "I cannot help but wonder how you acquired all those details about their individual backgrounds."

Jonathan's smile was washed away by a thoughtful frown. "I'm not sure how I acquired the information. I certainly didn't have it before I died." He shrugged. "I simply asked for it and it was given to me."

"Asked for it?" Darcy stared at him in astonishment. "I don't understand. Asked of whom?"

Jonathan hesitated for an instant, fully aware of how she might react, but he could not answer less than honestly. "My guide."

"Your . . . what?" she asked in a strained voice.

"My spiritual guide," he said. "He came to me after I refused the summons from the light."

"Came to you?" Now her voice had a rough and raspy edge of disbelief. "How?"

Jonathan exhaled. "All of a sudden, he was just there."

"He? A man, like you?" Darcy was looking at him in an odd way, wary and unsure.

"Yes . . . but . . ." Jonathan hesitated again, not quite certain exactly how to describe the entity. "He is also different." He moved his hand around, as if trying to pluck the descriptive words out of the air. "He is older, but eternally young, wiser by far than I, with depths of compassion and understanding that I, as so recent a mortal, cannot as yet comprehend."

"And he comes to guide you?" she whispered.

"Yes." He pondered a moment, then he went on, "I can see him as clearly as I see you. In appearance he is as other men. But he is not like other humans. His voice is soft, guiding, never directing; encouraging, never demanding. And his eyes . . ." Jonathan's voice revealed wonder bordering on awe. "His eyes are warm, filled with compassion and forgiveness and all-encompassing, eternal love." The awe in his voice gave way to amusement. "And still, he possesses an abundance of humor."

"I see." Darcy took a step back, against the window, as if needing to distance herself from him. Then, while her body remained absolutely still, her gaze swept the area around them. "Is . . . er, is he here, in this room, now?"

"No, Darcy, so please, don't look like that," Jonathan answered, smiling to reassure her. "Ah, how do I explain?" he murmured, sighing and shaking his head. "If I need him, all I have to do is think of him, and he is here." He raised his hand to tap one finger against his temple. "I can see him, but he is here, inside, with me."

Darcy didn't respond; she merely stood there, growing apprehension visible in her wide, staring eyes.

"There is no reason to fear, Darcy. He is good." Jonathan laughed. "He has even suggested to me a way in which I could remain here. Not as I am now," he said. "But in a fully physical, earthly manner."

"Resurrection!" Darcy breathed, her eyes going even wider, large and round.

Jonathan held up his hand, palm to her. "No, no, not at all," he assured her. Then he frowned, searching for a way to explain. "I'm not quite sure myself how it works, but as I perceive it, under certain circumstances, I could take over another's body and personality."

"Possession!" Darcy's eyes were filled with sheer horror.

"No. Definitely not," Jonathan shot back in tones of absolute certainty. "At least, not in the evil sense you are obviously thinking about."

"Then how?" she cried out. "I don't understand."

Regretting he had ever mentioned his guide, Jonathan groped for a way to calm and soothe her while attempting to explain to the best of his ability. "I don't either, not fully, but the process is not of the Devil, Darcy. As God is my witness, I give you my word on it."

Suppressing a need to go to her, enfold her within his protective embrace, thus comforting her, while comforting himself, if in a different way, Jonathan was reduced to offering her a smile for comfort. "All I know and understand of the process so far is that there must be some sort of mutual agreement, a soul or entity exchange, that can occur only under mutual and specific conditions."

"Oh, dear," Darcy murmured, going pale. "I . . . I think I had better sit down."

"Here, let me help . . ." Jonathan began, reaching for her. When his hand passed through her arm, he muttered a curse of frustration—yet still thrilled by the sensation tingling inside him. "I can't help, so please, don't faint again."

Darcy's head snapped up and she gave him a withering look, a look that told Jonathan in no uncertain terms that, unable—or unwilling—to accept the concept of soul transference, she had dismissed it, banished it from her consciousness.

"I'll have you know that yesterday was the first time I have ever fainted," she snapped, swinging away from him to stride through the room and into the sitting room. "And I have no intention of repeating the performance," she went on decisively—and unaffectedly—when he again suddenly materialized next to her.

"While I am delighted to hear you say that," Jonathan rejoined, fighting a grin of satisfied approval for her show of inner strength and determination, "I would, however, feel infinitely more assured if you were to sit down."

Although Darcy leveled a haughty look of disdain on him, she nevertheless seated herself on the striped satin settee. "All right, I am seated. Now will you please explain about yourself, how you got here, why you refused the light you mentioned, whatever that may be, and where you originally came from before you arrived here a year ago."

Having spoken, Darcy relaxed against the back of the settee, placed a hand on the delicately curved armrest, and betrayed her mounting impatience by tap-tapping her oval-shaped fingernails on the shimmery material.

Jonathan found himself hard pressed not to laugh aloud. Darcy looked so imperious, so skeptical, so teacher-like stern, and so very blessedly beautiful, he yearned to roar his appreciative joy to the heavens for the wonderful fact of her being.

But Jonathan didn't laugh, or even smile, because fast on the heels of his delight in her being came the sobering reminder of the very corporal quality of her person.

And the very ethereal quality of his own being. The urge to laugh had completely dissipated. In its stead grew a sigh of soul-shattering proportions. Jonathan looked away from her to hide the painful truth he felt positive shone from the depths of his eyes.

He was falling in love with Darcy.

"Well?"

"Well . . . what?" Jonathan turned without seeming to move. "I beg your pardon?"

Darcy gave him a cold, pointed stare. "If you do not wish to enlighten me as to the circumstances concerning your shadowy presence here, please say so."

"Oh, that," he murmured, inwardly chastising himself for getting lost in reverie. "Not at all," he assured her, assuming a languid position at the other end of the settee. "I . . . umm, was wondering where to start."

"The beginning?" she prompted.

"Very well. I was born in Virginia. My father was a schoolmaster, my mother his devoted helpmate. My father tutored me until he deemed me ready to attend seminary and—"

"You are . . . were a priest!" Darcy exclaimed, interrupting his narrative.

"A Protestant pastor," Jonathan gently corrected her. "On completion of my studies, I accepted a call from a small church in a town not too distant from my birthplace." His lips curved into a sad smile. "I had been ministering to my congregation less than a year when the hostilities finally broke into war between the States. Along with my father, I volunteered to serve the cause."

Darcy's eyes flickered with shock and surprise. "You, a man of the cloth, volunteered to fight, to kill in a war!"

"Soldiers need ministering to as much as if not more than civilians, Darcy," Jonathan softly chided. "In addition to my desire to offer comfort where possible, I firmly believed that the fabric of the Union must not be rent."

Darcy's expression revealed incredulity. "You, a Southerner, fought for the North . . . against your own?"

"I fought on the side of my conscience." Jonathan smiled with wry self-mockery. "Of course, I had no idea then that, although the North would eventually win, I personally would lose not only my father and my mother but my faith."

Her hazel eyes darkened with compassion and

pity. "Oh, Jonathan," she whispered. "I am so sorry."

Jonathan felt touched to the depths of his deathless soul by Darcy's response, and knew, were she in that unguarded instant to gaze into his eyes, she would witness the love for her expanding inside him.

"There is no need for you to feel pain for my loss," he assured her. "My parents are"—he smiled—"fine, as you can see I am." He shrugged. "But to continue. Having lost all faith, hope, reason for living when the war ended, I wandered . . . in my own wilderness, if you will, until I arrived here in Denver a year ago. I found myself reluctant to leave, as if something were holding me here, waiting for I knew not what."

"How very strange."

"Strange?" Jonathan chuckled. "No, Darcy, not at all strange. For, you see, now I do know what I was waiting for."

"What?" she asked eagerly.

"Purpose . . . partly." Jonathan gave way to laughter as new insight flooded his mind. "The purpose part came to me on the very same night I was roused by an altercation between two men in the bar downstairs and stood up at the precise moment to take a killing knife thrust into my chest."

"Oh! How ghastly!" Darcy's hand flew from the settee arm to cover her mouth.

"At the time, I suppose," Jonathan agreed with nonchalance. "In fact, I was furious, which, of course, is why I refused the summons from the light."

"The light!" Darcy pounced on the word. "Jonathan, what is it? What is this light you speak of?"

"Don't you know, Darcy? Search your soul," he murmured. "Can't you imagine?"

Darcy's eyes grew wide, fearful. "God?"

"Yes." Jonathan paused, then shrugged and smiled. "Or perhaps the ultimate consciousness."

"Oh, my goodness," she whispered. "And you dared to refuse that light?"

"I now feel, somehow know, positively, that force is never used, Darcy. All is choice, personal choice," he answered slowly, experiencing an expanding sense of inner wonder. "And infinite, indescribable, all-enveloping forgiveness and love."

Her eyes mirrored his sense of wonder. "But Jonathan, how could you refuse such a love?"

"Good question." Jonathan pondered a moment, then he nodded. "Initially, I refused out of outrage at being denied completing my renewed purpose."

Darcy's attention was riveted. "And what was that renewed purpose?"

"To teach Sarah how to read and write." Jonathan stared directly into her eyes and raised one, taunting eyebrow. "So, Darcy, are you still bent on deserting Sarah and the others by running back to Philadelphia to hide behind the formidable Miss Reinholt's skirts?"

7

The sound of gunshots shattered the breathless quiet and reverberated on the listless hot summer air.

Jack Pritchart, or whatever alias he had assumed, lay sprawled in the dust-stirred street in front of the saloon called the Last Chance.

Wade Dunstan stood, still and cold, in the street several yards away from the body. His right hand hung loosely by his side, next to his muscular thigh, his long fingers coiled around the butt of a Colt pistol. He held his left hand aloft, palm out, displaying his badge of office for the shocked eyes of the growing crowd of spectators.

"Marshal . . . ?" the bartender called out.

"Dunstan." Wade shifted his narrowed eyes from the body to the red-faced bartender.

The man nodded. "Heard of ya," he said, giving a judicious, knowing look to the man standing nearest to him. "He had a girl with him." He jerked his head at the victim.

"So?" Wade raised his brows in question.

"So I don't know what the hell to do with her," the bartender retorted. "She's only a kid, and she's up there in that room wailin' and carryin' on like she's bein' murdered."

Wade bit back a curse and managed to keep his voice even, disinterested. "What do you expect me to do about it?"

"Well, damnation, you're the law, ain't ya?" The bartender's face had gone a shade darker. "Hell, man, go collect her, take her home, or back to wheresoever he found her." He jerked his head again at the body.

Stifling a sigh, Wade concealed his irritated expression by lowering his head, monitoring the movement of his hand as he slipped the badge into his shirt pocket.

Damn, he grumbled in silent frustration, exhaling slowly. He had a job to do; the last thing he needed was to be shackled to, held up by, a kid . . . a female kid at that.

Nevertheless, Wade strode forward, toward the bartender standing just outside the swinging doors to the saloon. "Where is she?" he asked, brushing past the aproned man.

"Follow your ears," the man growled. "I ain't never heard such caterwaulin' afore."

The man had a point, Wade conceded as he pushed through the swinging doors. He grimaced at the harsh sound of deep-chested weeping permeating the place. Heaving a sigh, he crossed the packed-dirt floor and mounted the steps, following the increasingly louder assault of sobbing.

God, he hated to hear a woman cry. It always reminded him of that one awful time he had heard his Mary weeping as though her heart would break on the day she had miscarried their only child. Wade had hurt at losing the child too. But the sound of Mary's grief had hurt him even more.

The memory softened his impatience and annoyance enough that, when he reached the room from where the sound was coming, he raised his hand and tapped on the door, instead of flinging it open and walking right in.

"No! No, please!" a young, hysterical voice screamed from inside the room. "Don't hurt me nomore. Please, please, mister! Don't hurt me nomore."

Shit. What had the son of a bitch done to her? Wade raised his hand to knock again, and then a vision stabbed into his mind, drawing a sharp, painful gasp from his throat. As clear as if she lay before him, he could see Mary, the way she looked when he had found her, beaten and sexually mangled, lying in a pool of her own blood.

Goddamn. Without further thought, Wade kicked the door open and strode into the room.

"No!" the girl screamed, flinging her thin arms up around her head, while pressing back into the corner where she had been cowering at bay.

"It's all right, kid," Wade began in a soft, soothing tone, hoping to calm her down.

The girl appeared beyond calming. With harsh-sounding sobs tearing from her chest, she drew her knees up to her chin and crouched into the corner. "No! No!"

Disgust clutched at Wade's gut as he took in her appearance, or what he could see of it. She was naked as a baby—and little more than a baby at that. The skinny arms she had thrown protectively over her head bore the black and blue smudges of a man's gripping fingers. Her pitifully thin thighs, and what he could see of her buttocks, revealed long, crisscrossing welts, of the kind a man's belt would inflict.

But most damning of all in Wade's eyes was the infuriating sight of a stain of blood seeping into the bare floorboards from the girl's behind. He could clearly see that she had been sodomized.

Controlling a shudder of revulsion, Wade crossed the floor to her. "It's all right, kid," he murmured in a crooning voice. "The man who hurt you is dead."

"D-d-d-dead?" The girl lowered one arm, just enough to peer at him with one bruised and swollen eye. "De-dead? How did he get dead?"

"I shot him."

"Ohhhh," she moaned, burying her head again. "Are—are you going to shoot me too?"

"No, of course not," Wade assured her. The sight of her was getting to him, tugging at his sympathy. "Where are your clothes, kid? I'll get them for you."

She peeked at him again, giving him a one-eyed, fishy look. "You . . . you're tellin' me true? You're not going to shoot me, or hurt me?"

"I'm a United States Marshal," Wade answered, sighing. "I don't shoot kids. Now, you want to tell me where your clothes are?"

The girl lowered her arms as she raised her head to look at him. Wade had to bite back another curse. Her entire face was swollen, red from the stings of repeated slaps. Dried blood encrusted a split on her lower lip. She looked a heart-wrenching mess, and yet, Wade could discern the potential budding beauty of the girl.

Controlling the fury raging inside him was becoming more difficult with each new revelation.

"He . . . that man," she said tremulously. "He threw my clothes next to the bed." She shuddered and flicked her hand to indicate the far side of the narrow room. "Over there."

"Okay," Wade said, relieved to turn away. "I'll get your clothes and some water for you to clean up." He felt more relieved to note a pitcher and bowl on a rickety washstand. "Then I'll take you home." Bending, he scooped up the pile of clothing, which consisted of a boy's well-worn shirt and pair of pants and a scarred and split pair of boots run-down at the heels. Muttering a string of curses against the girl's obviously unconcerned parents, he swung around to walk back to her and came to a bone-jarring halt.

The girl had turned to brace herself on the windowsill to get up, her backside revealed to him. Wade's stomach muscles clenched at the sight of her blood-smeared bottom.

That cock-driven bastard. Railing inside at the man, Wade wished he were still alive, just so he could kill him again, much more slowly this time around.

"Are you all right?" he asked in a voice raw with anger and emotion. "I mean, can you get yourself cleaned up, dressed, and ready to go without help?"

"Y-yes, sir."

The girl turned fully around to face him, and Wade took a step back. She looked to be about twelve or thirteen and she was so damned thin; her shoulder, rib, and hip bones stood out. Her slight body was a mass of discolored bruises and angry red welts. Small, just forming mounds dotted her otherwise narrow, flat chest; the still tight buds of her nipples had a raw, chewed-up look.

The son-of-a-bitch, Wade thought, swallowing hard against a bitter taste of bile in his throat. Rage searing through him, he averted his eyes from the ravagement of her young body to the sad sight of her small oval face.

There was barely a spot that wasn't marked in some way, either by bruises or tear streaks through a coating of dirt and road dust. Her dark brown hair was lank and dirty, a tangled rat's nest. Yet even so, there was a near angelic beauty beneath the bruises, smeared blood, and grime.

Once again Wade was staggered by the vision of Mary, then his bride, weeping in his arms over the loss of their child. How long ago had it been? Ten years? Wade gave an inner, mental shake of his head. He knew exactly how long it had been. He was thirty-six now; he had been twenty-four, a U.S. Marshal for less than a year, at the time.

This ill-used girl was about the same age as his own child would have been.

Goddamn the man. The potent mixture of fury and disgust overcame Wade. Spinning on one boot heel, he strode to the door, needing the movement and escape.

"I'll be outside," he growled, nearly yanking the hinges loose with the force of pulling the door open.

"Marshal!" Panic swelled the girl's voice. "Please, don't go without me!"

"I said I'd be outside," he snapped, losing control for an instant. He paused, drew a breath, then continued, "I'll wait right outside the door."

She was quick. Very likely, Wade mused, because she was so very frightened. He had hardly had time to pace three strides back and forth in front of the door before she came scurrying out of the room, her wide brown eyes darting directly to him.

"I—I'm ready . . . er, to go, Marshal," she stammered, sliding a scared sidelong look at him.

"Good." Wade grunted, thankful she had stopped crying. Motioning for her to follow him, he strode along the narrow hallway to the stairs. "I want to shake the stench of this two-bit town off me."

The bartender still stood where he had been standing when Wade entered the saloon. The crowd of spectators was still milling around the corpse in the dust.

"Oh!" the girl exclaimed when she caught sight of the body. "Is he really dead?" Lingering fear trembled through her small, unsteady voice.

"Umm," Wade murmured, giving a brief nod of his head. "And hopefully frying in hell." Not even bothering to glance at the prone form, he grasped the girl's arm and started down the rough-boarded sidewalk, toward the rail where he had tied the reins of his horse.

"Hey! Marshal!" the bartender called out to him in a voice raised by surprise. "What about him?"

Tightening his fingers around the girl's arm,

Wade made a half-turn to look first at the body, then at the bartender. "What about him?"

The bartender looked blank for an instant, then he blurted out, "What should we do with him?"

Wade knew the smile that bared his teeth was anything but pretty. "Stick a bone up his ass and hope the dogs drag his carcass away."

Stunned silence trailed Wade to his horse, then a babble of irate voices broke the hot afternoon. Wade ignored the noise. He had more important things to do. He shifted his gaze from the girl to his horse, then back to the girl. Considering the condition her behind was in, sitting on a horse would be agony for her; but there was no help for it.

Exhaling a harsh sigh, he caught the girl around the waist and swung her up and carefully settled her into the saddle. She gasped as her rear made contact with the hard leather, but she didn't cry out or complain.

A sharp pang combined with equal parts of compassion and admiration for the girl twisting in his chest, Wade grasped the reins and mounted, settling his lean hips into the saddle in front of her.

"Hang on to my belt," he advised her, clicking his tongue at the animal to get him started. "Make tracks, Rascal," he coaxed, setting the horse into a canter. "I want to be long gone from this jerk-water town."

They rode in silence, each into their own thoughts, for close to an hour; Wade required the time to clear the rage from his system. He wouldn't have spoken then, except the girl began wriggling in the saddle.

"What's troubling you, gir . . ." He paused, frowning. "You got a name?"

"Betsy." He could feel the girl nod her head. "But mostly, people call me Betts."

"Un-huh." Wade made a sour face. "Well, I'm not most people. Name's Wade Dunstan. Is the pain getting worse, Betsy? Is that why you're squirming like that?"

"I . . . ah, no, it's not that," she answered apologetically. "But . . . I'm sorry, Mr. Dunstan, but I hafta . . . er, go . . . er, relieve myself."

Wade gave vent to a deep sigh of relief. "Okay, kid. I'll look for a place with some brush." He shot a glance at the mountains on the horizon. The sun was doing a shimmery dance along the jagged spires.

"Might as well make camp," he muttered, regretting the time lost on the necessity, while aware that the girl needed rest. "Get some grub together."

It was nearly dark and getting chilly by the time Wade unpacked his supplies and built a fire. The meager meal he prepared of thick pieces of bacon, canned beans, and coffee was consumed in silence. The girl dug into the food as if she hadn't eaten in days. Allowing her the larger portion, Wade slowly ate his food, while unobtrusively watching her gobble up every morsel on the tin plate.

"Oh, that was so good," she said in an uncertain, still fearful-sounding voice, avoiding his gaze by mopping up the juice with her grimy fingers. "Th-th-thank you, Marshal," she went on through teeth beginning to chatter from cold and—Wade suspected—physical discomfort and sheer exhaustion.

"Welcome," he muttered, rolling to his feet to walk to where he had dumped his bedroll. Untying the roll, he lifted his jacket, shrugged into it, then tossed the roll to the ground next to where she sat, all huddled together.

"Wrap yourself up in that blanket," he ordered, his voice curt in reaction to the feelings of sympathy undermining his determination to get her off his hands as soon as possible. "Get some sleep. I want to move out at first light."

"Y-y-yes, s-sir," she chattered, hurrying to obey and hide herself away.

Damn. Grumbling in silent commiseration, Wade checked the small fire, then stretched his long frame onto the cold ground, settled his shoulders and head against his saddle, and tugged the wide brim of his hat low over his eyes.

Sleep evaded him. His mind was too active, busy revising his plans.

Two down, and two to go. The thought was a source of inner warmth to Wade. Ignoring the surface chill, he stared up, into the star-strewn night sky, ruminating on the advance of his mission . . . his final mission.

Finding Jack Pritchart hadn't been as difficult as Wade had thought it might be. Owing to that bastard's unhealthy sexual appetites, he hadn't gotten to within a coupla hundred miles from Promontory, which now placed Wade closer to his next target—if the man was hiding out somewhere near Laramie.

The recent events unwound inside Wade's

mind, and set him pondering the role fate appeared to be playing in his drama of revenge and death.

By chance, late yesterday, Wade had come upon an old Cheyenne Indian in these same hills overlooking that town. The ancient one told Wade that, since he was the last of his family, he had come into the mountains to scratch out an existence from the earth until he closed his eyes forever.

Wade had decided on the spot to make camp for the night, and had invited the old man to share a meal with him. They had talked of this and that until long after darkness had spread its chill cloak over the landscape.

"You go to that town distant?" the old man asked from the folds of his sleeping robe, indicating the settlement nestled at the base of the foothills.

"In the morning," Wade answered, nodding.

"You . . . take some care," the old one cautioned. "There be a killer in that place."

Wade had experienced an uncanny sensation. Senses alert, he had questioned the Cheyenne. The old man's explanation was simple, to the point. He had watched a man, observing him in the way of his people, without being seen. The man had a furtive look about him . . . like an animal being stalked by man.

Chance? Wade smiled grimly into the night. Maybe so. But then again, maybe fate.

Wade had ridden into town, tied his horse, and was walking in the road toward the saloon when Jack Pritchart came tearing through the swinging doors. Wade had shouted for him to halt; Pritchart had stopped, and while spinning around, threw off a knife. Expecting it, Wade had leapt to the side, while pulling his gun. Jack Pritchart went into the dust with two bullets in his heart.

Two down, two to go.

Of course, Wade still had to return Betsy to her home and family—wherever in hell they were. Come morning, he decided, he'd have a talk with the girl.

Thinking of her drew his gaze to her huddled form. Betsy was coiled into a tight ball, yet even through the dimness of the dying fire, Wade could see that she was awake and shaking with cold. Another deep sigh escaped his guard.

"Bring the blanket and get over here, kid," he growled, shifting to one side to make room for her.

Betsy held back for a moment; then, as if afraid he'd come after her, she hastened to do his bidding. She curled up next to him and stared at him, eyes wide with fear.

"You—you goin' to fuck me good, Marshal?" she asked in a squeaky, terrified voice.

"*What?*" Wade jackknifed to a sitting position, his body rigid with shock.

"I . . . I asked if you was goin' to f—"

"I heard you," Wade cut her off with sharp harshness. "Where did you pick up talk like that?" he demanded, but continued on before she could reply, "Did that man back there say words like that to you?"

"Y-y-yes, sir," she said, clutching the blanket to

her shivering body. "B-But I heard the same before."

"When?" he snapped, anger flaying him again. "From whom did you hear it?"

She shrank back in obvious fear. "At . . . the farm . . . m-my uncle," she stammered.

Realizing that he was scaring her witless, Wade forced himself to calm down. He drew a deep breath before going on, in a soft, soothing tone. "I told you before that I won't hurt you, Betsy. I meant it. I only asked you to come over here because I could see that you are cold. Okay?"

Her wide-eyed stare remained fastened to his face. Something she saw in his expression, heard in his voice, must have reassured her, for she nodded and answered, "Okay."

Wade expelled the breath he hadn't realized he'd been holding. "Okay. Now, you say you live on a farm, with your uncle?"

Betsy nodded yes.

"Where are your parents?"

"Dead. Three years." Betsy gulped. "My uncle's my pa's half-brother."

"And he talks like that . . . to you?" Wade found it extremely difficult to keep his voice even; what he wanted to do was give vent to his anger with a string of vicious curses damning the man to an eternity of hell.

Betsy shook her head. "He never said that to me . . . yet. But I heard him near every night, sayin' that to his woman."

"Your aunt?"

"No." She gave another shake of her head. "She ain't my aunt. Ain't even the ma of my cousin, Billy." She frowned. "I don't rightly know who Billy's ma was."

"Billy's older than you?" Wade asked, frowning as he tried to get her disjointed story straight in his mind.

"Nah, he's a year younger, the pest." Betsy hesitated, then went on, "But he's bigger than me, and I'm glad of that, 'cause these here are his clothes." Opening the blanket, she tugged on the shabby shirt. "I stole 'em when I ran away."

"You ran away?"

"Yes, sir." Betsy bobbed her head emphatically.

"Why?"

" 'Cause I was tired of never havin' enough to eat, and Billy always whinin' and pickin' on me, and I hated bein' switched when the work wasn't always done on time, and hearing my uncle say . . . er, talkin' that way every night when he was ruttin' on that woman, and her, yellin' and hollerin' like she was dyin' or somethin'." She stuck her chin out belligerently. "I was just plain sick and tired of all of it."

"Sounds reasonable," Wade murmured, feeling his blood running hot with renewed fury. "Why did you steal Billy's clothes? Did you think you could fare better as a boy?"

"Dunno 'bout that." Betsy lifted her bony shoulders in a half shrug. "But I stole Billy's clothes 'cause I couldn't see no way to get mine from my uncle."

Wade started. "Your uncle had you running naked?"

"Each night, once I was inside after the chores was done. He said it was to keep me from doin' just what I did." Her small face got a tight, pinched look. "I didn't cotton to Billy grinnin' and grabbin' at my bare chest and trying to poke his finger into me down below neither."

Jesus Christ. Wade stared at the girl as determination firmed inside his mind. There was no way in hell he'd take this child back to those people. But that left the question of what in hell he would do with her. As if Betsy could read his thoughts, she pried into his mind with a determination of her own.

"I ain't goin' back there, Marshal. You can't make me go, not even if you was to beat me."

Wade had to smile, however faintly, at the set and dogged look on her little face. "I'm not going to beat you, or even try to make you go back there." His lips flattened into a hard line. "Come to that, as long as I'm around, nobody'd better try laying a hand on you."

The sound of her sigh wrapped around his heart. "Then . . . what are you going to do with me, Marshal?"

"Damned if I know, kid." Wade settled back against the saddle and drew her shivering, skinny body close to the warmth of his own muscular frame. "Go to sleep now, morning'll be here pretty soon and I want an early start."

"Where we goin', Marshal?" she asked around a wide yawn that revealed small and amazingly clean teeth.

"Laramie." Wade smiled as she snuggled trustingly against him. "I have some business to take care of. But first, maybe I can find a place for you there."

8

"Very fetching."

Darcy smiled, and turned to cast a side view glance at herself in the standing oval mirror. In all modesty, she had to agree with Jonathan's softly stated assessment; she did look rather good in the fetching outfit, but then, it had been her intention to appear as presentable as possible for her appointment with the personable young banker, Mr. James Singleton, and the solicitor, Mr. Mansford.

The afternoon dress of striped silk was her very best. It was also the newest garment in her wardrobe. Darcy had chosen it from the latest spring and summer patterns the dressmaker had received from Paris in the waning weeks of winter. She had taken delivery of the dress the week before receiving the fateful letter from the lawyer, Mr. Mansford.

Other than to try on the dress for fit, Darcy had not actually worn it until now.

And it *was* fetching, she mused, running a slow, sharp-eyed appraisal of the garment, from the open-sleeved, double-breasted jacket with its turned-down, fringed collar, to the tightly tucked waist above the full double skirt, which just brushed the floor, concealing her black satin day boots.

"Thank you," she belatedly responded, making a half turn to glance over her shoulder for a view of her back. The jacket lay smooth and unwrinkled over her shoulders, tapering neatly to the narrow velvet waistband of the skirt. A gentle gathering below the waist—the nearest to a bustle Miss Reinholt would ever countenance—enhanced her small derriere.

"That particular shade of amber in the stripe highlights the gold flecks in your hazel eyes," Jonathan observed. "And the primary color of bronze in the dress lends a becoming glow to your cheeks."

"Really?" Her eyes growing bright with pleasurable surprise, Darcy swished around to peer at her reflection. "Then . . . do you think I shouldn't need to pinch my cheeks to give them more color?"

"You never need to punish yourself by pinching your cheeks to give them color, Darcy," Jonathan replied in droll tones. "Just ask any one of the girls."

"*Rouge*?" Darcy's eyes flew wide beneath her raised eyebrows. "Miss Reinholt would be scandalized."

"Dare I remind you, Darcy, that Miss Reinholt is not here?" Jonathan retorted.

Chagrined, Darcy recollected that, in truth, Jonathan had dared to do much more than jog her memory throughout the previous two weeks. Ever since that day when he had dared to issue a challenge to her by tauntingly asking if she was going to run back to Philadelphia to hide behind Miss Reinholt's skirts, he had dared to instruct her, cajole her, tease her outrageously, and invade her privacy at will, morning, afternoon, and even in the middle of the night.

The very fact that she had not only accepted his challenge, against all reason and her better judgment, but had now not so much as flickered an eyelash at his comment when he had materialized in her boudoir while she was dressing, gave evidence of how quickly Darcy had become accustomed to having him suddenly appear out of thin air, and as suddenly disappear, right before her eyes.

No, Darcy mused, staring blankly into the mirror, the sight of Jonathan, the beguiling sound of his voice, no longer unnerved her. Quite the contrary. She was used to having him near—perhaps too used to his company.

Incredible, unbelievable, and as outlandish as she knew it to be, Darcy was very much afraid that she was falling, had already fallen, mindlessly and headlong in love with the specter of Jonathan Stuart, as ridiculous and impossible as she knew such a fruitless love to be.

"Whether or not Miss Reinholt is here, I absolutely will not resort to artifice," she finally responded repressively. "The world may accept me as I am, or it may reject me." She angled her delicate chin defiantly. "I care not."

Seemingly propped indolently against the fireplace mantelpiece, Jonathan threw back his head and let loose a roar of laughter.

Darcy's spine went stiff with indignation. "Do I

amuse you, sir?" she demanded, swinging away from the mirror to glare at him with eyes blazing fire.

"Yes," Jonathan answered, unabashed and still chuckling. "Despite all you have seen and learned since you arrived here, you are still such an oh-so-proper lady." He arched one—always the same one—winged brow in that now very familiar manner. "As tightly laced and securely buttoned as the formidable Miss Reinholt . . . hmmm?"

Darcy attempted to stare down her dainty nose at him; a frustrating endeavor, since he topped her by a good six inches, thereby making her look up to him. "I'll have you know," she said in gritty, crackling tones of ice, "Miss Reinholt is an exemplary example."

"Of what?" Jonathan's other eyebrow joined its counterpart midway on his forehead. "Repression? Subjugation? Self-immolation? Inhibition?"

"I am not repressed!" Darcy objected loudly and strongly, much too strongly, and not for the first time. She uncomfortably recalled objecting loudly and strongly to quite a few of his startling if not outright shocking comments.

"No?" Jonathan queried, smiling as he gave up the pretense of indolence to glide across the carpet to her.

Fighting an urge to back up in the face of his advance, Darcy held her ground, and clenched the muscles around her expectantly quivering stomach. Her breath caught and lodged in her throat as he raised his hand. Not once during the last two weeks had he attempted to touch her. Yet now . . .

Jonathan reached out, as if to stroke her cheek. The tips of his fingers hesitated a whisper away from her now flushed skin, hovering uncertainly a moment before, ever so slowly, carefully, he moved his hand forward.

Darcy felt . . . what? . . . a tingle, not an actual touch, but something, a sensation that caused a ripple of excitement cascading through her from her cheek to the very soles of her slim, delicately arched feet.

Shock, pleasurable and delicious, streaked like lightning along her nerve endings. Startled, confused, Darcy's gaze flew to the mirror. Her eyes grew wide with surprised disbelief at the sight of Jonathan's fingers appearing to be embedded within her flushed flesh.

The color drained from her skin, leaving it chalk white in contrast to the warm, seemingly vibrantly alive hue of Jonathan's hand and fingers.

Darcy's breath came out in harsh little gasps. Her bosom rose and fell in quick, short heaves. Her shoulders twitched and shook. Her spine stiffened. And yet, all the while, a thrilling warmth radiated from his fingers, sending shards of awareness into the very center of her being. Weak and quivering, she swayed toward the perceived strength of him.

"You feel it, too, don't you?" Jonathan's voice was low, gentled by compassion.

Darcy's gaze flickered to the soft gray eyes reflected back to her from the mirror. "I . . . I don't understand," she cried in a reedy whisper. "What is happening?"

"Ahhh, Darcy," Jonathan murmured. "You are

so very innocent." He drew his hand back, leaving her feeling cold and bereft. She shivered in reaction. A bittersweet smile played over his mouth; his eyes darkened. "The sensations are those felt when a man and woman are strongly attracted, both physically and emotionally, to one another."

Although she would have believed it impossible, Darcy's eyes grew wider still. "But . . . but you're a . . ." Her voice failed her, and she caught her bottom lip between her teeth.

"A shadow of the man," he finished for her. "Yes." He cocked that one eyebrow. "Interesting, isn't it?"

"Interesting?" Darcy stared at him in blank amazement. "How can you say that? It's . . . it's . . ." Once again she found herself at a loss for words. Her hand flailed in a gesture of helplessness and confusion.

"Love?"

That one murmured word caused a cessation of all movement. Darcy's hand hung in midair. For an instant, she couldn't breathe, she couldn't think, she couldn't talk. Even her heartbeat seemed to stop, before suddenly racing ahead again, banging a painful thrumming inside her chest.

The fact that she had secretly, in her private thoughts, feared she had fallen in love with him didn't matter. Jonathan was, or had been, everything she had ever dreamed a man should be, could be. Without substance, he still represented her ideal of the hero, his mind sharp, his wit quick. Never had she felt at once stimulated and secure while in the company of any other male.

Love. The word had been spoken. Hearing it openly expressed from Jonathan's lips brought the magnitude of the emotion crashing in on her. She couldn't deal with it, she would not deal with it.

"No!" Darcy cried the denial through bloodless lips. "I will not listen." Trembling, she spun away from him. "I . . . I must go." Her body stiff, her attitude unyielding, she walked to the bed to collect the gloves, beaded bag, spring straw hat, and frilly parasol laid out neatly for her. "I'll be late for my meeting with Mr. Singleton."

"Very well." Jonathan's voice held a wealth of understanding. "Run away, if you must." Without a visible show of movement, he was beside her, his presence more real than the room around her, the floor beneath her feet, the accessories clutched in her trembling hands. "I'll be here, waiting for you." He glided through the door before she could pull it open.

Darcy bit down on her lip to stifle an outcry of protest, not even knowing herself whether the protest was against his promise to wait, the unnatural appearance of his action, or her own inner state of confusion and upheaval.

Her silent wraith escorted Darcy down the stairs and to the burly man patiently waiting for her.

"Ah, there you are, lass," Clancy greeted her, swinging the front door wide in a natural and soothing manner. "I was just thinking I'd have to come for you." He shot a glance through the doorway into the dining room to the ornate grandfather clock standing tall against the far wall. "It's gone on to ten-thirty, you know."

"Yes, I know." Darcy managed a genuine if

rather weak smile for him. "Will we make it on time? I do hate to be late for an appointment."

"Aye, if we depart at once." Nodding, Clancy ushered her out of the house and into the open carriage waiting in the driveway. "The sun's blistering. You'd do well to shelter beneath that pretty hat and parasol," he advised, moving around the conveyance to step up into the driver's seat. He waited until she had anchored the hat to the curls piled at her crown with a long hat pin and had opened the parasol, then he collected the reins from the boy holding the horse steady. After the boy moved back, clearing the way, he smartly flicked a whip over the animal's tossing head.

As the carriage lurched forward, she turned her head to give a distracted smile to the boy, and a sidelong glance at the so-solid-looking spirit standing in the deep shade of the covered veranda, unseen by any living soul but Darcy.

Oh, Jonathan.

Darcy sighed and, forgetting every one of Miss Reinholt's strictures on deportment and proper posture, slumped back against the plushly padded carriage seat.

The July sun blazed overhead, scorching the earth and every living thing on it. Darcy barely felt the heat. Dust billowed in tan clouds from beneath the thudding hooves of the high-stepping horse. Darcy didn't see it. Nor did she take note of her surroundings, the bustle of the town, the congested roadways, the crowded streets, or even the curious glances sent her way by the pedestrians, some strolling, most rushing along the sidewalks. The raw vitality charging the hot, shimmering atmosphere escaped her notice.

Though staring straight ahead, Darcy was blind to the daily activity of the growing city, and all the attendant noise, odors, and hubbub. Her attention was directed inward, at her own thoughts and concerns, the multitude of events that had occurred during the previous two weeks.

After nineteen years of the disciplined life imposed by Miss Reinholt on the teachers as well as the students attending the girls' school, a life well ordered, almost free of disruptive incidents, Darcy had felt, continued to feel, swept along by the flood of new and unsettling events and information washing over her in billowing waves.

Perhaps she should have ignored Jonathan's challenge, commissioned the sale of the house to Mr. Mansford, and returned on the next train to Philadelphia, Darcy mused. But after that luncheon meeting with the women of the house, hearing their histories, she could not in good conscience desert them, leave them, as it were, to their own devices, of which, in fact, they could claim only one.

No, Darcy reaffirmed her decision to remain; she could not desert them. But what in God's name could she do to help them? Reopening the house, as Jonathan had originally suggested, was definitely out of the question.

The recollection of Jonathan's suggestion diverted Darcy's thinking process, stirring the memory of a later discussion they had had on the subject. Reliving the scene, she was unaware of the sway of the carriage as Clancy tooled the conveyance around a cumbersome wagon blocking the road, and deaf to the Gaelic curse that roared from his throat.

"So, you are set in your determination against reopening the house?" Jonathan inquired early in the evening of the day he had challenged her to stay.

Darcy didn't bother pausing in her trips between the bed and the dressing room to hang her clothing back in the closet. "Yes," she answered in an adamant tone. Returning to the bedroom after hanging away the last garment—the one and only evening gown she possessed—she stood, hands on her slender waist, regarding him quizzically. "What I don't understand, considering your past calling as a man of the cloth, and your . . . ah, present condition, is how you can blithely condone the profession of these unfortunate women."

"But I don't condone it," Jonathan said, a smile suspiciously tinged with amusement playing at the corners of his lips. "But neither do I sit in judgment and condemn it."

"But—"

"Darcy," he interrupted her before she could voice an argument. "As you heard this noon, these women have little choice in occupation." Although his eyes remained soft, his voice took on a faintly stern note. "Would you have me condemn them for being unfortunate and uneducated?"

"No, of course not," Darcy quickly denied.

He moved his shoulders in a light shrug. "Well, then, what else is there for them to do?"

Darcy had no answer for him . . . then. But the

problem had preyed on her mind throughout each successive day, each new and startling discovery.

The first of those discoveries came a few days after Darcy's initial luncheon with the women. Somewhat to her amazement, she found herself not merely in sympathy with them, but growing to like them as individuals.

From that enlightening point onward, the discoveries came, rapid-fire, one after the other.

In response to a note from Darcy requesting a meeting, Mr. Mansford arrived at the house to explain in detail the extent of Darcy's inheritance. The entire process required several hours, and by the time the solicitor had finished, Darcy had been reduced to a state of sheer astonishment.

"You did not know that your mother was a very clever businesswoman?" Mr. Mansford inquired when Darcy gaped at him in utter disbelief.

"I . . . I had no idea," she admitted in a subdued, obviously shaken tone of voice.

"Hmmm," he murmured. "Then I can understand why you are so taken aback. Through your mother's efforts and endeavors, you are now a very wealthy woman." He gave her a look that was at once both prissy and self-satisfied. "By prudently following Miss Flynn's investment advice, I myself am now financially independent."

Darcy had longed for an opportunity to get to know her mother, but had never for a moment had an inkling of the true depths of Colleen Flynn.

Darcy's mind whirled with the magnitude of her mother's estate. In addition to the house known as La Rouge, her mother had owned property both in the city of Denver and quite a bit of the land surrounding it. There were large shareholdings in one of the more successful mining operations, and even more shares of railroad stock. But Colleen's farsightedness had not been limited to projects west of the Mississippi. She had invested in prime real estate in New York, Philadelphia, and Boston, and held interests in shipping firms in all three cities. Her jewelry collection alone was worth a veritable fortune.

And Darcy was Colleen's sole heir.

The fact that she was indeed a very wealthy woman required several days' passage for Darcy to absorb.

Jonathan was there, materializing off and on, his soft gray eyes brimming with amusement, offering counsel and commiseration, and the occasional odd nudge to her conscience in regard to the lack of opportunity afforded to Colleen's "girls," throughout her period of adjustment to her improved status.

"It's such a huge responsibility," Darcy said as the reality of it all finally settled in her mind.

"But freeing," Jonathan observed, jolting her into awareness of the limitless possibilities available to her.

Darcy's eyes grew wide as she contemplated the extent of her options. "I could leave here, now, immediately," she murmured, not even aware of speaking aloud.

"Yes," he readily agreed. "Where would you like to go?" he then asked, in all apparent innocence.

"Where?" Darcy frowned. Where would she like

to go? she asked herself. Her mind went blank, devoid of an answer. "Why, I don't know," she replied.

"Have you longed for the bustle of New York City?" Jonathan inquired. "Or perhaps held a desire to see and taste the famed cuisine and wines of Paris?"

Darcy slowly shook her head. "No," she said, but went on to qualify, "Oh, I confess to having experienced the occasional moments of yearning to see the historic locations I taught my students about, but I have never harbored a burning need to go traipsing either around this country or the world."

"You were content?" he probed.

Darcy gave his question the consideration it deserved before responding in the affirmative. "Yes, I was content. More than content, I was happy."

"You derived pleasure from teaching?"

"Oh, yes," she answered without hesitation, and though he had posed the query in the past tense, she went on in the present tense. "I love teaching, opening young minds to the benefits of acquired knowledge."

"And you had thought to continue in the profession?" Jonathan probed, his tone bland, his expression unreadable.

"Yes, of course." Darcy frowned, wondering where his line of questioning might be leading. "Why?"

Jonathan didn't answer, at least not directly. "You did not dream of marriage? A husband? Children of your own to guide and instruct?"

Darcy felt her cheeks grow warm. Marriage. A

husband. Children. Yes, she had dreamed of having a family of her own someday. But the earth revolved, the years passed, opportunity dwindled—indeed, there had been no real opportunity, simply because she had had precious few occasions to meet young men. Now, at twenty-five, a spinster, she had put the dream behind her to squarely face the reality of her situation.

"For a time," she admitted, facing him as squarely as she had faced her reality.

"But no longer?" Jonathan persisted.

Darcy was growing impatient, and revealed it with a sharp shake of her head. "No." She gave him a tight, wry smile. "I fully realize that I am past the first blush, nearly middle-aged. Men want young brides."

Jonathan laughed. "That may be true everywhere else, but out here, where the males far outnumber the female population, a woman of almost any age can find a husband."

"If that woman is content to be little more than a convenient servant," Darcy retorted stiffly. "I am not. I much prefer a life of teaching."

"Following in the inestimable Miss Reinholt's footsteps," he said in a tone underlaid by a note of gratification that confused her.

"Yes," Darcy replied vaguely, pondering the cause of his oblique satisfaction. "And why not? Until two weeks ago, my world had been contained within the boundaries of Miss Reinholt's school for nineteen years. I had come to believe I would very likely live out the remainder of my life there. My only regret was that I had never had the opportunity to know my mother."

"She was a beautiful person," Jonathan said. "With a beautiful soul."

His assertion disconcerted Darcy. "How can you say that? She ran a house of ill repute. Was my mother not immoral . . . damned in God's sight by her own willful actions?"

"Ye without sin cast the first stone," Jonathan reminded her, his voice gentle, his eyes soft with compassion. "You have been agonizing over your mother's soul?"

Darcy bit her lip, and nodded her head. "Yes." Then she blurted out another concern. "She was laid to rest in unconsecrated ground. I fear for her mortal soul."

"Ahh, Darcy," he soothed. "There is no reason for you to fear. For you see, your mother's soul, indeed the soul of every living being, is not mortal but immortal." His one eyebrow inched upward. "Was redemption not promised?"

Redemption. Darcy's thoughts flew to the women of the house. Surely, she prayed, if any of God's creatures deserved redemption, these unfortunate women did, for as Jonathan had so effectively made it known to her, they had had little choice in their unsavory profession—except, of course, for Sally, who blithely confessed to liking her work.

Through getting to know the women, her discussions with them, Darcy had learned of her mother's kindness to them. Individually, they had made it known to Darcy that, although Colleen had employed them for the pleasure of her customers, she had also sheltered them, protected them, kept them secure, safe from the physical abuse, degradation, and brutality found in many of the other houses.

Honest by nature, Darcy conceded that at least a portion of her mother's great wealth had been garnered from the efforts of the women of the house. Now that wealth had come to her, and she had done nothing to earn it. The rigid moral strictures instilled in Darcy by Miss Reinholt rose to the forefront of Darcy's conscience, nudged along by subtle reminders from her soft-eyed resident specter.

"You are beautiful, educated, and rich. You may go . . . or stay, as you will. The choice is yours." His lips curved in a secret smile. "But then, the choice is always ours."

"I don't understand you," Darcy complained.

"Free will, Darcy," he explained. "Choice. Yours. Mine. I chose to stay."

"By refusing the light?"

"Yes." He once again arched that one dratted eyebrow. "Will you choose to go, thus refusing opportunity?"

Darcy was left to work out his meaning for herself since, simply by dematerializing, Jonathan refused to elaborate. It was yet another challenge offered to her.

It did not require mental strain for Darcy to conclude that the opportunity she would be refusing by deciding to leave would be the opportunity to make reparation to the women of the house for their contributions to the wealth that was now hers, through no effort of her own.

But how? Darcy's mind worried the question through many sleepless nights. Should she offer a settlement of a certain sum of money on each of the women, thereby enabling them to go their own way, free and independent? But if she did so, would they, could they, build a secure future for themselves, survive on their own?

The answer was too obvious; had Jonathan not enlightened her during that memorable luncheon? He had. Darcy accepted it with a sigh. The money would last only so long and then, uneducated, untrained, the women would be right back where they began, seeking a livelihood at the only profession they knew, very likely in much worse circumstances.

The seed of another idea, radical in concept, had begun germinating in Darcy's fertile imagination, slowly taking on form, when she made yet another discovery, a discovery so shocking it robbed her consciousness of all other considerations and concerns—at least for some days.

The discovery was of Darcy's mother's personal diary, which contained the crushing truth about her father.

Darcy had come upon the diary quite by accident a week earlier, while she was in the heart-wrenching process of going through her mother's personal possessions. Its contents spanning a period of more than twenty-five years, it was a small book, covered in supple black leather, innocent and unprepossessing in appearance. And in all innocence, Darcy had opened it and begun reading the lines written in her mother's delicate script, never dreaming the words inscribed held the power to pierce her heart.

Her beloved father, the handsome, laughing man Darcy had called Papa, and Colleen had called Stephen, the man whose full name Darcy had always believed to be Stephen Flynn, had never been her mother's husband.

His name was Stephen Darcy, and he had already had a wife when he first met Colleen Flynn.

Darcy faced the crushing fact that her beautiful mother had been Stephen's mistress, and she, Darcy, was the illegitimate result of their clandestine union.

The taste of salt on her lips jolted Darcy from her unhappy reverie. Bewildered for an instant, she raised her gloved hand to her face. The gloves came away bearing darkened moisture stains. Suddenly becoming aware that she was seated in an open carriage, her tear-washed face exposed to any and sundry who glanced her way, Darcy shielded herself behind the lowered parasol while she quickly wiped away all traces of tears. It simply would not do to have the general populace witness her despair.

Her composure once again intact, Darcy lifted the parasol, and her head, and sat erect, spine and shoulders straight, her posture correct, just as Clancy brought the carriage to a rocking halt in front of an obviously new two-story building bearing a sign over the door that proclaimed it to be the Citizens Bank and Trust.

Reminded of her mission, Darcy set the pain of her discovery aside and managed a smile for the man waiting for her on the sidewalk next to the door of the building.

9

Jonathan glided out from beneath the shaded porch and down the steps to the sun-drenched driveway.

Perhaps he should have gone with Darcy, he mused, watching the dirt churned up from the carriage settle back down, dusting the grass and shrubs bordering the drive with a coating of grayish film.

It was a bright, glaring day, sweltering under the relentless rays of the July sunshine; of course, Jonathan did not feel the physical effects of the gold disc in the sea of blue directly overhead. He had moved beyond the ordinary sensations of the physical plane.

And yet . . .

Jonathan's forward gliding motion ceased. He hovered, a frown of consternation drawing his brows together.

He had *felt*, experienced, sensation when passing his ethereal hand through Darcy's corporeal flesh. Was it possible, he reflected, to experience other physical sensations as well? Intrigued by the prospect, Jonathan called to mind the counsel of his spirit guide, to which, since it had been early on in his determination to remain on the earth plane, he had given scant attention.

In an interior-mind murmur, the guide had indicated that Jonathan could experience anything he desired, simply by desiring to do so.

With a mild start, Jonathan realized that he had, in actual fact, on numerous occasions, employed his guide's counsel without conscious thought, materializing and dematerializing, and appearing hither and yon, at will.

Jonathan arched one eyebrow. For example, he knew he did not need to glide along the driveway to reach the road. Testing, he decided to be there—and there he was, smack-dab in the middle of a large leaf tree standing sentinel to the side of the driveway along the road. He trembled to a thrill of awareness, a blending of his own essence and the vital and pulsating life force of the healthy tree. Mutely begging the tree's pardon for the invasion of his presence, Jonathan moved to one side.

Hmmm. Fascinated by the realm of possibilities apparently open to him, Jonathan decided to experiment further. Again with little conscious effort, he wished to experience the earth plane day, the myriad smells, the intense heat, the sweetness of the infrequent breeze.

At once, Jonathan felt the ramifications of his desire. The leaves hanging still and limp on the tree branches above gave little protection from the unrelenting and oppressive rays of the sun. The dry air parched his throat; he felt the weight of his jacket; perspiration beaded his brow.

The pungent odor permeating the heavy air

from a pile of recently dropped horse dung directly before him in the road assailed his senses. Jonathan's nostrils twitched; a smile lifted the corners of his mouth.

He wished his jacket gone—it disappeared, and he hovered there, in his shirtsleeves, savoring the feeling of dampness in his armpits.

Food. Could he experience hunger? Jonathan's stomach growled before the thought had finished forming. Hunger—of a sensual nature? Jonathan gasped as physical desire slammed into his ethereal form.

He wanted. He wanted.

Darcy.

Not now.

Jonathan laughed aloud as the desire suddenly vanished.

Why had he ever feared death? he chided himself. He felt more alive now than he ever had while carrying the heavy weight of a dense physical body.

Except—

Jonathan's smile fled. Except for the earthly reality of Darcy's solid corporeal form.

Jonathan exhaled a very physical-feeling sigh. Darcy continued to exist in the density of the earth plane, no more alive than he, perhaps even less so, but separate and apart from his realm of existence.

The essence of her filling his mind, Jonathan was reminded of Darcy's appointment, and pondered her purpose for requesting the meeting with the banker and the solicitor.

What had Darcy decided to do about the house and the situation thrust upon her? Jonathan wondered, not for the first time. Although she had reached her decision two days earlier, Darcy had not confided in him, but had promised to do so after meeting with Mr. Singleton and Mr. Mansford.

Unbeknownst to Darcy, Jonathan could have invaded her thoughts, if he had wished, thereby garnering her plans. But he had declined to do so, on principle. He would no more invade her mind against her will, than he would her body.

Perhaps he should have gone with her, Jonathan reiterated his thought of moments before.

He could have advised her, guided her, in a manner not unlike that of his own—

Your emotions are engaged. You would have been tempted to lead her along the path of your own interests.

The distinctive sound of the voice of his spirit guide murmured inside Jonathan's consciousness.

Yes, Jonathan acknowledged in silent truth. He would have been tempted to impose upon Darcy his own interests. He wanted her to choose to remain in Denver, to in some manner fulfill his own predeath wish to help young Sarah—indeed all the women of the house of La Rouge. Knowing this, he had determined not to accompany her to the appointment.

Not that Jonathan couldn't follow her anywhere in the world she chose to go, should she decide to act on her original declaration to sell the house and return to Philadelphia, or go traveling the world now that she was financially independent. He knew, intuitively, that he could, so long as he refused the ecstasy offered by the light.

But as both a mortal and eternal being, the

choice was Darcy's to make. Jonathan could do no more than offer suggestions, pointing out the options available for her consideration and ultimate choice.

He had chosen the only proper course in remaining behind to await the outcome of her meeting, her decision.

Darcy would be arriving at the bank about now, he judged, aware of the passage of earthly time. Waiting for her return, and her decision, would require patience.

Staring down the road in the direction taken by the carriage, Jonathan was struck by a very human sensation of uncertainty and anxiety regarding Darcy and her choice.

"Good morning, Miss Flynn," Mr. Mansford said, removing his hat as he rushed to the side of the carriage to assist her in alighting from the conveyance.

"Good morning, and thank you," Darcy replied, accepting his hand as she stepped from the vehicle to the sidewalk. "I'm sorry if I've kept you waiting."

"Not at all," he hastened to assure her. "You are precisely on time," he said, proving his assertion by plucking a large timepiece from his vest pocket and displaying it to her. "I was a trifle early."

And perhaps a trifle anxious about the portent of this meeting? Darcy reflected, suppressing a smile and turning to the brawny Irishman in the driver's seat, stoically waiting for instructions from her.

"Is there someplace you can wait, Mr. Dugan?" she asked, glancing along the noisy, dust-clogged street congested with the traffic of wagons, buggies, buckboards, and horsemen. "Someplace out of the direct sunlight?"

"There's a stable in back," Clancy answered, jerking his head to indicate the location. Not that it was necessary; the odor hung heavily on the hot, still air. "Mr. Singleton will have me alerted when you're ready to leave."

"Very well." Darcy made to turn away, then paused to suggest, "Perhaps there's a place where you can procure a drink to wash the road dust from your throat."

"Aye, lass, there's a place," Clancy said, flashing a grin of gratitude. "Nearby too."

"Very well, feel free to quench your thirst." Darcy turned away to join the solicitor, adding a note of caution to him over her shoulder. "But mind you keep your senses about you, Mr. Dugan."

Clancy chuckled. "I always do, ma'am." He ran a skeptical look over the lawyer and the building the two were about to enter. "And might I be speakin' out of line by taking the liberty to offer you the same advice?"

"Yes," Darcy tossed back. "But I shall endeavor to follow it, nonetheless."

Clancy's hearty bark of appreciative laughter could still be heard by Darcy even after Mr. Mansford had pulled the door of the bank shut behind them.

James Singleton stood waiting for Darcy and the solicitor in the open doorway of his private office.

A warm and charming smile split his attractive countenance as Mr. Mansford escorted Darcy through the bank, directly to him.

"Ah, Miss Flynn, welcome," Mr. Singleton greeted her in tones of genuine, if a bit flowery, pleasure. "It's truly a delight to see you again. I have been looking forward to this meeting ever since I received your note requesting it."

"How very kind," Darcy replied, returning his smile as she offered her hand to him. "Thank you." Her soft, even voice and her serene appearance concealed mounting inner trepidation and uncertainty.

Not that Darcy suffered one moment of doubt concerning her decision; she did not. Her resolve was as solid as the ground the building sat upon. Her sense of trepidation and uncertainty centered on how her decision would be received by the two gentlemen ushering her into the office.

"May I offer you refreshment?" James nodded to indicate a serving tray set on a small table next to his large, neat desk. "Tea, or a cool glass of lemonade?"

It was only then that Darcy noticed how dry and scratchy her throat felt from the heat and road dust. "Tea would be lovely," she said with gratitude. "Thank you."

While he turned to the table, Darcy's thoughts returned to the shadow she had left standing in the shaded porch.

Jonathan.

Had he ridden beside her in the carriage, invisible to her sight, following the ribbon of her unwinding memory? she reflected, certain in her own mind that, should he wish to do so, Jonathan possessed the ability to listen in on her thoughts, discern her emotions.

Was he here now, in this very room?

Darcy went still inside, receptive to awareness of him, his spirit essence, if indeed he was there.

She felt nothing, not the tiniest quiver indicating his nearness. Oddly, she felt positive he had not sojourned from the environs of the house.

Repressing a combined sense of relief and regret, Darcy marshaled her thoughts, preparing her arguments, if they should prove necessary, as James Singleton poured out tea for her and lemonade for Mr. Mansford. Then, when they, and the proprieties, were served, she immediately launched into an explanation for requesting the meeting.

Between delicate sips of throat-soothing, and surprisingly delicious, English breakfast tea, she briefly and concisely outlined her carefully formulated plans for the future, her own, as well as that of the women of her house.

"And so you see, gentlemen," she said in summation, "I requested this meeting for the express purpose of imploring your assistance with the practical arrangements."

Not unexpectedly, Darcy's recitation was received in stunned silence. Both the banker and the solicitor stared at her with like expressions of shocked disbelief. The banker was the first to recover his voice.

"But . . . but, Miss Flynn," James protested in a choked near whisper. "This . . . this is—" he broke off, shaking his head, as if unable to articulate his objections.

"Unusual?" Darcy returned the now empty cup to the tray before continuing. "Yes, I am aware of that but, however unusual, or unorthodox, it is what I have determined to do."

Perhaps because of his years of close association with Colleen Flynn, Mr. Mansford recovered his aplomb more swiftly than the banker.

"You are your mother's daughter." Untinged admiration colored his quiet tone. He gave her a wry smile. "I assume you do realize that there will be opposition, an outcry of public objection?" Although it was more a statement than a question, Darcy nevertheless responded.

"Yes, I do."

"I don't understand, Miss Flynn." James Singleton's voice matched his baffled expression. "You are obviously a cultured woman. Why would you so much as dream of taking on such a task, not to mention the good ladies of the city."

Darcy suppressed a sigh, managing to smile instead. She really did not relish the probability of clashing with the "good" ladies of the city, but should a clash prove inevitable, she was determined to persevere.

"I am a teacher, Mr. Singleton," she replied. "And in this instance, I feel a moral obligation." She smiled with gentle reproof. "Can you suggest a better way for me to discharge my duty to these women?"

"But there is absolutely no reason for you to feel obligated," he insisted. "None whatever."

"I disagree."

James betrayed the extent of his agitation by raking a hand through his neatly brushed hair, and turned to the solicitor for assistance. "Paul, tell her she is mistaken."

The lawyer slowly shook his head; his smile spoke of acceptance. "It would be to no avail, I fear. If I learned nothing else during my years of association with Colleen Flynn, I learned to simply hang on when she ran with the bit between her teeth." He gave a fatalistic shrug. "If, indeed, as I suggested, Miss Flynn is her mother's daughter, then I must further suggest that you and I are merely along for the ride."

James Singleton looked thoroughly deflated.

Darcy felt thrillingly elated—though she did contrive to contain her victorious feelings, presenting to the two gentlemen a facade of proper composure.

Miss Reinholt would most definitely have approved.

"Thank you, sir," she said to the resigned-looking lawyer. Then, turning to the banker, she offered a conciliatory smile. "I will need advice on how to proceed."

James exhaled a sigh of surrender. "As you wish," he agreed, working up a faint smile in return. "I would suggest we begin with a complete review of your financial standing here at the bank." He drew a large ledger front and center of his desk. "As I told you when I stopped by to offer my condolences," he went on, opening the ledger to a marked page, "I personally administered the allowance account your mother opened for you soon after she arrived here in Denver."

"Yes, I understand and—"

"But that was not the only account in your name of which I maintained exclusive control," he continued, interrupting her in an apologetic tone.

"Not the only one?" Darcy said in bewilderment. "My mother opened more than the one account?"

"No, not your mother." James gave a brief shake of his head. "Your father."

Darcy felt suddenly cold, and knew her face had gone pale. Anxiety clutched at her throat. "My—my father?" she repeated, in a choked, breathy voice.

"Yes." The expression of compassion in James's eyes told her in eloquent silence that he knew of her illegitimacy, knew and sympathized with her distress. "Your father, Mr. Stephen Darcy, opened the account on the same day as your mother did. Not an allowance," he clarified, "but a trust."

"I . . . ah . . . see." Darcy's face was now hot, flushed by mortification and humiliation. Somehow, knowing that the banker had known all along of her illegitimacy made the fact more demeaning, harder to bear.

James Singleton avoided her eyes. Ruddy color rose from his neck to his cheeks. He appeared uncomfortable, shifting restlessly in his chair.

After a taut moment of uneasy silence, Mr. Mansford cleared his throat. "Er . . . yes, well, James, could you be a little more specific concerning the details of this trust?"

"Yes! Yes, of course," the banker eagerly replied, obviously relieved by the suggestion to end the embarrassing moment. "As I said, Mr. . . . ah,

Darcy came to me soon after Miss Flynn opened the allowance account. He set up the trust, with precise instructions on exactly how it was to be administered." His tone took on a cool, professional clip. "I followed his instructions to the letter, prudently investing in what I believed to be the most solid of ventures." His smile revealed his self-satisfaction. "As a result of my management, the value of the trust today is more than ten times the original amount." He stated a dollar figure, then sat back to enjoy the mirrored expressions of astonishment on the faces of both Darcy and the solicitor.

Bereft of speech, Darcy sat, numb in body and mind, staring at the banker in stunned disbelief, robbed of thought, feeling, reaction by the sheer extent of wealth that was apparently now hers.

"Miss Flynn?" Concern shaded James Singleton's voice. He sat forward in his chair, peering into her ashen face. "Are you all right?" he asked anxiously. "Can I get you some more tea? A glass of water?" His voice faltered, and he shifted his alarmed gaze to the equally alarmed-looking lawyer.

"No, thank you," Darcy said, her voice hardly above a strained whisper. "I . . . I'm fine."

But she most obviously was not at all fine, and both men knew it. Her eyes were dull, devoid of their bright hazel sparkle; her skin had a sickly pallor, washed of its natural translucent glow; her posture was not merely correctly straight, but stiff, rigid, taut with tension.

Mr. Mansford again cleared his throat, this time in nervous agitation. "Miss Flynn," he said in a kindly, avuncular manner, "Would you prefer to end our meeting now, postpone it until after you have had some time to assimilate the information Mr. Singleton has imparted to you?"

Darcy shook her head, snapping herself out of her daze. She had come here to implement her plans, and hopefully win the assistance and support of these two men. Inside her head, it was as if she could actually hear Miss Reinholt's austere voice reminding her of her duty to represent the standard of conduct set by her mentor.

It would not reflect well on her character if Darcy were to use the ploy of a gentlewoman's sensitivity. Whereas she was feeling quite unwell from shock, she certainly was not about to indulge herself with a fit of the vapors.

"No," she answered, exerting her willpower to collect herself. "Although I do thank you for your solicitude, sir, I would prefer to continue."

Deferring to her wishes, the banker and the lawyer sat patient and alert, listening as Darcy succinctly outlined her plans for their edification.

Feeling exhausted, Darcy sat in the carriage, listening to the repetitive, mind-soothing cadence of the horse's hooves and the revolving carriage wheels.

The meeting between Darcy and the banker and solicitor was at last over. She had succeeded in eliciting their pledges to assist her with her plans. Yet Darcy enjoyed no feeling of elation or even satisfaction over her success. Her victory had been tarnished by the introduction of her father's name into the discussion.

Her father.

Darcy shuddered beneath the relentless rays of the midday summer sun. She had completely forgotten to raise her parasol for protection. It didn't matter; lingering shock had inured her to the heat, the noise, the sights and sounds of everyday life proceeding around her.

As clearly as if she held her mother's diary in her hands, Darcy could see the lines of elegant script Colleen had set down in the sporadically kept journal.

The first notation to capture then rivet Darcy's attention had been entered on a date preceding her birth.

I met the man I love today, Colleen Flynn wrote. *He came into Papa's shop while I was alone behind the counter. His name is Stephen Darcy. He is the most handsome and charming man I have ever met.*

The very next notation was dated some weeks later. The content of the two baldly stated, damning sentences pierced Darcy to the heart.

I do not care that Stephen is already married. I love him beyond the constrictures of convention, and I am proud to be carrying his child.

Stricken by the words, Darcy had closed the diary, only to immediately open it again, dreading the truth yet needing to know. She found her truth three pages farther along in the journal.

Stephen has purchased a beautiful house for me and our precious daughter, Darcy. He visits us whenever he can get away from his demanding family. Meanwhile, I have given shelter to four ladies of genteel birth but no money or prospects, forced to support themselves in the only manner available to them. Stephen is not happy

*with my decision to house these women, yet how can he
object when, as his willing mistress, I myself am merely
one step above them?*

I am content, Colleen had ended, boldly under-
lining the declaration.

Reading the script twenty-odd years later, Darcy
felt positive that, since the diary was private, secret
unto Colleen, her mother's assertion had been a
flash of bravado, written to assure and convince
herself.

Her illusions shattered, her pride lacerated,
Darcy had nevertheless continued to read the in-
scriptions to the very last one, dated two days before Colleen's demise.

Through her mother's words, she learned that
it was her father, Stephen Darcy, who had taught
Colleen the intricacies of financial investment. It
was also Stephen, certain of the imminent conflict
between the North and the South, thus concerned
for Colleen's safety, who had insisted she sell the
house in New Orleans and relocate in the West.

According to Colleen's account, Stephen had
visited Darcy's mother in Denver on an average of
four times a year. Reading of the joys of their brief
reunions caused incredible pain for Darcy, for
with all his traveling, he had never taken the time
to visit his daughter in Philadelphia.

And yet, in the last entry she had committed to
the diary, Colleen wrote of his enduring love for
her, and the child conceived and born of that love.

"Miss Flynn?" Mr. Dugan's voice broke through
the haze of misery clouding Darcy's consciousness.
"We're home."

Home. Darcy blinked to dispel the stinging mist filming her eyes. No, she thought, silently correcting the former bouncer. This house was not her home. The only home she had known for nineteen years was an institution in Philadelphia. But she would endeavor to make this house into a home, she vowed, raising her chin in determination.

"Yes," she responded, managing a smile for Clancy, who was eyeing her with concern. "We're home."

"Jonathan?" Darcy softly called upon entering her bedroom. "Are you here?" Tossing her gloves, hat, parasol, and beaded bag onto the bed, she walked to the standing mirror to inspect her eyes for traces of tears.

"I'm here." And he was, in an instant, as he had been earlier, seemingly lounging against the fireplace mantlepiece. Well, not quite as he had been earlier; his jacket was gone, and his white shirt gleamed in the afternoon sunlight.

Darcy's eyes widened in surprise . . . and a twinge of sensuous shock at the hint of flatly muscled chest and broad shoulders beneath the soft-looking material. "You are in your shirtsleeves?" she blurted out thoughtlessly.

"I'm sorry." Jonathan grimaced as he glanced down at himself. "I forgot. I'll remedy—"

"No, stay as you are," Darcy said with a sharp head shake. "I am surprised, not offended."

"Thank you." His soft gray eyes flickered over her face, and darkened as they delved into the windows of her soul. "You've been hurt, deeply," he said, drifting over the carpet to stand beside her, teasing her senses with his nearness. "Who is to blame for the pain in your eyes?"

"It's nothing." Darcy dismissed the subject, and tried to change it. "I have asked Mr. Dugan to inform the women of my desire to meet with them in an hour to discuss the plans I have made for the future."

"Indeed?" Jonathan arched that one same brow. "And am I invited to attend this meeting?"

"Yes, of course," she said at once. "After all of your efforts to impress upon me the extent of my responsibilities in the matter," she went on chidingly, "I would not dream of excluding you." She gave him a look both droll and wry. "Not that I could, even if I wanted to."

Jonathan appeared to look chastised and amused at one and the same time. "I accept your most gracious invitation," he murmured, executing a half bow. Then, as he floated upright, he fixed a probing stare on her. "Now, tell me who, or what, caused the pain you are attempting to conceal."

Darcy turned away, denying him access to her eyes, the depths of despair lingering there. "Jonathan, please, I really do not wish to discuss it."

"Your father?"

A simple question. Just two words. And yet those words, the gentle understanding contained in his soft voice, held the power to wrench a muted cry from her aching throat.

"You know?" Darcy spun around, and gave an

involuntary gasp at the sight of him, standing so very close to her.

"I'm sorry." Jonathan sighed. "I didn't mean to startle you. I thought you had grown used to my sudden materializations. But to answer your question: Yes, I know your father, Stephen Darcy, was not married to your mother." His smile held a hint of gentle reproach. "They truly loved one another, Darcy. But your father could not deny the legal rights of his wife. He paid the price of his love in anguish over what he believed to be his loss of honor and integrity."

"I am illegitimate!" she cried.

"Only in the eyes of mortals," he said. His gray eyes took on a teasing gleam. "I consider you quite legitimate."

Darcy was not consoled; quite the contrary. A wave of rejection and soul-deep longing swept over her, washing away her normal reticence. "He did not love me!" she choked out around a sob rising in her throat.

"Ahh, Darcy, you are wrong." As soft as it was, Jonathan's tone commanded her attention. "Your father loved you more than you could ever know."

"But he abandoned me," Darcy said. "He never came to see me after I was installed in Miss Reinholt's school."

"And that's how very much he loved you," he insisted. "Stephen Darcy loved you so much, he denied himself the child of his heart as well as his loins, to maintain your appearance of legitimacy. Had he visited you, he would have had to give Miss Reinholt his name. For you see, despite belief, your father was an honorable man. He was scrupulously honest."

"But he lived a lie!" Darcy exclaimed.

"No, he did not. He told his wife about his love for your mother before entering into a liaison with her. He begged her to release him. She refused, telling him that so long as she retained her position in society, he could do as he pleased, but she would never release him."

"Oh, Papa," Darcy whispered. "And Mother. How terrible to be forced to live like that because they were in love."

"They were not unhappy, Darcy. They were saddened by their decision to send you away from them, but they were determined to protect you from the taint of their love."

"And yet . . ." Darcy paused, glancing around the room. "She ran this house."

"Ran it, yes," he concurred. "But she never entertained or made herself available to the customers. Your father was her only love, and lover."

His assertion reminded Darcy of the relief she had felt when Jonathan had assured her he had never shared Colleen's bed. And now, she understood what he had meant at the time, when he had confused her by swearing he had not been offered that singular privilege.

Experiencing an infinitely deeper sense of relief, Darcy closed her eyes. A sensation, a touch, yet not a touch, shivered through her from her cheek to the base of her tingling spine. Jonathan! Her eyes flew open. His arm was raised, his hand moved, as if in stroking her face. Her breath caught, lodged in her throat at the sight of his expression.

Jonathan's beautiful soft eyes stared into hers with pure, unadulterated love for her blazing from their gray depths. "Darcy, I know how they felt, Stephen and Colleen. I know the power, and the beauty, and the agony of a love that consuming. I never felt love's sting in life. I feel it now."

"Oh, Jonathan, no!" she cried, backing away from him, the beguiling lure of his eyes, his touch that was not a physical touch, but more intense, more frightening.

"You feel it too."

Her father's child, Darcy could not, would not lie to him; he'd have known anyway. "Yes, I feel it. But Jonathan, it's wrong."

"Love is never wrong."

"In this instance it is! You know it is!" Spinning around, she fled to the window. Feeling as fragile as the glass pane, she wrapped her arms around her middle and held on, as if afraid she'd shatter like glass should she let go.

"No, it is not."

Darcy didn't respond. Restless, still clasping herself, she began to pace, numbering the reasons why their feelings for each other were impossible.

In the first place, a shared love between her and Jonathan was hopeless. He had no substance, for all he appeared more real to her than any *living* person. There was no future for them, could never be any future for them—Jonathan was of the past, his own past.

The thoughts, fears, objections whirled inside Darcy's mind, bringing her up short to stare in mute appeal at the shade of the man she had grown initially to like, then to appreciate, and finally, with alarming ease, to love.

"Darcy?" Jonathan's soft call drew her from her disquieting introspection.

She blinked, dispersing the warm rush of moisture to her eyes, uncaring of the overflow trickling in an increasing stream down her cheeks.

"Don't cry, love," he pleaded, his strained expression revealing the depths of his concern for her and their unusual, unearthly situation. "I did not speak of my love again to upset you. But I needed to tell you. Wanted you to know how very much I have come to love you."

Darcy wanted to protest, disagree, argue, but in truth she could not. How did one contest an absolute? She loved, he loved, hopelessly but absolutely.

"You feel the same, don't you?"

Darcy's drooping shoulders betrayed her flagging spirit. Her tears proved her inner turmoil. Her innate honesty demanded nothing less than truth.

"Yes," she answered in a whisper. "I do love you."

Jonathan's tender smile broke her heart. "And yes, I do love you." His avowal sealed her fate.

A soft but telling sigh whispered from Darcy's lips. "We are lost, aren't we?"

"Oh, no, Darcy," Jonathan replied quite seriously. "For all mortals despair for their souls, one is never lost."

"But you're talking about souls," Darcy cried. "I'm talking about love, our love, our hopeless love."

"Love is never hopeless," he said. "Never. Love is, and always will be."

"I seek answers," she protested. "And you offer me religious platitudes."

Jonathan shook his head. "I offer you truth, Darcy. The truth that love is universal. It knows not the boundaries of life and death. It is diverse, with many forms, all equal in value. The romantic love we share is as strong, as genuine as any other expression of love."

"But there can be no future for us." A sob tore from Darcy's throat. "We cannot *share* a lifetime."

"Not this one, no, because mine is over." Jonathan's voice was so low, Darcy barely heard him. "Although . . . my guide has said there is a way."

Darcy was no longer listening. Distracted, desolated by the futility of their love, she turned away to pace the room in restless agitation. "Jonathan, this love is impossible. There can be nothing between us. Nothing substantial. No tomorrow. No marriage. No children."

"I know." His immediate presence beside her no longer held the power to startle. "All we have is the here and the now. The present. But then, in truth, the present, each separate moment, is really all we ever have."

Pondering his assertion, Darcy continued to pace the comfortable room until it was time to join the women, accepting without question his superior knowledge and understanding, and his ethereal form gliding beside her.

10

The women looked bored, restless, edgy.

Darcy felt edgy as well. The turbulent emotions aroused by her discussion with Jonathan continued to churn inside her, disrupting her thoughts.

And from the expressions on the faces of every one of the women, Darcy knew the instant she walked into the dining room, where they had gathered for the meeting, she needed to be alert and clear-headed.

"I sure hope you called this meeting to tell us you're going to reopen the house." Sally took the initiative as first to speak. "The customers are getting mighty damned impatient about this long mourning period."

Relegating the disrupting considerations of love for an elusive shadow to the very fringes of her mind, Darcy stared into the shrewd, hard eyes of the fresh-faced, sweet-looking young woman and knew she had been robbed of the opportunity to gradually present her case, hoping thereby to win their acceptance of her plans. Challenged, she drew a quick breath, exhaled, and slowly shook her head from side to side. "No. As long as *I* own this house, it will never be reopened as a house of ill repute."

Her pronouncement was met with incredulous stares and stunned silence for some seconds, then the room reverberated with the sounds of their exclamations.

"What?"

"But why didn't you say somethin' sooner?"

"It's been two weeks!"

"How are we supposed to earn a living?"

"You shoulda told us!"

"Well, goddamn!" This came from Sally, and had surly, intimidating connotations.

Feeling under siege, Darcy took a step back, then was brought up short by a spectral voice inside her mind.

Do not retreat now. Tell them of your intentions.

Drawing a vision to her mind of her mentor, Darcy straightened her spine, squared her shoulders, and lifted her chin. "If you will give me the courtesy of your attention," she said in perfect imitation of Miss Reinholt's sternest and most austere tones, "I will endeavor to explain."

The effect of Darcy's voice, the intonations, on the women, mirrored precisely the effect Miss Reinholt had maintained on her staff and students; it cut through the babble like a knife through butter. The women were rendered wide-eyed, slack-jawed, and silent.

"Thank you." Sparing a cool smile, Darcy proceeded into the room, to take her seat at the head of the long dining room table. "Please, if you will be seated?" She inclined her head, inviting the two women still standing to join the assembled group. Then, while Sally and Katie moved to comply, Darcy raised her voice a notch to summon the cook from the kitchen and Clancy from the bar/gaming room.

"Dora . . . Mr. Dugan, please join us. This concerns the two of you as well as the ladies."

Darcy ignored the exchange of mutters around the table, and the silent shadow hovering by her side, sitting erect, hands folded on the gleaming tabletop, drawing the fluttering shards of her composure together as she waited with what appeared to be calm and limitless patience.

The heat in the room bore down upon her; beneath her dress, perspiration trickled along her breastbone to pool under her breasts. Darcy ignored the discomfort as well. Not so much as the faintest zephyr of a breeze bestirred the lacy curtains hanging limp and wilted at the open windows. The hum of bees and the fragrance of honeysuckle teased her senses, along with the clattering sound of a passing wagon and the unmistakable scent of animal droppings.

Soothed by the very normalcy of the smells and noises, Darcy gained command over her emotions by the time the obviously baffled cook scurried in from the kitchen and the mildly curious-appearing Clancy sauntered in from the bar.

"Well, now, lass," he drawled, coming to a stop behind Molly's chair. "And what's this all about?"

"The future," Darcy replied succinctly. "Mine. Yours. And every woman here." She swept the encircling faces with a cool, calm gaze. Inside, every nerve in her body quickened in readiness for the task facing her.

"What future do any of us have here if you're not going to reopen the house?" Sally demanded.

"Hopefully, a better future than if I were to reopen the house as it used to be," Darcy shot back at her.

"Well, I don't see how—" Sally began in argument.

"If you'd shut up," Katie inserted with gritty impatience, "maybe we'd all hear what Darcy has in mind."

"Yes, do be quiet, Sally, please," Jane said in her carefully acquired ladylike tones. "The rest of us would like to hear what Miss Flynn has to say."

Sally appeared on the point of further argument, but at the sight of the emphatic nods of agreement from the others, she subsided, her expression mutinous.

"After some necessary refurbishing, I intend to reopen the house," Darcy said. She held up her hand, beseeching quiet, when several of the women began questioning her. "Not as a house of pleasure," she went on, her raised voice slicing through the chatter. "But as a private school."

"A school!" Sally repeated, her voice harsh, her lips twisting in a sneer of disgust. "What kinda future is there for any of us in a school?"

"A future free of the bondage of prostitution," Darcy responded at once. "A future independent of the base and often cruel appetites of men."

"But . . . how?" Katie asked, frowning. "I mean, how would your school help us?" She indicated her companions with a wave of her hand. "We must earn a living."

There ensued a murmur of agreement from the

group, which Darcy again penetrated by slightly raising her voice. "And you shall, eventually."

"Eventually?" Young Sarah shook her head. "I don't understand what you're getting at, Miss Flynn."

"With your consent," Darcy said in her normal, softer tone, "I am proposing to educate every one of you, thereby preparing each of you for future respectable employment."

Ahhh. Jonathan exhaled in a purring sigh of satisfaction and approval.

Darcy felt a shiver at her nape, almost as if she could feel the warmth of his breath wafting over her skin. The sensation induced a weakness, a melting, a yearning for a deeper, more intense contact with him. Ensnared by the closeness of his essence, she lost the thread of the discussion in progress, the discussion she had initiated.

Darcy. His soft voice swirled inside her head. *The ladies are fairly bursting with questions.*

Her reverie shattered, Darcy became aware of the amusement lacing his tone, and the uproar around the table. The "ladies" were chattering away nineteen to the dozen, tossing queries at her and each other. Grasping at the broken thread, Darcy latched on to one such query.

"You wanna teach us to read and write?" Sarah's eyes and face were aglow with hope and wonder.

"Yes, and speak correctly," Darcy answered, smiling to ease the bite from her remark, while underscoring her response with a determined nod of affirmation. "Among other things," she went on, her voice gathering strength.

"What other things?" Sally asked, her attitude now openly belligerent.

She had already lost Sally; Darcy knew it as well as she knew her own name. Quashing a pang of disappointment, she girded herself to fight to hold on to the others.

"All the subjects taught in an institution for young ladies," she replied. "And perhaps a few more," she continued with a burst of inspiration.

"But . . ." Katie began, frowning. "It seems to me that what you're describing sounds mighty like a private school for young ladies."

"Precisely."

"But don't private schools like that cost a lotta money?" Sarah's visible chagrin stole the light from her eyes. "I . . . I ain't got no money."

The young girl's obvious disappointment was mirrored in the expressions of most of the other women.

"Nor have I," Jane said, her carefully maintained posture surrendering to drooping shoulders. "We all felt so safe here, with your mother." She glanced at the downcast faces around her. "There seemed no need to squirrel away our earnings."

Her statement received nods and murmurs of agreement from the others.

"You will not need money."

"But then . . ." Katie started, then paused to shake her head, as if to clear her thoughts. "How?"

Prepared for the question, Darcy leaned forward, poised to put forth her evolving plan, the flowering of her original seed idea. Jonathan forestalled her by once again whispering directly into her mind.

Do not offer them charity.

Do you truly believe that I am a fool? Darcy demanded in sudden, if silent, irritation, hard-pressed to keep from snapping the protest aloud.

She had been trained by an expert in the art of observation—an art imperative for a teacher of young girls adept at inventive mayhem and imaginative mischief. Despite all the mental distraction caused by the stunning revelations of her parentage and the enormous wealth bestowed upon her, Darcy had not been blind to the observation of the emerging individual talents possessed by each of the women. The method of exactly how to utilize those talents had slowly formed over the previous weeks, dawning full-blown in her mind mere moments ago.

Now, angry with her spirit companion, her mind ticking like a precision timepiece, Darcy mentally dismissed Jonathan and launched herself into her presentation.

"You will earn your tuition by filling the double roles of students *and* teachers."

"Teachers!" the women exclaimed simultaneously.

Sally followed through with a raucous peal of ridiculing laughter. "I have heard enough," she announced, pushing her chair away from the table. Then, standing, hands planted on her well-rounded hips, her laughter replaced by dripping sarcasm, she mocked her professional sisters. "Fine bunch of teachers of young women any of us would make." She made a rude snorting sound.

"Hell, we could get arrested for the only thing any of us could teach anybody."

"You are quite wrong, Sally," Darcy said with soft insistence. "Please, won't you sit down again, hear me out?" she pleaded.

"No, ma'am." Though Sally's voice had modified to a tone of respect, it remained adamant. "Your mother was kind to me, and you've been kind to me, too, and I thank you for that. But I know what I am." Her gaze was direct, unflinching. "And I like what I do." She tossed her head in defiance of the judgments of others. "I can go to any number of houses for employment, so I'll be leaving this house today yet." With that, she turned and marched from the room.

Rising, Darcy extended her arm, palm up, as if in anxious supplication, ready to make another plea to call Sally back, reason with her, but an inner whisper kept her mute.

The choice is hers.

"Sally's made her decision." Clancy unknowingly reinforced Jonathan's edict. "Don't take it so to heart, lass. Let the girl go her own way."

With a soft sigh of acceptance, Darcy sank back onto her chair and turned her attention to the remaining tenants of the house, belatedly noting the fact that both the cook and the bouncer were still standing.

"Dora, Mr. Dugan, won't you be seated?" she implored the pair. "This may take some considerable time."

Instead of moving to comply, Dora fixed a probing look on Darcy's pale face. "Did you eat anything today?" she asked with sharp impatience.

Darcy couldn't deny a faint smile; Dora had proved such a mother hen. "No," she confessed. "But I'm not—"

"Horsesh—er, shoes," Dora cut her off, shaking her head in despair. "If, as you say, we're going to be here a spell, I'm going to make some coffee and some sandwiches." She heaved a mighty sigh as she turned toward the kitchen, mumbling, "You'd think an educated lady would have the sense to know a body needs food to keep going."

The cook's practical statement galvanized the other women who, until then, had appeared content to sit, watching the drama unfold and waiting for whatever came next.

"I'll help," Sarah offered, scrambling up and away from the table. "I'm kinda hungry too."

"Yeah, come to think of it, I didn't eat anything neither," Daisy said, surprising everyone, since Daisy, hungry throughout every one of her years at the orphanage, never missed a meal or a chance to snatch a snack. "I'll help too."

June and Molly—encouraged by a nod from Clancy—followed in the wake of the other two.

The two remaining women, Katie and "Lady Jane," sat back, relaxing and exchanging glances before bestowing smiles of satisfaction on Darcy. Clancy chuckled, drawing puzzled looks from the three smiling women. "Well then, lass," he addressed himself to Darcy. "Seeing as how none of these other girls saw fit to leave with Sally, I'd say you've got yourself at least six student-teachers for your new school."

I'd say he's right.

"Teachers." Jane smiled. "This should prove

rather interesting." Her attractive, so-cultured-sounding voice drew Darcy's attention away from the wryly stated comment whispering through her mind.

"I beg your pardon?"

Jane executed an elegant shrug. "Forgive me, but I simply cannot imagine . . ." Her voice faded and she stared at Darcy in patent bemusement.

"I will explain presently," Darcy said, a soft smile of encouragement curving her lips. "I feel certain you—all of you—will be pleasantly surprised."

"I'm already surprised," Katie said in a dry-sounding drawl. "I'm more than surprised; I'm flabbergasted."

"Now, Katie girl," Clancy chimed in chidingly. "After all the time you were here, in this house with Colleen, *I'm* surprised that any little thing could surprise *you.*"

"You've got a point there," Katie allowed, laughing. "Our Colleen never was any too predictable."

Darcy leaned forward, about to ask Katie to elaborate on the unpredictability of her mother, when the other women swept into the room from the kitchen, carrying large serving trays and chattering away like magpies.

Clancy sprang to his feet and charged around the table, rushing directly to Molly to relieve her of the heavy tray, laden with two huge agate coffeepots. Steam curled upward from the wide spouts on the pots, permeating the still air, and tantalizing Darcy's senses with the aromatic scent of freshly brewed coffee.

Suddenly feeling ravenous, Darcy shifted her glance to peruse the contents of the other trays. Her gaze merely skimmed over the tray in Daisy's capable hands. The tray held only plates, saucers, and a neat stack of linen napkins; no nourishment there. Likewise the tray in June's hands, which was filled with cups, cutlery, a sugar bowl, and a jug of cream.

Her avid gaze searching evidence of sustenance, Darcy rose along with Katie and Jane to assist them in transferring the burdens from the trays to the table.

"Hmm," she murmured as her gaze settled on the tray set in the center of the sparkling white cloth that Katie spread over the tabletop. The tray was piled high with sandwiches, filled with thick slices of baked ham and roast beef. Her mouth watered in anticipation as, from the corner of her eye, Darcy caught a glimpse of the desserts on the tray in Sarah's hands. There was a three-layer vanilla-frosted cake, a spicy-smelling apple pie, and a basket mounded with fresh-baked oatmeal cookies.

Dora brought up the rear of the group, bearing a wide-mouthed cream-colored crock of pickles, a beaming smile lighting her heat-flushed face.

"Help yourselves," she announced, raising her voice above the clatter of the trays Clancy was stacking on the sideboard. "No need to stand on ceremony."

Taking the cook at her word, everyone, including Darcy, if in a genteel manner, attacked the food. Laughing and jabbering away, they quickly passed out plates, cups, and cutlery, and followed up with the sandwiches and pickles. Hefting the heavy pots, Clancy poured out the coffee.

The noisy chatter subsided to low, appreciative murmurs of conversation while the meal was consumed. Adding little but the occasional comment of agreement, Darcy was content to appease her hunger, and attend the remarks Jonathan whispered into her now receptive mind.

It only appears that they are all eating in a normal manner, he observed, a thread of amusement running through his deep tones. *In truth, you have practically got the lot of them eating from your hands.*

Startled by his assertion, Darcy came dangerously close to responding aloud in denial of his claim—thereby running the risk of casting doubt into her companions' minds concerning the extent of her mental stability.

Sounding happy, supremely satisfied, and in a teasing frame of mind, Jonathan continued in the same vein throughout the relaxed, impromptu meal.

From the collective display of evident gusto, one might presume that laughter and excitement sharpen the appetite, for mental as well as physical sustenance.

Darcy sent a deceptively casual-looking glance around the table, noting the animated expressions and bright eyes of every one of the assemblage, and found herself forced to agree with his assessment.

Even the tough former bare-knuckle prize fighter appears eager and excited. Jonathan's whisper sparkled with barely contained laughter. *But on reflection, I can't help but wonder if Clancy's bright-eyed gleam is due to your proposal, or to the blushing young woman he seems unable to drag his attention as well as his soulful gaze away from.*

Though Darcy nearly choked on a morsel of ham at the droll humor in Jonathan's voice, she agreed with him with a barely perceptible nod of her head, and gazed in benign approval at the couple seated opposite one another at the far end of the long oval table.

When all that remained of the hastily assembled luncheon were a few pickles, a handful of cookies, a small wedge of cake, a sliver of pie, and the dregs of the coffee, Katie reintroduced the original subject into the conversation.

"All right, Darcy, we're all fed, watered, calmed, and ready to listen," she said in her usual blunt and straightforward manner. "Are you now ready to explain to us this teacher-student idea of yours?"

"Yes, of course," Darcy replied at once, sitting erect and folding her hands on the tabletop. "It is quite simple, really." She smiled at the skeptical expressions washing over every one of the faces turned to her. "First, let me begin by explaining that my school will differ somewhat from the private schools back East, insofar as the curriculum is concerned."

"I'm sorry, Miss Flynn," Sarah piped in, looking embarrassed. "But I don't even know what a curriculum is."

"A course of study, Sarah." Darcy gave the girl an understanding smile. "In most private girls' schools, in addition to the primary studies, the curriculum usually includes instruction in deportment, manners, and the accomplishments associated with society's definition of a properly educated and well-trained young lady."

"Like yourself," Clancy inserted in a low-voiced, absolutely convinced observation.

Darcy inclined her head in acceptance of the compliment, then went on to expand her explanation. "The difference I intend to implement in my school is the inclusion of several other courses which, in my opinion, will deal with the practical elements necessary to any woman living here in the West, practical elements each one of you is familiar with."

She paused to look directly into each woman's face in turn before continuing. "In the two weeks I have been here, I could not help but notice the talents each one of you possesses," she asserted. "And so my idea is that, while I instruct each of you in the basics of formal education, you ladies can earn your place here by instructing one another, sharing those individual talents and skills with one another."

"Huh?" Sarah blinked.

"What skills?" June frowned.

"What talents?" Daisy giggled.

"What do you mean?" Molly looked blank.

While Clancy remained mute but attentive, Dora appeared confused. Katie expressed her doubts in silent eloquence by arching her eyebrows.

It was therefore left to Jane to articulate the overweening question in the minds of all of them.

"Might I suggest that you elaborate more fully, Darcy," she said in carefully modulated tones. "Precisely to what talents and skills are you referring?"

"Your skill with decorum and correct speech, for one." Darcy smiled. "I've been given to understand that you acquired the skill by observing then emulating my mother." She raised her brows. "Is that correct?"

"Yes, but—"

Darcy silenced Jane with a brief headshake. "Could you not then instruct the others in the speech and behavior patterns of a proper young lady?"

Jane appeared not so much startled as pleasantly surprised by Darcy's suggestion. "Why, yes, yes, I could," she answered after mulling over the concept a moment. A controlled grin tugged at her lips. "It might prove quite enjoyable."

Until then, Jonathan had been content with the position he had assumed to the right and just slightly to the rear of Darcy's chair; a stance suitable to Darcy, since she could not see, thus be distracted by the sight of him.

Now, appearing every bit as solid to her as any of the others in the room, and more attractive than any man she had ever looked upon, attired as he still was in his chest- and shoulder-revealing shirtsleeves, he drifted around the room, studying the various expressions on the faces of the group.

"I feel positive it would be," Darcy responded to Jane as she took note of the effect on some of the others of Jonathan's closer presence.

June shivered and glanced at the window as he passed behind her chair. A frown drew her brows together when she saw that not a hint of a breeze ruffled the curtains.

"I feel strange," Sarah said in a small, fearful voice.

"Yeah, and me!" Daisy exclaimed. "Almost like I'm being watched or something."

"I feel it, too," Molly whispered, her wide-eyed gaze seeking the reassuring bulk of Clancy.

"Now that I think on it," Dora said, glancing around uneasily. "I've been getting this same kind of feeling every so often lately."

"Are you thinking the place is haunted, then?" Clancy asked in a teasing tone, obviously attempting to lighten the suddenly somber atmosphere.

"Haunted!" Sarah's eyes grew as round as the plates cluttering the table.

"Don't be silly," Katie admonished the girl, scowling at the grinning Irishman before turning to Darcy to ask hopefully, "Could we get back to the business at hand?"

"Certainly," Darcy said briskly, suppressing an urge to mirror Katie's scowl, but aiming it in warning at Jonathan instead of Clancy.

As if he could read her mind, Jonathan chuckled, but obliged by zipping back to his former station, behind her chair. The languid hot air in the room was disturbed by the sudden sigh of relief that issued simultaneously from several throats, including Darcy's own.

"Now you, Katie, have demonstrated a distinct skill in handling a pistol," Darcy went on, determined to ignore her playful specter. "And since it appears to me that a young woman has a need of such knowledge here in the West, you could fulfill your teaching duties by giving all of us instructions on the proper use of the weapon."

"All?" Katie raised her eyebrows. "You also?"

"Yes," Darcy said solemnly. "After that unpleasant incident soon after my arrival here with that dreadful and offensive man, I feel compelled to learn how to defend myself should the need again arise."

"All right, I'll do it," Katie agreed. "It seems a small price to pay for an education."

And so it went, Darcy pointing out individual talents and skills as each woman in turn claimed not to be in possession of the same.

She complimented Daisy for her instinctive talent for style and design, and the ability to unerringly judge what fashions would and would not becomingly suit any figure.

She commended June for the cooking and housekeeping skills she had so aptly learned from her mother, and regularly displayed by helping Dora in the kitchen and the rest of the house.

She praised Molly for the deft talent she revealed with a needle and thread whenever she was called upon to close a seam, repair a garment, or even, as Darcy had witnessed, create a complete outfit that rivaled any constructed by a professional seamstress.

Each of the women in turn happily agreed to teach her unrealized talents and skills to the others in payment for the opportunity to receive instruction of a more formal educational nature from Darcy.

Each, that is, until Darcy leveled her eyes on Sarah. That young woman bit her lip, blinked against the tears misting her eyes, and shook her head.

"I can't do any of those practical things, Miss Flynn," she wailed. "I don't own any suchlike talent."

"Indeed?" Suppressing a compassionate smile, Darcy slowly raised her arm, drawing their attention to her hand as she touched her fingers to the shining curls cleverly arranged at the top and back of her head. "Did you not dress my hair for me this morning," she inquired, arching her brows, "as you have most mornings since I've been here?"

Sniffing, Sarah bobbed her head. "Yes, but—"

"Sarah," Darcy gently interrupted the girl. "Let me assure you that the ability to dress hair so beautifully is definitely a talent, a skill envied by many." She appealed to the others for confirmation. "Am I not correct, ladies?"

Their response was immediate and gratifying.

"It sure is," Daisy chirped. "Just look at me. If I had half your skill, I wouldn't always be looking like the rag mop Dora uses to do the floor."

The comments from the rest, though briefer, were basically along the same line.

"But . . . it's so easy!" Sarah exclaimed, shaking her head as if unable to believe what she had heard. "I could teach anyone, all of you, to do it."

"Precisely." Allowing herself a self-satisfied smile, Darcy gazed at the startled girl, who had unknowingly just proved the point Darcy had tried to make.

The smile that swept over Sarah's pretty face banished the expression of sad vulnerability. "You mean, just by teaching everyone to dress their hair, I can stay here with you, Miss Flynn, learn to read and write?"

"Yes, of course," Darcy assured her, and with an encompassing glance, the others. "We will all be busily employed teaching one another."

"And what about me?" Dora's voice broke into the din of excited chatter that ensued.

"Why, you will continue in the position of cook and housekeeper," Darcy replied. Then she frowned. "You do wish to stay with us, don't you?"

Dora beamed. "You just try to get rid of me!"

Laughter and chatter erupted again from the ladies; this time it was Clancy's voice that broke through.

"And me, lass? I can't see that you'll be needing a bouncer in a school for ladies."

"You are quite right, Mr. Dugan, I will not require a bouncer," Darcy concurred, suppressing a twitch at the corners of her lips at his crestfallen look. "But this will still be a house of females, in need of protection," she continued. "Can I prevail upon you to stay on in that capacity?"

Pushing his chair back, Clancy stood and made her a respectful bow from the waist. "Ah, lass," he crooned as he straightened. "I would count myself honored to do so."

It was settled. Exhaling a deep sigh of relief, Darcy sat back in her chair. "There is a lot to be done before we can begin in earnest," she told them. "I am counting on all of you to help me prepare the house, change it into a school . . . She paused, then added strongly, "And a *home.*"

11

Heaving a sigh of relief, Darcy slumped back against the bedroom door. Closing her eyes, she rested her head against the solid wood panel, and sent up a silent prayer of thanks for the successful conclusion to the seemingly endless day; had it really only been some twelve or thirteen hours since she had awoken around six-thirty that morning?

Darcy opened her eyes to glance at the delicate porcelain clock on the mantel. The hands read six forty-two. A long day indeed, beginning with her meeting with Mr. Mansford and the banker, Mr. Singleton, and ending with her meeting with the residents of her house.

And even though Darcy regretted losing Sally, she was encouraged by the enthusiasm of the others. After winning their support of her plan of turning the house into a private school, they had all remained in the dining room, discussing ideas and suggestions for refurbishing the house. As the supper hour approached, they had moved as a group into the kitchen, still voicing their thoughts while assisting Dora in the preparation of the evening meal.

Now, early in the evening on the longest day of Darcy's life, her sense of triumph was slightly tinged by exhaustion, for although she had won the first battle in her secret war to reclaim the lives of the women of the house, the initial victory had taken its toll. She felt drained, physically and emotionally.

Darcy wanted nothing more at that moment than to drop onto the bed and lose herself in the nothingness of unconsciousness, if only for a little while. The temptation was so strong, she actually pushed herself away from the door, moving like a sleepwalker toward the inviting bed.

The sound of activity and splashing water brought her to a halt mere feet from her goal.

A weary smile tugged at Darcy's lips. The heat throughout the day had been beastly, the air heavy and stifling. Before taking her leave of her companions, Darcy had spoken aloud her longing for a bath.

"It's yours, lass," Mr. Dugan had promised, flashing a grin as he strode from the room.

Clancy was now engaged in the process of fulfilling his promise, by filling the tub in Darcy's dressing room.

The anticipation of submerging her sticky, grubby-feeling body into a tubful of soothing clean and scented warm water banished a measure of the utter weariness pulling at Darcy's depleted spirits.

Drawing a deep, reviving breath, she raised her hands to the row of buttons on her dress; Darcy had discarded the overjacket soon after the impromptu luncheon. Memory nudged, stilling her fingers on the third button.

"Jonathan?" she softly called, skimming her gaze around the so silent room. "Are you here?"

There was not so much as a whisper of response, no sudden spectral appearance.

Releasing yet another sigh, Darcy resumed removing the perspiration-dampened garments from her tired, overheated body. Then, clad in a thin but concealing wrapper, and carrying a summer-weight cotton nightdress, she eagerly crossed to the dressing room. Discarding the wrapper, she lavishly sprinkled bath salts into the steaming water and stepped into the tub, sighing with sheer pleasure as she slid down into the deliciously warm liquid.

A bright flash of lightning immediately followed by a deep rumble of thunder startled Darcy out of the doze she had been lulled into. She shivered, but not only because the bath water had cooled considerably. The air in the room was also noticeably cooler.

Another sharp crack of thunder brought her surging upright in the tub. Lapping water sloshed over the metal rim onto the floor.

The room was nearly dark, the air, though cooler, was oppressive from the storm approaching over the mountains from the west. Another brilliant streak of lightning accompanied by booming thunder sent her scrambling from the tub.

Irrational, unreasonable, senseless as she knew it to be, Darcy was terrified of thunderstorms.

Her eyes wide, her heart pounding, she grabbed the towel folded neatly on the stool next to the tub, and quickly ran it over her body, leaving most of the surface slick with beaded moisture.

A gasp lodged in her tight throat and her gaze flew to the bedroom doorway when another streak of lightning flashed, momentarily illuminating both the unlighted bedroom and the dressing room. A gust of wind swept through the open bedroom windows and the doorway into the dressing room to swirl around her body, chilling her flesh.

Snatching up her nightdress, Darcy pulled it over her head and tugged it down over her trembling form. The soft, finely woven cotton pasted itself to the damp patches of skin, revealing the contours of her figure.

Unmindful of the gown clinging to her, Darcy dashed into the bedroom and directly to the windows, cringing and crying out as a crooked bolt of lightning rent the roiling black storm clouds and thunder boomed overhead as she reached for the sash.

"There's nothing to be afraid of."

Darcy let out a screech and spun around to confront the soft-voiced man behind her. "Jonathan!" she exclaimed, once she had succeeded in catching her breath. "Will you please stop creeping up on me like that."

"Creeping?" Jonathan arched a familiar eyebrow. "I never creep," he said, blatantly suppressing a smile. "I may drift. I may glide. I may even float. But I never creep. Creeping lends bad connotations to the good name of spirits."

"How very amusing," Darcy snapped, shuddering at yet another ear-splitting crack of thunder. Spinning around, she grasped the window and shut it with a resounding crash. "Nevertheless," she went on in a repressive tone, while making a dash for the other open window at the front of the house, "I would appreciate it if you would not do it again. It's unnerving."

"Your wish is my command," he said, bending low from the waist in an elegant, old-worldly bow. "What would you prefer I do in future to announce my approach?" Jonathan's voice was dry, his tone droll. "Whistle? Hum? Sing, perhaps?" As usual, that one blasted eyebrow peaked into a quizzing arc.

Feeling easier for having shut herself inside, away from the worst of the storm's noise, Darcy found herself able to smile, at herself and her own irrational fears, and for him, and his attempt to relieve her unreasonable fright.

"Do you possess a good singing voice?" she inquired, retracing her steps to his side. "Or would the sound of it grate like a nail scraped against slate?"

"I have received compliments on the full richness of my baritone voice," he answered solemnly.

"Indeed?" Darcy mirrored his eyebrow arch with one of her own. "Received from whom?"

"Members of my former congregation," he replied, his twitching lips belying his solemnity. "I always joined my voice with theirs in the singing of hymns."

"Sending your praises to heaven . . . so to speak?"

"So to speak," he agreed, giving her a bone-melting grin. "And speaking of praises," he went on, "I give you mine, in grateful abundance."

Praises for her? Darcy frowned. "I'm afraid I don't understand," she said. "Praises for what?"

Jonathan's grin curled into a soft, breathtaking smile. "Why, for your decision to remain here, in Denver, in this house. But primarily for your brilliantly conceived idea to turn the house into a school." His eyes glowed with approval. "Your dedication to, er, *saving* these women from a life of sin and degradation is commendable."

Darcy had not missed his brief hesitation over the word *saving*. Nor had she been unaware of the tinge of amusement coloring his tone. Confused by it, she felt compelled to challenge him.

"Are you laughing at me, my intentions to help these women?" she demanded, hurt and angry.

"Not at all," Jonathan said at once. "You, of all people, should know better, for you alone, of all mortals, know that my sole reason for resisting the light was my strong desire to teach Sarah to read and write."

Not fully convinced, but willing to be, Darcy gave voice to her suspicions. "Yes, at least I believed that to be so. But why, then, did you place emphasis on the word *saving* in regard to my intentions concerning the women?"

Jonathan's smile took on a chiding tilt. "Ah, Darcy," he gently scolded. "I begin to suspect you haven't heard or believed a word I've said."

"But that's not true!" she denied. "I just told you I believed your stated reason for remaining earthbound, or however you refer to your presence here."

"Earthbound will do."

"But then why . . ." Darcy broke off, raising her hands in a gesture of confusion and defeat.

Jonathan shook his head, in a manner indicating despair. "Didn't I also tell you that no soul is ever lost?"

Darcy frowned in incomprehension. "Are you now telling me that my efforts designed for redemption and reparation for these women are unnecessary, even superfluous?"

"In regard to their souls, yes," he replied bluntly, but then immediately softened the verbal blow by adding, "but in regard to their mortal existence, no. As I already mentioned, your efforts and intentions are highly commendable, and will not go unnoticed."

Darcy was almost afraid to ask, and yet she had to know. "Unnoticed by whom?"

"The light," he answered simply.

"God?" she asked in an awed whisper.

Jonathan inclined his head. "If you will."

A feathery shiver stole up her spine, and Darcy cringed, just a bit, as lightning flashed and thunder roared directly over the house, and visibly shivered as a strong gust of wind rattled the windowpanes. The onslaught of driving rain had further cooled the air in the room, dropping the temperature by some thirty degrees. Darcy shivered again, this time from the effects of the much cooler air penetrating the damp nightdress plastered to her body.

"You are cold?"

"Yes," she confirmed, but unwilling to admit to the deeper spiritual reason for the inner thrill, she opted instead to admit to the surface effects. "After the heat of this afternoon, the contrast is chilling. Don't you feel it?"

"Only if I choose to," he said, giving way to a teasing smile tugging at the corners of his mouth. "It's one of the advantages of being dead."

Darcy shivered once more, but once again not from the surface chill. "How can you joke about being dead?" she asked in a strained whisper.

Jonathan laughed, an easy, pleasant sound. "Maybe because the joke's on me," he answered, still chuckling. "And for the most part, I'm rather enjoying myself."

Darcy could do no more than stare at him in disbelief, so disturbed by his attitude she was unfazed by yet another display of brilliant lightning.

"You're so very beautiful."

Coming so abruptly on the heels of his teasing, the sudden serious sound of Jonathan's low-pitched voice startled Darcy. "Wh-what?" she said, staring in blank confusion into his soft gray eyes.

"I said you are beautiful." A smile every bit as soft as his eyes played over his attractive, masculine lips. "Do you, I wonder, realize that your gown is clinging to you, outlining every alluring curve of your body?"

"Oh!" Darcy's hands flew to her gown, pulling the damp material away from her form—now shivering in response to an intense awareness, of herself as a woman, of him as a man.

"Darcy, Darcy." Murmuring her name, Jonathan raised his hand to her flushed cheek.

Darcy gasped. As had happened before, his fingers sank into her flesh; she didn't have to see it as she had in the mirror that morning. She could feel it, the same sensation of warmth, excitement, arousal streaking through her with more effect and fury than the lightning streaking through the massive storm clouds darkening the evening sky.

"Am I frightening you?" His voice was sad; his eyes were sadder still; his smile was saddest of all. "I'm sorry." With a whispered sigh, he began withdrawing his hand.

Darcy shook her head in quick denial. "No, Jonathan. I'm not frightened," she said, unconsciously lifting her hand to cover his. Her flesh sank through his.

Jonathan's response was immediate and visible; he shuddered and groaned. "Oh, Darcy, why, why did I have to die before meeting you?" An agony of despair and remorse weighted his emotion-raspy voice. "As you said this morning, there can be no future for us. I want to offer you marriage, and I cannot. I want to offer you joy of communion, and I cannot. I want to offer you children, and I cannot." His eyes betrayed his inner pain. "I love you, and I should not."

Darcy felt and shared his pain to the very depths of her heart and soul. "And I love you," she confessed in a whispered cry. "And I care not what should or should not be."

Jonathan closed his eyes, as if overcome by hearing her confession. When he opened them again, all traces of the pain were gone. Only the sadness remained. "If you are willing, I would love you, make love to you, join with you in celebration of our love."

Darcy's eyes flew wide in surprise. "Can you?"

Her voice quivered with questioning disbelief—and her pulses raced with wildly burgeoning hope.

"No, not in the normal, mortal way," Jonathan answered, shaking his head. Like a column of smoke, he drifted to the side of the bed. A smile illuminated his face. Unconditional love glowed in the depths of his eyes. "But there is a way." He extended his hand, palm up, to her. "Come, trust me, be with me, love me, Darcy," he murmured. "Let me demonstrate, to the extent that I can, my love for you."

Because she did trust him, utterly and completely, and because she did love him, with every fiber of her being, Darcy did not hesitate for an instant.

Boldly, bravely, proudly, she walked to the bed to stand facing him. "I love you, Jonathan," she said with quiet simplicity. "Tell me what to do."

A flame leapt to life in his beautiful eyes, revealing a depth of passion she would have thought impossible for an ethereal being. His visible response caused a corresponding flare of passion inside Darcy, stealing her breath, creating a painfully pleasant tightness in the fountainhead of her femininity.

"I would see you in your mortal glory but, though I would rejoice in the task," he said, smiling ruefully, "I cannot remove your gown."

Again Darcy reacted without hesitation. Gathering the damp folds of her nightdress in her trembling fingers, she drew the gown slowly up her body and over her head, then let it float unnoticed to the floor.

The flame erupted into a blaze in his eyes as he

drank in the beauty of her slender form from the auburn mane on her head to the delicate toes of her narrow feet.

"Loosen your hair, please," Jonathan said in a low, strained plea. "I long to see it wild and unfettered."

Fully aware that by granting his request she would be presenting for his inspection her full, tightly nippled breasts, Darcy raised her arms to bring her hands to her hair. Heat, intense and urgent, raced through her at the expression of adoring hunger that swept over Jonathan's face as his eyes feasted on her upthrust breasts.

He did not touch the flesh he so obviously desired; he could not touch her—and yet, and yet, Darcy's flesh quivered, as if from an actual physical caress, as his smoky gaze devoured her pale, satiny skin.

Darcy's fingers fumbled with the pins anchoring the coils Sarah had fashioned at the top and back of her head; then, finally, she drew out the last one. Her glorious mane of auburn hair tumbled around her alabaster shoulders and down her back.

Jonathan raised his eyes to the shimmering tresses; a sigh whispered through his slightly parted lips.

"So very lovely," he murmured. He reached toward her with one hand, then paused, long fingers visibly trembling. "May I?" he asked in a low, strained voice.

"Can you?" Darcy replied in a reedy puff of exhaled breath. "Can you feel . . . anything?"

"Oh yes, I can feel," he answered, moving his hand to her hair. "Can you?"

Darcy's eyes grew wide with shock and delighted surprise for, though she could not see his hand, she felt it sink, blend with the silky strands of her hair. The resulting sensation was elemental, electrical, quite like, she suspected, being struck by lightning. She felt singed, burned, in a most arousing way, to the very core of her femininity.

"Oh, Jonathan!" she cried, shuddering in reaction to his touch that was not a touch.

His eyes, so adoring, so intent, took on a light of teasing deviltry, creating a gleaming glow that sent another bolt of turbulent excitement streaking through her entire being. Darcy moaned in response to the emotions quaking through her. She felt weak, drained. Her knees buckled, and swaying, she reached out to grasp him. Her hands, then her wrists, then her arms went straight through him, and she cried aloud again, this time in frustration and despair.

"I know, I know." Jonathan's voice betrayed his own frustration. "I cannot hold you, support you." He hesitated, as if unsure. Then, softly, uncertain but hopeful, he suggested, "If you would lie down on the bed?"

Darcy was way beyond the point of pausing to consider, reflect, or even question. She began to turn toward the bed before Jonathan had finished speaking. She drew in a sharp breath as his arm passed through her face, and felt him draw his arm back, leaving a coolness where there had been a delicious sense of warmth.

Her breathing shallow, her pulses pounding,

her blood seemingly racing through her veins, Darcy sank onto the feather mattress, then shifted until she lay full length, trembling from a dizzying combination of apprehension and anticipation. Lowering her eyes, she peered at him through the screening fan of her thick lashes, watching, waiting with bated breath, and heated flesh, to see what he would do next.

What Jonathan did set her eyelashes to fluttering and her heartbeat into a gallop. Without uttering a sound, or making a move, or blinking an eye, his clothing vanished in an instant, revealing a beautifully formed male in full, throbbing, and thrusting arousal.

Darcy had never in her life seen a naked man, let alone one sexually aroused. Awed by the sight of him, the sheer masculine strength exposed, she stared at him in unabashed and blatant curiosity and fascination.

"Don't be afraid, Darcy. I won't hurt you." Though firm with reassurance, Jonathan's tone held a hint of disappointment. "Your maidenhead is safe, for in truth, I cannot hurt you in the mortal rite of piercing to deflower."

Though Darcy was innocent and untouched, she was by no means unaware of what occurred between a man and woman during the act of physical lovemaking. And Jonathan had asked her to be with him, make love with him. But, she queried in silent confusion, if he could not, then . . .

"You'll see," he murmured, answering the question filling her mind before she could give it verbal substance. "Do you love me, want me, trust me?"

"Yes," Darcy answered at once, raising her arms to him in surrender and acceptance.

"Darcy, my love." Even as he spoke, he moved, floating through air until he hovered over her, his head even with hers, his eyes gazing into hers. "This is all as new to me as it is to you," he murmured, smiling down at her. "Shall we experiment? Explore the possibilities?"

"Yes," she agreed, never pausing to think or doubt, lost in the enfolding depths of his soft eyes.

Jonathan lowered his head, bringing his ethereal mouth to hers. There was no pressure, no feeling of physical contact, and yet sensation shot like a skyrocket through Darcy. Yearning, she parted her lips, and gasped, shuddering, as a searing flame seemingly swept into her mouth, seeking to brand every sweet inner inch as its own.

Her breathing grew uneven, ragged; her heartbeat a frenzied tattoo at every pulse point; a melting heat invaded her limbs, her stomach, her very core.

Craving, aching for some undefined something, Darcy raised her arms to reach for him, draw him closer. Then, recalling that she could not, but needing to hold on to something solid, she thrust her arms out to her sides and grasped the coverlet, digging her fingernails into the soft material.

The spirit kiss lasted an eternity, and ended much too soon. Darcy uttered a deep-throated moan of protest when Jonathan lifted his head, but the moan became a cry of pleasure when the flames that were his spirit tongue licked a trail of stinging sparks down her arched throat. Her mind splintered when his tongue of fire circled, then flickered over and ignited her passion-tightened nipples.

"Jonathan! Jonathan!" Darcy's voice was raw with desire. Her chest heaved with each panting, labored breath. Her body twisted with restless abandon.

"Part your legs for me, my love."

Jonathan's whispered plea pierced the sensuous fog clouding Darcy's mind. Without a cautioning thought, she complied at once, desperate to experience more of his fire. Eyes wide, she watched as he floated into the cradle of her quivering thighs.

"Are you sure, my love?" he murmured, hovering over her, not touching—but sensed by her to the marrow of her bones.

"Yes, yes." She sobbed, drawing her knees up to brace her feet on the bed, and arching her body in silent supplication and acceptance of his.

"Darcy, I love you." Jonathan moved as he softly uttered the solemn-voiced vow.

True to his promise, Darcy experienced no sense of penetration, no piercing of her maidenhead. There was no pain, no discomfort, but a sense of wonder and awe. For this time, the flame was a column, a pillar of fire entering her body, filling her with an all-consuming blaze. The pillar moved with ever-increasing urgency, enticing Darcy to move in time with it, matching her body to the rhythmic cadence.

The dance of mortal and specter spun along an ever-diminishing spiral of tension, playing out the bowstring of an age-old waltz. Sensation whirled in flashing lights inside Darcy until the

music attained a crashing crescendo, and the
string snapped, flinging her into a vortex of exquisite, shattering, pulsating pleasure.

Yet still, it was not over.

Barely conscious, Darcy murmured when Jonathan moved, unwilling to relinquish the warmth
of his fire.

"We are merely together, my love," he murmured soothingly. "Now I seek to make us one."

Not understanding, Darcy observed him through
confusion-clouded eyes as Jonathan floated above
her. Then, extending his arms to align with hers,
and measuring his length to hers, he began a slow
descent.

Darcy's eyes and mind expanded in growing wonder as Jonathan's ethereal form sank, blended, then
meshed with her, mingling their separate entities
into a single essence.

A sensation of sheer joy and exaltation swept
Darcy from physical reality into a realm of incredibly beautiful spiritual union of two entities fused
by the power of pure love into one complete soul.

Soaring through time and space with her eternal soulmate, Darcy drifted on a wave of absolute
fulfillment into peaceful unconsciousness.

12

The earth lay sear and parched beneath the unrelenting rays of the brassy early September sunshine. In a near pasture, a small herd of cattle grazed on the drying grasses. All was still, quiet, the bird song hushed by the reverberating crackle of recent gunfire.

Wade Dunstan stood tight-lipped and narrow-eyed, staring down at the body of a man sprawled out on his back, his blood seeping into the thirsty ground from the twin bullet holes in his chest, directly above his heart.

The man had called himself Daniel Clemmens. Wade neither knew nor cared if the name had been the man's own or just one of a string of aliases.

The corner of Wade's lip curled into a faint unpleasant smile of satisfaction.

Three down and one to go.

"Ah . . . Mr. Dunstan?"

The hesitant, uncertain sound of Betsy's voice drew Wade from his contemplation of the carcass at his feet.

"Yeah?" he growled, tearing his gaze from the body to glance at her. "You okay, kid?"

"Uh-huh." She gave a jerky nod. "Now what?"

"Huh?" Wade tilted his head to frown at her.

"Now what do we do?" Betsy stared back at him, her little face pale, pinched with strain. Though Wade had given the man an even chance, going so far as allowing the killer to get off the first shot before firing himself, her expression revealed shock at the entire incident, culminating with the shootout, and Wade's close brush.

"About what?"

Betsy flicked one small hand at the body. "You can't just leave him layin' here . . . can you?"

"Why not?" Wade's shrug conveyed unconcern. "The buzzards have to eat too."

The girl shuddered and cast her gaze at the brilliant blue sky, squinting at the dark shapes of the scavengers already circling overhead. She made a face of disgust and shuddered again.

"They . . ." She indicated the lowering birds, and swallowed. "They'll tear him apart."

Wade shifted a hard-eyed glance to the dead man. "He won't feel a thing," he drawled.

Betsy made a choking noise, deep in her throat. "But that don't make it okay to just leave him," she said in a whispered protest. "I mean . . . it's . . . it's not Christian, or not human, or somethin'."

Justice? Wade kept the observation to himself, and heaved a tired sigh of surrender; considering her contribution to his cause, she had a right to demand concessions from him. "Okay, kid, we'll stop by the ranch house of this"—he aimed a sour look at the body—"this animal's friends, and tell them where to find him." His voice grew an implacable edge. "But that's as far as I'll go."

A tiny smile, sweet and heart-touching, tugged at Betsy's tender lips and, as had happened often lately, at his emotions. "So long as somebody knows where to find him, that's far enough. Thank you, Mr. Dunstan."

"Yeah," Wade grunted, jerking his head at the two horses and a placid pack mule grazing a few feet away. "Let's get moving." He strode to the smaller of the animals to stand waiting for her, impatience scoring his trail-drawn features. "I want to cover some ground before sunset."

"Where we goin'?" she asked, scurrying up to him and raising her arms trustingly. "Laramie?"

"No need now." Wade shook his head as he grasped her around the waist to swing her up into the saddle. "After what that sodbuster back aways said about there being no place to speak of for me to leave you in Laramie," he said, sighing again as he turned to walk to his own horse, "I suppose we might as well head straight for Denver."

"I'm sorry."

Scooping up the mule's lead line, Wade thrust a booted foot into a stirrup, and swung a long leg up and over the horse, while tossing a droll look at the girl. For all the sound of meek contrition in her voice, Betsy wasn't sorry by a damn sight, and he knew it.

Shaking his head, he made a low, clicking sound with his tongue to get Rascal moving. Betsy imitated the sound, bringing the mare alongside him.

The docile mule fell into a trot, bringing up the rear.

That's the way it had been for the last three weeks, ever since he had struck a deal for the mare and the mule with the owner of the horse ranch they had come across located in the foothills of the mountains. The drill was always the same: Wade leading out, Betsy falling into line beside him, the mule bringing up the rear.

Wade slanted a quick glance at the girl, and immediately wished he hadn't.

Damn, the kid was a true beauty, in temperament as well as appearance.

His Mary would have rejoiced in her.

He sighed. He had to find a place for Betsy, a safe place, where she could hopefully be educated while she completed the natural process of growing up.

Wade knew that finding a safe haven for the girl was the right thing to do; and yet he hesitated, grasping at any excuse to put it off, just as he was now using the excuse handily given to him by that sodbuster.

Hell, for all he knew, the farmer didn't know a damn about the existence, or lack thereof, of decent orphanages or boarding schools in Laramie. And they weren't all that far away from Laramie, just a few miles as the crow flew.

And it wouldn't cost him all that much in time wasted either, Wade mused. A day, two, three at most.

Yet with a leaping surge of relief, Wade had jumped at the opportunity to circumvent Laramie and head straight for Colorado. Oh, Wade had come up with plenty of rational reasons for his eagerness to take the word of the farmer, every one of them as convenient as it was sensible.

They had some miles to cover, and though the weather remained mild and summery, the bite in the night air warned that fall would soon be upon them. Wade knew too well how capricious the weather could be on the plains and in the mountain country. One day a man could be basking in the soft breeze and the very next day find himself shivering in a sudden snowstorm.

An excellent, logical reason for pushing on, Wade reflected, slanting another glance at his companion.

Catching his hooded gaze, Betsy smiled, lighting up her entire face—and the dark interior of his heart.

Wade exhaled a silent sigh. There, in her face, shining from her eyes, was the true reason he so willingly put off getting shut of the kid. For although she was fourteen, and not the twelve he had at first judged her to be, Betsy, or a child very like her, might have been his.

And Wade rejoiced in the sight of her.

How had it happened? he pondered, content with the steady, loping pace of the animal beneath him. How had this scrap of young humanity wormed her way into his heart and emotions so quickly, so decisively?

"You busy into your own thoughts, Mr. Dunstan?" Betsy's voice was soft, not at all intrusive.

"Yes."

"Okay." She fell silent, a tiny smile of understanding curving her tender young mouth.

How had it happened? Wade smothered a snort of self-derisive laughter. He knew exactly how it had happened. And it hadn't taken long either.

With nothing more pressing to do other than guide Rascal in the right direction, Wade let his thoughts meander back in time—four weeks in time, to that first morning after he had dispatched the second of the four killers of his wife.

Wade came wide awake as usual when the pearl-gray of predawn tinged the horizon. A half grimace, half smile twitched his lips at the sight of the kid curled into him for warmth, still dead to the world in sleep.

God, she looked a mess. Compassion stabbed at his heart at the sight of the rainbow-hued bruises discoloring her pale face. He didn't dare even think about what the rest of her skinny body might look or feel like.

The son of a bitch.

Silently condemning the man who had inflicted the injuries, mental and physical, on the girl, Wade attempted to ease away from her without waking her. Betsy's eyes popped open with his first tentative move.

"Don't leave me alone here, Marshal!" she cried in a voice made squeaky from fear.

Wade didn't know the first damn thing about children, but his years of following the law had given him a perceptive insight into people in general, and a real understanding of fear. Gut instinct told him that this kid's fear was running dangerously close to the edge of terror.

"Easy, girl," he said in a soft, soothing tone, patting her awkwardly on the shoulder. "I'm not going anywhere. Why don't you go back to sleep while I fix breakfast."

Betsy kept her gaze fastened to his, and gave a jerky shake of her head. "I . . . I'll help," she said, trying to conceal a grimace of pain as she scrambled up to shift restlessly from one foot to the other. "Soon's I . . . ah . . . I hafta . . . er."

"Go on," Wade cut her off, flicking a hand at the bushes. "I'll fetch water for coffee."

"Ye-yes, sir."

Wade stepped out to head for the small mountain stream he had discovered some distance from the camp, but paused at the glimpse he got of Betsy from the corner of his eye. The pang twisted deeper into his chest at the sight of her stiff, obviously painful progress.

The kid was hurting, bad.

Muttering a curse, Wade strode to the stream, now reduced to little more than a trickle in the midsummer heat. Damn, he had intended to move on right after breakfast, make tracks for Laramie, find a place to house the girl, then get on with his death hunt.

But the kid needed to rest, to heal . . . at least the surface scrapes and bruises. Only God knew how severe the interior wounds were, or when they'd heal, if ever.

Impatience crawled through Wade, twanging on his nerves with clawing fingers.

Damn it to hell, he railed, scooping water into the battered coffeepot from a shallow pool at the base of a short decline of the stream down the side of a hill. He wanted to be on his way. He had a man to find, the third man of the four who had destroyed his life along with his Mary's . . .

Grasping the pot, Wade went rock still and closed his eyes, envisioning the gentle face of his wife. Sheer agony scored deep lines into brackets around his tight-lipped mouth; despair locked his strong, raw-boned features.

He had a man to kill . . . but his Mary would be shocked, saddened by his disregard of the girl's injuries.

Opening his eyes, Wade worked his features, loosening the lock, and with a sigh of acceptance, quashed the rage of impatience gnawing inside.

The man would keep. For now, young Betsy came first.

One very like her might have been his.

"You asleep?" Betsy's voice was little more than a breathy whisper, but it was strong enough to draw Wade from the depths of reverie.

"No." Shaking the memory cobwebs from his head, Wade angled a droll look at her. "I'm resting my eyes."

Betsy grinned.

Wade laughed. From the look of her now, it was hard to believe she was the same shivering kid he had found sobbing and cowering in a corner of a rented room in that two-horse, two-bit excuse for a town.

Bright-eyed, bushy-tailed, and feisty as all hell. The descriptive phrase sprang into his mind, bringing another laughing chuckle to his throat.

And all it had taken was three short days of rest and healing time in the mountains.

As he had been then, Wade was struck anew at the resiliency of the young.

Betsy had slept through much of those three days, allowing nature to take its healing course. While she slept, Wade had roamed close to their campsite, hunting small game to supplement his dwindling food supply.

After breakfast the second morning, before she had a chance to dive back into the healing arms of slumber once more, Wade had tossed his extra shirt at her, along with quiet but determined instructions.

"Get out of those filthy clothes. You can wear my shirt while I wash 'em."

While she slept, he had kept busy, first beating the hell and grime out of the tattered clothes, then enlarging the pool of water at the base of the incline.

When Betsy woke up in midafternoon, he led her to the pool, handed her the sliver that remained of his bar of soap, and pointed at the water.

"You reek damn near as bad as those clothes did, kid," he said bluntly. "Get into that pool and take a bath, all over, including your head. By the time you're finished, those rags you were wearing should be dry, and supper done." As he turned away to leave her alone, he tossed over his shoulder, "You can use my shirt to dry off . . . then wash it. That way, you, your duds, and my shirt will be clean."

She cleaned up pretty good too.

He felt a softening sensation inside, not at all unpleasant, as recollection swamped his senses.

Despite the bruises, Betsy looked like a different kid when she returned to the camp after her bath. Her soft brown eyes, so similar to those of a timid doe, were bright, alert, the darkness of pain and memory washed away by the cool waters of the mountain spring.

But her hair was still a tangled mess, only now it was a dripping wet rat's nest. Heaving a sigh, Wade turned and strode to his saddlebags to dig out his comb, which was not too clean and missing a few teeth.

"Come over here, kid," he ordered, settling his butt on a flat-topped rock.

A thrill of something—satisfaction? gratification?—shot through him when she obeyed without hesitation, displaying her trust in him.

"Yes, sir?" she asked, coming to a halt before him.

"Plunk yourself down on the grass here, between my knees," he directed her, motioning at the spot with the comb. "Somethin's gotta be done with that sopping mop of yours."

This time, Betsy wasn't as quick to obey. "Is it gonna hurt?" she said, eyeing the comb warily as though it were an instrument of torture.

Somehow, Wade had suppressed the laughter that rose to his throat at the look of horror on the girl's face. After what she had been through, the very idea that she feared the tug of a comb on her scalp struck him as damn near hilarious.

"More'n likely," he admitted in a choking drawl, giving way to a grin. "Be brave, kid," he advised in a teasing tone. "Just grit your teeth and bear it."

"I ain't gonna cry," she muttered, gingerly settling her smarting rump on the grass.

"That's good, for I sure hate the sound of a wailing brat," Wade told her, laughing to himself.

And she hadn't cried, not as much as a whimper. Which raised his opinion of her grit more than a notch.

It took a good while to rake the tangles from the thick mane, but the results were well worth his efforts. When he was at last satisfied, Betsy's hair hung in smooth strands halfway down her back, the dark brown color gleaming in the long golden rays of late-afternoon sunlight. To keep it neat, he had separated the still damp tresses into three clumps and plaited them into one long, fat braid.

Betsy replaited the braid every morning from then on before stuffing it beneath her hat.

Wade slid a slower, more comprehensive look at the girl. Even dressed in the boy's garb of flannel shirt, rough, shapeless pants, boots, and the almost new hat he had bought for her from the same sodbuster who'd sold him the mare and mule, her attractiveness shone through.

Lordawmighty, he thought, examining her soft, clear skin and delicate features. Betsy already showed signs of beauty. In a few more years she would be a stunning young woman.

Beautiful and brave, he mused, for she had proven her courage to him several times over.

Not once had Betsy uttered so much as the mildest complaint about her injuries during those three days at the campsite, or later, while bouncing in the saddle behind him as they made their way down out of the mountains.

And considering how that bastard had used her, Wade recalled, he knew her ass had to be extremely tender. Yet she had maintained a stoic silence, which had earned for her both his approval and his admiration.

Then, just yesterday, Betsy had gone a step farther in proving her courage by slipping away from their night camp before dawn and boldly setting out on her own in an attempt to glean information about the man Wade was hunting, to see if he was in the vicinity.

Damned if she hadn't been successful, too, Wade thought, laughing to himself. And she had accomplished the coup by questioning the children from the tiny nearby community as they converged on the crude schoolhouse.

Hell, he'd never even thought of questioning the local youngsters, he admitted ruefully. He'd have gone to the one and only saloon in that cluster of houses too small to be called a town. And probably learned nothing, Wade figured, since the bartender turned out to be a suspicious, surly, and close-mouthed son of a bitch.

Wade shot a glance at the girl humming to herself as she rode beside him. Seeing her now, looking so young and innocent, who would believe that she had set herself up for him, using herself as a decoy to expose the supposed hired hand at that ranch for the killer he was?

Passing strange, he reflected, how fate and females seemed to be playing a hand in his death quest. First he'd had help from Maybell, the whore in the Last Ditch saloon. And now Betsy had played her role.

He sent another glance her way; she caught it and sent him a sweet smile in return.

Beautiful and brave. Admirable in a youngster. In a woman, a tempting combination.

He'd have to stand guard over her with a gun.

The consideration brought Wade up short.

What in hell was he thinking? He wouldn't be around in a few years to stand guard over her. He had a man to find and kill, and then . . .

Mary.

But first he had to find a place for Betsy, a place where she could be around other girls her own age, a safe, decent place where she could be educated and learn female things while she finished growing into womanhood.

A bigger town, a vital, growing city would have more than one such place.

Wade clicked his tongue, urging Rascal into a faster, ground-covering gait.

"What's the hurry, Mr. Dunstan?" Betsy asked, nudging the mare into position alongside him. "Where're we goin'?"

Wade didn't look at her, he wouldn't allow himself to look at her. His course was set, and no kid, no matter how appealing, was going to change it. Wade's determination hardened his low, terse voice.

"Denver."

13

She was so achingly lovely in sleep.

The observation brought a faint, bittersweet smile to Jonathan's lips, and a twist of very real-feeling flutter of near pain to his chest.

It was early; the first probing pink fingers of morning were spearing through the pearl gray of predawn. The air wafting through the open bedroom windows was deliciously cool, a harbinger of approaching autumn.

Stretched out in a reclining position, elbow bent, head propped on his open palm, Jonathan floated a millimeter above the mattress, as comfortable as if he were resting on a large fluffy white cloud.

The chill in the air lacked the power to draw goose bumps on his skin, even though he was as naked as a newborn. Jonathan chose to be nude. However, he did not choose to suffer the discomforts attendant to the condition.

He did not wish to be distracted from his contemplation of the woman lying asleep beside him.

Darcy.

Thinking her name caused another, stronger flutter of sensation inside Jonathan's chest.

In sleep, Darcy was so unbelievably beautiful, vulnerable with her features softened by relaxation, her glorious hair freed from the pins anchoring clever twists and curls, fanning out around her head, a mass of deep red strands appearing like flames in contrast to the white pillowcase and the paleness of the delicate skin of her face.

God, he loved her.

"Darcy." Though he uttered her name aloud, Jonathan spoke in a mere whisper, obeying a need to say it, yet not wanting to disturb her rest.

Nevertheless, the muted sound of his voice must have reached her on some level, insinuating into her dreams, for Darcy murmured in her sleep and her soft full lips curved into a tantalizing smile.

It would appear that her dreams were pleasant, Jonathan mused, resisting an impulse to kiss the sweet curve of her enticing mouth.

A longing sigh heaved itself from his suddenly tight throat. How he yearned to kiss Darcy, really kiss her, experience the earthly thrill of physical flesh pressed to physical flesh, not only of mouth to mouth but of body to body, his mouth, his naked body, to her mouth, her naked body.

A cry of protest swept Jonathan's consciousness, a protest against the hand of Fate that had projected that flashing knife blade directly into his chest, ending his earthly sojourn mere days before Darcy had appeared on the scene.

Darcy.

Her name reverberated throughout Jonathan's entire being, a silent moan of agony.

Your choice . . . if not a physically conscious one.

The gentle voice of Jonathan's spirit guide tolled softly inside his head.

I know . . . now . . . too late, Jonathan responded in silence, and acceptance.

It is never too late. All is infinite. There are no boundaries. Everything is choice.

And I choose to remain with, be with, Darcy, Jonathan replied to the inner voice.

And so you are. And so you have been. Have you not?

Yes, he answered. But . . .

Have you not experienced the deepest sense of satisfaction? the voice persisted. *Deeper and infinitely more satisfying than any experienced while in the physical reality?*

Yes, yes, Jonathan admitted, thrilling to the memory of blending his very essence with Darcy's. But . . .

But?

I want to hold Darcy in my arms, he cried in silent supplication. I want to feel her arms clasping me to her breast. I want to caress her soft skin, stroke her hair, kiss her lips, know her body, feel her caressing, stroking, kissing, knowing my body in return. I long to be with Darcy in a physical manner, not only in an ethereal, spiritual sense.

You are requesting life on the earth plane.

I know. Jonathan sighed. And my life is over.

Yes . . . but . . . there is a way.

So you've said before, Jonathan thought, frowning. But I'm not sure I understand the process.

Then I shall endeavor to explain. The voice paused, then resumed in a cautioning tone. *You must understand that there are certain conditions that ap—*

"Jonathan?" Darcy said in a sleep-fuzzy murmur.

The guide's voice receded. The interior dialogue ended. Jonathan felt no concern; all he had to do was ask, and the guide would return to resume his explanation.

"Yes, my love?" Jonathan answered Darcy, smiling into her morning-bright hazel eyes.

"Is it time to get up?"

"No. It's still early, barely five o'clock," he said, frowning at the dark smudges of weariness under her eyes. "Go back to sleep for an hour or so."

"All right," she agreed readily, closing her eyes and snuggling deeper beneath the covers. She was fast asleep once more within moments.

A tender smile touched Jonathan's lips as he continued to study her features in repose.

After the near frantic pace she had set, for herself as well as every other member of the house, throughout the previous month, Darcy was tired and it was beginning to show. There were those dark smudges under her eyes, and tiny new lines had recently appeared to bracket her mouth.

Little wonder, he mused, considering the strides she had made in reorganizing both the house and the women in it.

In Jonathan's admittedly biased opinion, Darcy had proved herself something of an organizing marvel. To his way of thinking, her accomplishments of the last weeks were only slightly less than amazing.

With the single-minded purpose of a commander readying green troops for battle, Darcy had drilled the basic precepts of private school customs and regulations into her small army of females, and two males—the stalwart Clancy, her right hand in evidence, and Jonathan himself, her constant, if invisible, second in command.

Then, besides working with the house residents, Darcy had also keenly monitored the progress of the men James Singleton had hired to renovate the interior of the house, as well as the crew he had also employed to construct an extensive addition to the existing structure.

In consequence, Darcy had portioned herself very thin between instructing the women, Clancy, and her companion spirit, and overseeing each and every step of the interior and exterior work in progress on the house.

With nothing better to do, while his beloved lay gently cradled in the soothing arms of Morpheus, Jonathan let his mind drift back in earthly time, reviewing the chain of events of the previous month.

"Out."

The echo of Darcy's voice, firm, decisive, brought a chuckle to Jonathan's throat, which he suppressed with a quick glance at Darcy. But instead of the face of his slumbering adored one, he saw the way she had looked that morning, weeks earlier.

Darcy had been standing in the foyer, chin up and tilted at a determined angle, her back straight as a poker, one arm outstretched, slim finger pointed at the painting of the reclining nude on the wall.

"Mr. Dugan," she said in an imperious tone that brooked no arguments. "I want that . . . that . . .

thing out of here." Making a sharp half turn, she directed her finger toward the bar/gaming room area. "The one in there as well."

"Yes, ma'am." Though he had grinned, Clancy had moved at once to carry out her orders.

"It'll leave a large clean spot on the wall," Jonathan had observed in a teasing drawl.

"And when you're finished with that," Darcy continued, ignoring her shadow's comment, "I want you to remove and destroy all the alcoholic beverages on the premises."

Clancy paused in midstride, and spun around to stare at her in shock. "Now, lass, be reasonable," he protested. "Your sainted mother stocked some excellent whiskies and brandies. 'Twould be a crying shame to pour them away."

Darcy's expression set into obstinate lines. "Nevertheless, I want the spirits gone from here."

"Does that include me?" Jonathan had inquired, laughing outright. "Or just the liquid spirits?"

Unable to reply, as of course he was well aware, Darcy made her impatience with his teasing evident with a dismissive, regal toss of her head.

"Even the wines?" Clancy asked plaintively. "The cellar is stocked with some vintage labels."

"Surely not the wines?" Feigning astonishment, Jonathan reinforced the bouncer's disbelief. "Shouldn't they be kept for special occasions and celebrations?"

Beginning to look harried—or haunted—Darcy had relented and given in gracefully. "All right, you may leave the wines, but everything else must go."

Now, recalling how Clancy had fairly turned the air blue with his curses as he had destroyed bottle after bottle of the potent spirits, Jonathan was forced to choke back the chuckle tickling his throat.

The memory scene shifted, this time to an equally amusing confrontation less than a week before between Darcy and the formidable wife of a pillar of the community.

"I am Mrs. Albert P. Parkingham." The dour-faced woman had announced herself as self-importantly as if she were the wife of Albert the Consort, and not merely the spouse of a minor municipal official.

"Yes, ma'm?" Clancy stood four-square in the open doorway, blocking entrance, appearing neither impressed nor intimidated by the haughty female.

"And *this* is Mrs. Samuel Denton," the self-anointed woman of substance went on, indicating with an imperious movement of her head a small, birdlike woman hovering to the side and halfway behind her generously proportioned, tightly corseted form.

"Uh-huh," Clancy grunted, not budging by as much as a hair from his blocking position. "And how can I be helping you . . . er . . . ladies?"

Mrs. Denton began in a nervous and squeaky-sounding twitter, "We . . . ah, wish to—"

"We demand an interview with Miss Darcy Flynn," Mrs. Albert P. Parkingham interrupted her companion.

"Demand, is it?" Though the brawny Irishman's eyebrows arched, his voice was as smooth as glass, and as incisive as a sharp edge of that brittle material.

"Yes." The sizable lady—whom Jonathan uncharitably and unrepentantly likened to the ungainly, ironclad Merrimack—thrust her double chin out pugnaciously.

"I see." Clancy's smooth-as-glass voice took on a serrated edge. "Well, then, ma'am, in that case, I feel duty bound to inform you that Miss Darcy Flynn does not give interviews . . . on anyone's demand."

"Now see here, my good man," the Civil War battle wagon sputtered, bristling like a riled porcupine. "I'll have you remember to whom you are speaking."

"I know too well to whom I am speaking," the bouncer retorted mockingly. "I know your husband . . . very well." His lip curled in derision. "That selfsame upright, sanctimonious minion of the community was a frequent visitor to this—"

"Mr. Dugan." Darcy's cultured, schoolmistress tones cut across Clancy's low-pitched snarling voice.

"Aye, lass?" The abrupt change in the Irishman's voice was startling, as was the rapid shift in his facial expression from surly to tenacious to conspiratorial when he turned his head to flash a grin at her.

"I will speak with the ladies," Darcy said repressively, though obviously fighting the smile twitching at the corners of her soft lips. "Admit them, please," she directed, moving across the foyer. "And show them into the parlor."

Now, more than a week later, Jonathan's smile

softened, as it had then, at the note of pleasurable pride in Darcy's voice in referring to the former bar/gaming room, which had been fully renovated and transformed into an elegant, proper parlor that any woman could be proud to call her own.

Walking with the erect, graceful bearing of a genuine queen, Darcy preceded Clancy and the two visitors into the tastefully appointed room, then turned to face them, her expression calm and serene.

Drifting along with Clancy, Jonathan felt a sensation of purely human admiration for Darcy, and vindication for her at the awed expressions on the two other women's faces as their avid gazes examined—and very likely priced—every stick of furniture, wall decoration, and piece of bric-a-brac in the room.

"Won't you please have a seat?" Darcy graciously invited, indicating the groupings of obviously brand-new chairs and settees, covered in equally obviously expensive plush velvet in a deep claret color. "Will you take tea—or coffee, perhaps?"

The aristocratic overtones of her voice, her phrasing, her well-bred demeanor set the two women aback, rendering both of them speechless for some noticeable seconds. The war wagon was the first to regain a portion of her dissipated steam.

"No, thank you." The woman's ample bosom heaved and her long, narrow nose grew pinched, as if in defense against an offensive odor. "This is not a social call."

Jonathan smiled in remembrance of how he had been visited by an unspiritual impulse to freeze his essence and slowly glide through the woman's overendowed body, thus introducing her to the thrill, and chill, of being haunted.

"I . . . see." Darcy shifted a quick, narrow-eyed, cautioning glance at Jonathan, silently telling him she also saw his unholy intent, mutely warning him not to implement it.

He shrugged.

Darcy returned her full attention to her unsocial guests. "In that case, may I ask the purpose of your call . . . ladies?" Her hesitation before the term of address was as brief, and insulting, as Clancy's had been earlier.

"We have been given to understand that you are planning to open a private school for young ladies in this . . . this establishment." Mrs. Parkingham's tone rang with righteous indignation. "Is that correct?"

"No, I am not planning on opening a school." Darcy met the woman's glaring stare with unruffled calm. "I have opened the school." Ignoring the gasps of shock issued simultaneously from both women, she continued unperturbed, "Classes began over three weeks ago."

"Oh, my goodness!" The timid, up until now silent Mrs. Denton exclaimed in a muffled squeak.

"But this cannot be tolerated!" the more forceful Mrs. Parkingham declared in protest. "This . . . this establishment has an unsavory reputation as a house of ill repute."

"No longer," Darcy gently corrected her. "This

establishment is now, and will remain, an institution of learning."

"But we will not allow this!" the now irate woman cried. "We are not deceived by your attempt to conceal the true purpose of this establishment, nor will we tolerate the corruption of innocent young girls under the guise of education!"

"Indeed?" Darcy arched her perfectly shaped eyebrows. "And who, precisely, are we?"

"Why, the good and decent women of this city. The members of the Ladies' Society of Community Standards." She gave an audible sniff of disdain. "I think you will find, to your dismay, Miss Flynn, that your school will not be allowed to continue in operation." Her expression grew smugly baleful. "We wield some considerable power, since our husbands control the running of this city."

"And I think you will discover, to the dismay of every member of your Community Standards Society, that my school will not only be allowed to continue in operation but in fact has been encouraged to do so, under the auspices of your members' husbands, the gentlemen who control the running of this city." Darcy rose as she was speaking, her expression conveying dismissal. "Good day, ladies, Mr. Dugan will show you out."

Now, recalling the aghast looks on the two women's faces, Jonathan nearly strangled on the laughter trapped inside his throat. And yet, as amusing as Darcy's encounter with the pompous woman had been, the most amusing incident, or string of incidents, of all had been occurring at regular intervals during the previous month, and every one involved the budding romances unfolding between Molly and Clancy and June and the banker, James Singleton.

Not that Jonathan considered the concept of the romances laughable, because he did not. He heartily approved of them, most especially in the case of James and June since, at first, he had suspected James's sudden need to visit had more to do with his interest in Darcy than his stated reason of needing to discuss with her the work to be done on the house. And knowing he could not interfere if Darcy reciprocated that interest, Jonathan felt a sense of near physical relief when it early on became obvious exactly where and with whom James's interest lay.

Freed of personal concern, which he knew as well he should not be feeling, Jonathan nevertheless derived amusement from the tongue-tied and awkward approach of the two supposedly adult men in question.

At the clumsy and hesitant rate of speed with which Clancy and James were progressing, poor Molly and June might well succumb to old age before they ever got a chance to succumb to the mates of their choice.

One incident in particular sprang to mind. Jonathan really didn't want to recollect the scene that had unfolded just yesterday, but it was too late; he had recalled it, and there it was, inside his memory, in all its uproarious color.

James had presented himself at the door early in the morning, as clean and sparkling as the new day. Fortunately, June answered the door, since she was crossing the foyer at the time, on her way to conduct her morning deportment class. As it turned out, she never did conduct the morning class.

Jonathan was witness to the encounter because, though unbeknownst to June, he was accompanying her as an interested observer to the class.

"Good morning, Mr. Singleton," June greeted the banker in her very best prim and proper imitation of her new mentor, Darcy. "Please, come in."

"Thank you, miss, ah—may I call you June?" James asked in a stilted, hesitant manner, initiating Jonathan's amusement, because Jonathan knew that James didn't know June's last name. Come to that, neither did most members of the house.

"Please do," June replied, a trifle breathlessly, stepping back to allow him entry.

"And will you please return the gracious favor by calling me James?" Removing his beaver hat as he stepped inside the foyer, he then proceeded to circle the curled brim with nervous, unsteady fingers.

"I would be honored . . . James." A flush of pink complimented June's lovely face.

Jonathan had begun to have hope for them. But alas, perhaps prematurely.

A silence ensued, during which James shuffled his feet, June stood poised like a statue, holding the door wide open, and Jonathan hovered near her right shoulder, rolling his eyes and despairing for the both of them.

After a lengthy interval, June cleared her throat in a ladylike manner and finally broke the taut silence.

"It feels a bit cool and autumnal this morning, does it not?" She gave a dainty shiver.

Jonathan groaned—to himself.

James coughed—discreetly—before managing a response. "Why, not at all." He frowned. "I was just thinking that it's quite warm for September."

The weather. Jonathan shook his head. What a beautifully conceived conversational gambit. His hope for progress from the couple withered like the summer flowers.

"Well, actually, I had thought it rather warm earlier myself," June came back with the scintillating rejoinder. "But now I feel a definite chill."

"Oh." James looked crestfallen. "I pray my unexpected visit has nothing to do with your chill."

It has to do with my presence, you blockhead, Jonathan said in scathing silence, drifting back, away from June. Look at the woman, man, he mutely urged. Her feelings for you are written plainly in her soft eyes.

"Oh, no, sir!" June hastened to assure James, and hope renewed inside Jonathan. "I . . . I . . ." She sputtered to a halt; so did Jonathan's glimmer of hope.

"I'm relieved to hear you say so," James confessed, taking a cautious step closer to her.

Expectation blossomed in Jonathan.

June took a maidenly step back, thereby halting James's advance. He looked chagrined.

The blossom died inside Jonathan, killed by the frost of his unholy sense of humor. In his admittedly biased opinion, their situation was ludicrously funny.

The thought was Jonathan's undoing. No

longer able to contain his laughter, it sprang forth, rich and deep.

"What are you laughing at?"

Berating himself for his carelessness, Jonathan sobered and focused his gaze on Darcy's wide-open, confusion-filled eyes. "An amusing memory," he explained contritely. "I'm sorry for disturbing you."

"I'm not disturbed," Darcy said, moving her lithe form in a sinuous, senses exciting way beneath the covers. "I was merely curious."

"You know the old saying about curiosity, don't you?" he asked, taking delight, as usual, in teasing her.

"Umm. but I'm not a cat." Her white arms appeared from beneath the covers to be curled above her head in a luxurious stretch.

Jonathan felt the now familiar flame of desire uncoiling in the center of his being. "No," he agreed in a low, rough-edged voice. "But you move very like one."

Her eyes, also feline in appearance, glittered with sparks of fire. "You've made a sensualist of me," she accused in a throaty murmur. "If she could see me with you, Miss Reinholt would be scandalized."

"Or envious," Jonathan opined. "Exploring the senses is a natural part of the human condition," he said. "Repressing the inclination is very likely the reason why Miss Reinholt is so hidebound and straitlaced."

"It appears to be a part of the nonhuman condition as well," she said, letting him know she was aware of the smoldering intensity of his regard.

"Yes." Jonathan shrugged. "At least, it is in the case of this nonhuman."

"Is it time for me to get up?" Darcy asked, the gleam in her eyes flashing a message to him.

"Not yet," he murmured, lowering his hand from his head and drifting into position above her. "It is time for me to love you, mesh with you, blend with you."

"Yes, please." A slumberous expression, unrelated to sleep, darkened Darcy's eyes. Lowering her arms, she grasped the covers and tossed them aside, revealing her slender nude form. "Love me, Jonathan," she pleaded, stretching her arms out to either side to grip the bedclothes for something to hold on to, because she could not hold on to his insubstantial image.

Jonathan felt a searing twinge in his heart, and his conscience. He was being unfair to Darcy by remaining with her, and he knew it. She was beautiful, inside as well as out, and she deserved better than what he could offer her, even if his offering consisted of his absolute love for her, resulting in ecstasy of essence.

Darcy deserved a flesh-and-blood man. A man she could hold fast in her empty arms. A man to marry her, give her children, protect her while they grew old together.

They had been lovers, in the only way they could be lovers, for over a month now. Though he had never so much as contemplated doing so, Jonathan did not need to invade her mind to know her thoughts, her feelings.

He knew that Darcy loved him with every fiber of her being. And yet, Jonathan knew as well that there were moments when, caught overtired or unaware, she suffered the wounds inflicted by clawing doubts, despair, and frustration.

He was without substance. A ghost. A shadow of the man he had been while on the earth plane.

Darcy was a living, vibrant, earthbound entity.

Their love was hopeless.

And yet they loved.

Jonathan felt anguish for those moments when the hopelessness overwhelmed the love Darcy felt for him.

"Jonathan?" Her soft voice penetrated the darkness of his remorseful thoughts.

"Yes, my love?"

"Do not despair for me," she said, revealing the closeness of their unusual union by correctly reading his emotional conflict. "I knew and accepted the boundaries of our association from the beginning."

"But you deserve so much more," he said in rueful self-condemnation.

"Darling, come," she whispered. "Love me, join with me, set my spirit free by mingling your essence with mine. I truly do not know if I could bear any more."

His conscience somewhat appeased, and his desire for her dominant, Jonathan slowly lowered his head.

It was then, at that exact moment, that Jonathan experienced a strange, uncanny sensation, a shiver-inducing portent of something happening in some distant somewhere, something that would affect him in some inexplicable way.

A flash of insight told him it had something to

do with a man's death. No, the death of several men.

But how could the deaths of several men affect him? Jonathan wondered, confused by the inner knowledge.

The sensation was too strong, too certain to be denied. In addition, there was more to it than the deaths of some unknown men. He could feel, sense it, but . . .

The never before experienced sensation gave him momentary pause. What could be the cause of this eerie, nearly precognitive feeling? How could something happening in some distant place, to some unknown men, have such an odd effect on him?

Then the sensation was gone, as quickly as it had struck. Dismissing the strange feeling, Jonathan brushed his mouth over Darcy's parted lips in a ghostly parody of a physical kiss.

14

Darcy shivered in response to the fiery sensations caused by the heating of her lips from the
flicker of Jonathan's seeking spectral tongue.

"Jonathan. Jonathan." Her voice was as nearly
without substance as his being, and yet, she knew
he heard, understood, as well as she felt, compre-
hended, the passion and love he was conveying to
her.

"My soul burns for you, my love." His voice sank
into her, became a part of her. "Give yourself, your
essence, your spirit to me. Join with me. Be one
with me."

"Yes. Yes." Eager to experience again the shattering sensations only he could give to her, Darcy
parted her thighs and arched her hips, even
though she knew he could not in reality settle into
the cradle of her invitation, penetrate the mem-
brane of her maidenhood, fill her womb with the
proof of his masculinity, any more than he could
bestow upon her the physical kiss that she had
never experienced.

Jonathan's smile warmed her, preparing her for
the mind-divorcing thrill of sensual sensations in

store for her. He hovered above her for a moment, drawing the tension to a fever pitch inside her.

"Jonathan, please," Darcy cried, fingers spading into the mattress as she arched her sensation-hungry body higher. "What have you done to me? I can't bear the wait. I feel wanton, mad with desire for you, your special essence. I need it, crave it. Please, my darling, fill me with your fire."

"Ahh, my love, my love," he whispered directly into her mind. "Your pleasure is my pleasure."

Darcy shuddered as his spiritual being slowly lowered, blending, merging, becoming one with hers.

"Oh. Oh, sweet Lord!" Darcy moaned. "If this is death, I welcome it with all my heart."

"No, my love," Jonathan murmured. "This is not your death. This is my taste of life. And the taste is unutterably sweet and addictive."

Caught within the beauty of a sensual cataclysm, which was not yet a physical release, Darcy did not, could not, reply for long, earthmoving seconds, unending moments of rapture and incredible joy, wherein she soared, swaying to the harmonic rhythm of the universe, waltzing to the symphony of the infinite forever.

When the music thrummed its final note through her being, and she felt lucid enough to speak, her voice was weak, heavy with the lethargy of timeless completion.

"I love you, Jonathan," Darcy murmured, offering him a soft smile as she closed her weighted eyelids. "I love you with my heart, my soul, and my body."

* * *

Darcy was awakened by the ringing sound of hammers striking nails into siding planks.

The building workmen were on the job; it was time—past time—for her to be up and working too.

Still, Darcy lingered, luxuriating in the warm cocoon of blankets and euphoria.

Jonathan. A muzzy smile curved her sleep-softened lips, and she opened her eyes and turned her head to bid him a grateful good morning.

The curve on her lips turned downward, and a crease marred the pale smoothness of her brow. The space on the bed beside her was empty of the free-floating image of her spirit lover.

"Jonathan?"

"Good morning, my love." Jonathan materialized next to the bed before the echo of her plaintive call faded on the cool morning air.

"Where were you?"

He gave her a heart-wrenching grin. "It's a beautiful, brisk morning. I was outside, with the men."

The clear sight of him brought a sharp pang to her chest and a lump to her throat. Even though his company with the construction crew was silent and unseen, Jonathan had whimsically chosen to clothe himself as they were dressed, in flat-heeled, scuffed boots, rough pants, and a plain, collarless shirt. He had left two buttons unfastened at the neck of the shirt, and rolled the sleeves up to his elbows.

However, unlike any of the workers Darcy had observed since their arrival on the scene over a month ago, in the common garb Jonathan presented a picture of devastatingly attractive masculine virility.

The tightness in Darcy's throat expanded into a painful sigh of longing for what might have been, had she been given the opportunity to meet Jonathan before his lifeline had been so abruptly and cruelly severed by a carelessly aimed and thrown blade.

Her sense of euphoria crushed by the weight of reality, Darcy clenched her teeth to deny expression to her sigh, and tossing back the now confining covers, she rose from the bed to face another busy day.

"Am I terribly late?" she asked in an enforced businesslike tone, turning away to conceal from him her growing sense of hopeless yearning.

She should have known better, should have known by then that nothing about her escaped Jonathan's notice.

"My love, my love," he murmured. "I have hurt you, continue to hurt you with my defiance, my selfish self-indulgence. If I were to be fair, I would leave you to—"

"Don't say it." Unmindful of her nudity, flushed pink by the slanting rays of morning sunlight, Darcy spun to face him, her eyes wide, her voice low, imploring. "Please, my darling, please don't ever speak of leaving me." Her eyes welled with hot, stinging moisture, and she blinked, spilling over a flow to run unchecked down her cheeks. "You are my love, my only love. If you were to leave, or be called to the light, I would willingly die to be with you in the wonder of its glow."

"No." His smile sad, Jonathan skimmed across

the floor to her. "No, my love, you shall not die, whether or not I am called away. You have found your mission here"—his smile tilted to a whimsical angle—"shepherding all of these lost sheep in female clothing."

Darcy shook her head with determined vigor.

"No, if you should leave, I wouldn't want to go on. This place, the task I have set for myself, would mean nothing."

"Nothing?" Jonathan arched that very same brow in silent chiding. "No meaning? And how about young Sarah? She has already made great strides, mastering the writing of her name, the reading of simple words. But there is still a long way for her to go. Could you desert her now, condemn her to a life spent earning her keep on her back?"

A measure of her determination visibly drained out of Darcy. Her shoulders drooped for an instant, then they squared as a gleam of challenge flared in her hazel eyes.

"By your own admission, you refused the light because of your strong desire to help Sarah achieve her full potential," she reminded him.

"That's correct," he readily agreed. "And now you have assumed the burden of my desire, which is why I insist you will remain, continue on, even if I should surrender to the light, to the call home."

"Home?" Darcy blinked, thrown off balance by this newly introduced concept. "What do you mean?"

Jonathan shrugged. "So far, I have only a glimmering of this state of afterlife, but I am somehow filled with the certainty that this plane of existence in between our sojourns, or incarnations, on the earth plane is not merely a resting place between lives, but our one true home."

Darcy's eyes were dark. "You confuse me when you speak of it . . . that place."

"I'm sorry."

She shivered.

Jonathan smiled. "Are you chilly?"

"Yes," she confessed.

"Perhaps . . . if you'd dress?" He ran a slow and deliberate glance the length of her body, bringing her to startling awareness of her natural state.

"Oh!" Darcy exclaimed, blushing from her hairline to the soles of her dainty feet. "Oh, heavens!" Belatedly fumbling to conceal her nakedness with her hands, she whipped around and dashed into the dressing room.

Jonathan's deep, rich laughter slipped beneath the hastily shut door to nip at her heels, and cause an altogether different kind of blush to pinken her warm flesh.

Darcy emerged from her bedroom ready to face the day some thirty-odd minutes later. Jonathan drifted along at her side, traces of amusement lingering at the twitching corners of his attractive mouth.

"I must admit that I prefer you *sans* attire," he observed drolly, raking her form, now respectably concealed by the garments she referred to as her working clothing.

Deigning not to respond, Darcy gave a delicate sniff, and smoothed a palm over one hip, satisfied with the tactile contact with the servicable material.

The suggestion for the ensemble had been hers. Recollecting the uniforms worn by the students of Miss Reinholt's Academy, Darcy had conceived the idea to require such outfits at her school, only broadening the concept to include teachers as well as students—since, to date, the only students were performing as teachers as well.

Molly had carried through on Darcy's idea, producing a simple costume consisting of a pale blue cotton blouse, severely tailored along the lines of a man's narrow-collared shirt, and a plain, full, bustle-free skirt of sturdy poplin in a contrasting dark blue.

With a display of ingenuity, Molly had incorporated her uniform project into her sewing classes, thus killing two birds with one stone by instructing the other women in the fine art of stitchery by having them make their own costumes.

Darcy was no exception to the class; the skirt and blouse she had donned were the second, and infinitely better looking, of the costumes created by her own efforts.

While fully aware that she would never make a fashion modiste, Darcy was nevertheless both proud of and satisfied with her accomplishments.

The same could be said of the other women, whose achievements ranged from adequate to exemplary. Either way, all agreed to feeling a deep sense of gratification upon having successfully produced their own uniforms.

A small achievement, perhaps, but one Darcy felt boded well for future projects, and for the future of the school in general.

Owing to the lack of classroom space, the classes

conducted thus far had been limited. With Sally's departure, Darcy had had her bedroom emptied and the gaming tables brought in to be used as sewing tables, thus creating a temporary sewing classroom, which Molly conducted each morning. During the afternoon, between the midday meal and dinner, Darcy used the dining room table to hold rudimentary classes in the basics of reading, writing, and simple arithmetic. Jane held forth throughout the odd moments of the day with lessons in speech patterns and deportment.

It was a makeshift arrangement at best, Darcy knew, but one that would suffice until the completion of the addition to the existing building, which would contain classrooms, sleeping quarters, and a large dining/common room.

And then, as soon as the addition was finished, the workmen were to begin building a small cottage on the far front corner of the property. Darcy, deciding she would feel safer with a caretaker close to hand, or cry for assistance, had requested the house to be built for Clancy Dugan.

Jonathan had immediately informed her that by her action, Darcy had as much as indentured Clancy to her for life—willingly, of course.

Darcy didn't know about the veracity of Jonathan's claim. What she did know was that she would be happy to have the big Irishman spend the rest of his years in her employ. The man was honest, trustworthy, good-natured, and diligent in his duties, primarily in regard to protecting Darcy.

Darcy slid a sidelong glance at Jonathan as she descended the stairs. Her spirit lover was handsome, charming, and a delightful companion;

but lacking physical substance, he could do little to protect her from the very real dangers present at any given time. Living in the West bore precious little comparison to the cloisterlike existence Darcy had known in Philadelphia.

The raw, untamed quality of life in Denver was a fact of that life. In Darcy's opinion, only a foolish woman would attempt to function unprotected, and Darcy was anything but foolish—thanks to inherited intelligence, and the dedicated instruction of her mentor, Miss Reinholt.

Darcy loved Jonathan with every fiber of her being and every cell of her brain, but loving him had not rendered her senseless. And so she took actions designed to keep the brawny Mr. Dugan in her employ.

Besides, she genuinely liked the man, even though he was at times a mite overprotective.

The chatter of animated conversation wafted to Darcy from the dining room as she attained the foyer. There was a sudden indignant outburst . . . from Molly? Then a sharp question from Katie, followed by a deeper-voiced comment from the man recently uppermost in Darcy's thoughts.

"Sounds like a storm brewing in there," Jonathan observed, turning to frown at her.

Darcy felt a chill of premonition. "Yes." Her sigh was soft, but telling. "I was afraid things were moving along too smoothly," she said, recalling the unpleasant visit paid to her by the "decent" ladies of the city. Had the good ladies come up with some nasty business for her to deal with?

"Don't anticipate trouble," Jonathan advised. "Just go in there and find out what's going on."

Squaring her shoulders, as if steeling herself for battle, Darcy crossed the foyer to the dining room. She was noticed the minute she stepped into the room.

"Here's Darcy now," Katie said in a tone of suppressed wrath. "She'll know what to do."

"Do about what?" Darcy asked, keeping her voice even, while bracing herself for bad news.

"It's about this kid!"

"We've got to do something."

"She's little more than a child."

"It's just not right."

"A crying shame."

The comments flew at her in a jumbled mass and from different directions. Feeling besieged, Darcy held up her hands defensively and begged for order. "One at a time, please." Her questing gaze settled on Katie's sternly cast features. "Katie, please explain what has you all so upset."

"Sally was here early this morning," Katie began, then paused to exhale harshly in exasperation.

Darcy frowned. "Seeing Sally upset you?"

"Oh, no!" Sarah exclaimed.

"Not seeing her," Katie went on, giving a quick head shake. "We were upset by what she told us."

"Well, go on," Darcy urged, her impatience tempered by relief that the uproar did not concern the machinations of the malicious "good" ladies of the city. "What did Sally tell you?"

"She told us about this girl her new boss just bought," Molly blurted out heatedly before Katie could reply.

"Bought?" Darcy pounced on the word, feeling a sick sensation invade her stomach.

"Yes, bought," June said, her voice quivering with fury. "Sally said the girl's father has gold fever real bad. He sold the kid for a grubstake."

Darcy was appalled. "But . . . how? I mean, a man can't sell a woman into prostitution."

"Ah, lass, sad to say, but it does happen." Clancy's tone was grim.

"But what about the authorities?" Darcy exclaimed, incensed by the very idea. "The law?"

"Sometimes there's a conspiracy of silence," he said. "And the authorities don't know."

There was a snorting sound from one of the women, and the others all wore mirroring expressions of disdain.

Clancy lifted his massive shoulders in a shrug. "And sometimes they look the other way."

Sheer outrage seared through Darcy. Her hazel eyes glittered. Her face went dead white. A tremor twitched her fine nostrils.

"Sickening, isn't it?" Jane murmured, her normally modulated voice cracking with emotion.

"Unconscionable," Darcy agreed, shuddering.

Tears ran unchecked down Molly's face. "My folks left me to go chasin' the gold rainbow," she said unsteadily. "And that was bad enough. But at least they didn't sell me."

"And my pa threw me out," Sarah muttered. "But even he didn't try to sell me, like a piece of meat."

"Sally said this girl is only eleven or twelve," Katie said, grimacing in disgust.

"This cannot be tolerated." Darcy shook in reaction to the outrage searing through her. "Where is this . . . this house? And who is this woman who buys children?"

"You're going to try to do something for the girl, Darcy?" Jane asked, voicing the hopes of the others.

"No." Darcy's eyes narrowed. "I am not going to try to help. I am going to take that child out of that house."

"It won't be easy, lass," Clancy said. "That house is up in the hills, in a shack town in the gold fields." He shook his head. "How do you plan to get her out, go in there blasting away with a shotgun?"

Good point, Darcy silently conceded, pondering the problem of how to rescue the girl.

Money is always a good bargaining tool.

Jonathan's voice whispered through Darcy's mind, bringing a smile to ease the tightness of her lips.

"I doubt gunplay will be necessary, Mr. Dugan," Darcy replied. "My choice of weapon will be gold."

Clancy grinned. "You're gonna buy the kid from the whore?" he asked, beginning to chortle.

"Precisely."

"What's your limit, then?" Clancy rubbed his large hands together in anticipation. "I'll go to the, er, woman, and make your offer."

"No," Darcy said with firm determination. "I'll go confront the woman myself."

Clancy frowned. "But I'll be going with you." His tone matched hers in determination.

"And so will I," Katie said flatly. "I know that shack town, and that woman." Her right hand slid down to cover the slight bulge in her skirt pocket. "When do you want to go?"

"I'll be ready to leave in half an hour," Darcy said, whirling around and heading for the door. A smile curved her lips at the calls of encouragement that rang out behind her from the other women.

Exactly thirty minutes later, Darcy stepped onto the shaded veranda, resplendent in full female battle array. She looked every inch the proper lady, from the elegant hat perched atop her gleaming auburn hair, to the nipped-in waist and ruffled jacket over her afternoon walking skirt, to the soft kid shoes on her slender, delicately boned feet.

Were she there to see her former student, Miss Reinholt would have been justly proud of Darcy.

Gliding along by her side, Jonathan also felt the human emotion of pride in his beloved.

But in tandem with the pride, Jonathan was subject to apprehension. Like Katie, he knew the environs of the shack town, and the rough, often violent occupants of the makeshift community. Bravely but innocently, Darcy was embarking on what could be a very dangerous mission of mercy.

If anything should happen to harm her in any way . . .

Jonathan leveled a stern look on Clancy as he settled beside the former bouncer. Were she to come to harm, Jonathan vowed he would haunt Clancy until the day he gave up the ghost.

15

Unlike the better planned and constructed towns at the base of the mountains, the shack town appeared to cling precariously to the sloping side of a foothill.

The ramshackle structures huddled together along the narrow, rutted roads, which became quagmires in the spring and fall rains, and nearly impassable with the heavy winter snowfalls.

On the crisp September air, the stench of the place was an assault to the senses and sensibilities.

Gasping, Darcy raised her gloved hand to cover her nose. "Of all the places Sally could have gone to," she muttered, turning a dismayed look on Katie. "Why in heaven's name did she choose this awful town?"

Katie's mouth twisted wryly. "Gold," she said distinctly. "And a lot of men with it in their pockets."

"Yes, of course." Darcy sighed, resigned to the unsavory fact of Sally's choice of employment.

"This . . . woman Sally works for, do you know her?"

Katie gave a short, unpleasant laugh. "Oh, yes, I know her. I don't know what her true name is, but she calls herself Queenie Jones. She's greedy and mean and hard as the ground under the wheels on this carriage."

At that moment the carriage jolted and rocked, as if to confirm Katie's assessment of the earth beneath it.

Darcy threw her a shrewd glance. "You're also familiar with this town, aren't you?"

"Yes," Katie answered. "I lived here, in a one-room shack on the edge of town while my husband prospected for gold up farther in the hills." Though her expression remained calm, her agitation was betrayed by the nervous clicking of one fingernail against another. "He was killed in a fight over mining rights. After he died, I was destitute." She paused, swallowed, then went on without inflection, "I had nowhere to go, no one to turn to, no training to earn a living." She paused again and drew a deep and harsh-sounding breath, her voice growing equally harsh. "So I went to work for Queenie."

Darcy gave no indication that she had already heard Katie's history from Jonathan. "I see," she murmured, trying to equate the way Katie might have looked at the time with the genteel appearance she made now.

Although Katie had not changed out of her shirt and skirt uniform, she had draped a short cape around her shoulders and pinned a fashionable hat—one that had belonged to Colleen—atop the cluster of curls on her head. Regular hours had eased the taut strain of weariness and hopelessness from her face, and Darcy believed she looked younger, prettier.

"I hated her and the place." Katie's voice was not pretty; it was raw, ragged with memories. "Most of her customers are brutes, animals." A sad smile softened her pinched lips. "Going to work for your mother saved my sanity, if not my life."

A tightness swelled Darcy's throat at the mention of her mother, and the realization struck her that she was, in effect, following Colleen's example, if in a different way. From all accounts, Colleen had been fierce in her determination to protect the women who worked for her, and Darcy was equally fierce in her determination, not only to protect the women she had inherited along with the house but to rescue the child Queenie Jones had bought from the girl's avaricious father.

"We're almost there."

Katie's observation drew Darcy from introspection, making her aware of the sights, sounds, and pedestrians around the slowly moving carriage.

For the first time since entering the miserable town, Darcy noticed the gawking stares following the vehicle's progress down the narrow road, and the number of people, mostly men, trailing along behind them.

A nervous sickness roiled in her stomach and her muscles quivered with tension. Meeting, dealing with this Queenie person would be bad enough, she thought, steeling herself as the carriage came to an abrupt stop. Having an audience of avidly interested, ill-bred miners heightened the nervous tension scouring her body, abraded her mental process.

What would she do, what could she do, if Queenie Jones refused to release the child?

She had no influence whatever with the authorities . . . if indeed there were any local authorities in this depressing excuse for a community.

Darcy's gaze shifted to monitor the crowd pressing closer, their expressions intent.

Incipient panic clutched at her throat.

The sight of the brawny Irishman and her ever-present spirit companion alighting from the driver's seat lent a measure of reassurance to Darcy's determination. The strength of Mr. Dugan's hand as he assisted her from the carriage onto the rutted road steadied her nerves. Yet the most calming, soothing effect of all came from the soft voice that whispered through her mind, reining in her racing thoughts.

I am here, my love.

Her flagging spirits bolstered, Darcy looked at the building Mr. Dugan indicated with a hand movement, and experienced a sensation like the bottom of her stomach falling away.

The sagging, two-story building looked to be on the verge of collapsing in on itself. The elements had taken a damaging toll on the inferior building materials used in its construction; it appeared grimy, dilapidated, and unfit for occupation, by either humans or animals.

Denying an urge to scramble back into the carriage and order Mr. Dugan to return at speed to the safety of her own beautiful house, Darcy gathered her composure together, straightened her shoulders, lifted her chin, and strode with apparent fearlessness into the forbidding building.

The interior of the place was even more unsettling than the exterior. In the confined space, the combined odors of stale beer, human sweat, and years' worth of uncleaned dirt struck Darcy like a physical blow.

Her stomach revolted, sending a protesting gush of stinging bile to her throat. Swallowing the sour surge, Darcy narrowed her eyes, raised her chin another notch, and swept a haughty glance around at the gaping faces of the customers seated at the crude tables and standing at the rough-hewn bar.

Obviously her entrance had not gone unnoticed—or unreported to the proprietress.

"Well, Katie, ain't you the grand-looking one?" The drawled observation came from a large, over-blown, overdressed, overpainted woman standing in a doorway in the back of the room, just off the far end of the bar. "Who's that high-toned woman you got in tow, the First Lady of the land?"

Even with the length of the room separating them, Darcy could hear the disparagement in the blowsy woman's voice. Anger flashed, and Darcy was on the point of delivering a scathing setdown, when Jonathan's calm voice once again whispered through her mind, cooling her ire.

Softly, my love. Remember, more flies are caught with honey than with vinegar.

"I think you know well enough who she is," Katie replied, her tone laced with revulsion.

Taking the initiative, Darcy cut a swath through the room, ignoring the stares and offensive remarks from the disreputable customers as she made straight for the large woman. Jonathan

glided along at her side, while Katie and Mr.
Dugan followed in her wake.

"I am Darcy Flynn," she told Queenie in a softly
pitched tone of voice. "I have come here to discuss
a business transaction." She flicked a gloved hand
to indicate the slack-jawed onlookers. "In private,
if you please."

"And if I don't please?" Queenie jibed, heaving
her overendowed bosom in a huffing breath.

Darcy favored the woman with a gently chiding
smile. "The matter is of a delicate nature but"—
she lifted her shoulders in a dainty shrug—"I will,
of course, abide by your decision." Continuing to
smile, though the effort was a strain, Darcy waited
for a reply with seemingly endless patience.

Queenie's eyes narrowed, her lower lip curled,
and then she burst into raucous laughter. "Damned
if you ain't every bit as hoity-toity, and shrewd, as
your mother ever was," she said between gasps for
breath. "I like guts in a woman, she went on, wiping
her laughter-moistened eyes with a pudgy hand.
"Come on into my office," she invited, jerking her
head at the room behind her. "We can talk in private there."

"Thank you," Darcy murmured, stepping forward and edging around her considerable bulk.

"But leave your watchdogs out here," Queenie
ordered, barring entrance to Katie and Clancy,
both of whom immediately squawked a protest.

"It is all right," Darcy said, cutting through
their angry voices. "I will be fine," she assured
them, slanting a glance at her grinning spirit companion, who could not be barred from going anywhere he chose to wander. She compressed her

mouth against a smile at the sight of the visible shiver that shook Queenie as Jonathan floated through her into the room.

Leaving Clancy and Katie muttering dire threats should any harm befall her, Darcy sauntered into Queenie's dirt-encrusted, sparsely furnished office.

"Take a load off your feet," Queenie said, briskly rubbing the goose bumps on her fleshy arms before waving Darcy into a rickety ladder-back chair set in front of a scarred, paper-strewn desk. Plopping her wide bottom onto a swivel chair behind the cluttered desk, the madam fixed her with an assessing stare. "Hang me for a horse thief if you ain't the image of La Rouge," she said, shaking her head in wonder.

Darcy had by now heard about her resemblance to her mother so often she no longer bothered to refute the assertion, although personally, she still could not see the likeness. Accepting Queenie's observation as a compliment, whether or not the woman intended it as such, she murmured her gratitude, then changed the subject by going straight to the point of her visit.

"Miss Jones, information has come to me about the sale of a young girl to you," she said bluntly. "Is that information correct?"

Queenie's expression grew wary. "Who gave you this information?" she demanded, bristling.

Darcy gave her a faint smile. "I think you know I will not tell you that."

"It was Sally, wasn't it?" Queenie snarled. "I shoulda known better than to take her on. All she's done since she came here is fill the other girls' heads with how wonderful it was to work for your mother, how good and kind she was to her girls." Her shrewd eyes studied Darcy. "Sally says you closed the house to customers, and that you've turned the place into a school for young ladies— that true?"

"Yes."

Queenie hooted with ridiculing laughter. "You ever hear the saying about not bein' able to change a sow's ear into a silk purse?" she taunted, choking back the laughter. "The same goes for a whore into a lady."

"You've seen Katie," Darcy said simply.

"Yeah." Queenie made a sour face. "But lookin' like a lady don't make a body one."

"You're quite right." Darcy surprised the other woman by her ready agreement. "I have met some of the decent, upstanding women of Denver."

Queenie was silent a moment, digesting Darcy's observation. Then she nodded. "You're right, they ain't none of them ladies, neither."

"Which is beside the point," Darcy said, steering the conversation back to the reason for her venture into the hills. "Although I am fully aware that the buying and selling of human beings is both immoral and illegal, I came here to make you an offer for the girl."

"You want to buy her from me?" Queenie said, an avaricious smile twisting her scarlet-painted mouth.

"I want to buy her freedom," Darcy corrected her. "Are you willing to . . . barter?" she asked, unwilling to utter the word *sell* in regard to the girl.

A sly, calculating expression washed over Queenie's face. "I don't know. She's prime. A virgin. I've got customers chompin' at the bit for a piece of her."

Darcy could barely contain the sense of outrage and revulsion that swept through her. Suppressing a shudder, while hoping the woman's contention that the girl was still untouched was the truth, she drew a quick, steadying breath, but before she could speak to make an opening monetary offer, Jonathan's voice, sharp and concise, rang inside her mind.

Don't dicker with the woman. Appeal to her greed with an offer she won't be able to refuse.

I have no experience of this unspeakable kind of business, Darcy responded in frustrated silence. *What sum can I offer her that she won't be able to refuse?*

Ten thousand in gold.

Darcy had to steel herself against starting in sheer astonishment. Ten thousand dollars! Good Lord.

What is mere money compared to a human life?

"Well?" Impatience riddled Queenie's voice. "Are you goin' to make an offer or not?"

Darcy didn't hesitate any longer. "Yes. I will give you ten thousand dollars in gold for the girl."

Queenie's eyes popped wide open. She gasped and her jaw dropped, slack and loose, causing her double chin to jiggle. "Did you say ten thousand?" she asked in a disbelieving croaking whisper. "In gold?"

"Yes." A surge of confidence shot through Darcy, bringing a note of command to her voice.

"That is as high as I will go. Will you accept the offer?"

"Will I accept?" Queenie let out another burst of laughter. "Do I look tetched in the head?" Her eyes glowed with a money-hungry light. "O'course I'll accept."

"Very well," Darcy said in precise, businesslike tones. "I will meet with my banker and make the arrangements. Mr. Dugan will deliver the gold to you in exchange for the girl." Both her tone and eyes went hard. "I fully expect the girl to be untouched, with not so much as a mark on her."

"You have my word on it," Queenie promised. "For ten thousand in gold, I'll guard her night and day."

"Then we are agreed." Standing, Darcy extended her gloved right hand. "I'll have your hand on it."

Rising, Queenie grasped Darcy's hand and gave it a firm shake. "A deal," she repeated in evident satisfaction. "Now, will you have a drink on it?"

"No, thank you," Darcy declined, repressing a shudder at the thought. "Katie and Mr. Dugan are waiting . . . anxiously, I imagine. I must be going. Good day, Miss Jones." Giving her skirt a gentle shake, she turned and walked to the door.

"Good day to you, Miss Flynn," Queenie called after her. "It's a real pleasure doing business with you."

Three days later, Clancy escorted Sue, the wide-eyed, obviously frightened girl from the shabby saloon in the shack town to the large house on the outskirts of Denver City.

Predictably, like all morsels of information too rich to be kept secret, the tale of Darcy's trip into the mining town, and the reason for it, spread like a prairie fire, the details leaping from lips to ears throughout the mining towns and into Denver and its environs.

As autumn advanced with its vanguard of biting winds and chilling rains, the dire straits of other girls and women, young and not so young, were brought to the attention of, and subsequently alleviated by, Darcy's intervention.

By the time the work was completed on the addition to Darcy's house, there were five females waiting to occupy the dormitories, all of whom had been sleeping on pallets hastily made up in the existing bedrooms in the original house.

And by the first light dusting of snow on the ground, Darcy's name and deeds had become legend in the vicinity, her reputation deemed sterling by most residents.

In consequence to Darcy's bold actions, and the growing understanding of her high moral standards, her school was accorded credibility, and her former prostitute-students a grudging measure of acceptance, by the majority of the citizens of Denver.

The "good" ladies of the city were left with little choice but to offer Darcy a smile—if tight—and a "Good day"—if strained—when passing her on the sidewalk.

Clancy and the women were bemused by the results.

Darcy was faintly amused by it all.

* * *

For his part, Jonathan felt a deep satisfaction with the course of events and the progress Darcy was making; distance aside, she had come a long way from Philadelphia.

His love for her, and his pride in her, were ever more consuming, to the extent that Jonathan no longer questioned the rightness of his association with her. After much soul-searching, he had decided that, so long as Darcy was content to exist within the limits of the love they shared, willingly forgoing the broader spectrum of experience to be found with an earthbound man, he would continue to resist the promise of universal love and spiritual paradise.

Possibly recognizing, and thus becoming resigned to, his determination, Jonathan's guide had ceased in his efforts to lure him into the light.

In truth, Jonathan was thoroughly enjoying his . . . death. Or at least, he would have been, if not for the ever-increasing sensation of the importance of something . . . or someone.

With growing frequency, Jonathan felt a strange stillness within, immediately followed by a sense of urgency, of destiny closing in on him.

By early November, the sensations were so intense, so disturbing, that Jonathan, frustrated by his inability to discern the cause of them, called out to his spirit guide for an explanation of the odd feelings.

He is coming.

He?

Jonathan went blank for an instant, then he began to quiver, his mind expanding with wondrous speculation.

The second coming?

No. The guide's voice was gentle in soft denial.

Then who? Jonathan demanded with crushed disappointment.

The man bearing the gift of the possibility for you to reexperience the earth plane.

Once more Jonathan went blank for a moment, then his mind filled with eager expectancy and hope.

Life?

The possibility. The guide's voice held an understanding yet cautioning note.

When?

Soon. You will know when the time is nigh. But remember, the entity must be willing.

But I'm not sure I understand how the process works, Jonathan cried, afraid of losing his opportunity through ignorance.

All will be made clear . . . if the possibility comes to fruition.

And if it does not? Jonathan asked, feeling a decidedly human, sinking sensation.

You can always come to the light.

16

The mid-November damp seeped up through the loose, uneven boards of the saloon floor, permeating the room with a moist and musty earth smell. The odor seemed right at home with the rundown, filthy place, and the scruffy appearance of the customers, bartender, and cheap-looking women plying their trade.

Dunstan had seen cleaner pig sties . . . and cleaner pigs.

Hat pulled low on his forehead, shoulders hunched against the penetrating cold, Wade sat at a crude table, sipping raw whiskey from the chipped glass cradled in his gloved hands and staring at the foul-mouthed man in a corner, fondling a whore between swigs from a mug of beer.

The dirty, rudely dressed man was Dunstan's quarry, the last one of the four men who had murdered his wife. Dunstan had tracked the man through three mining towns before catching up to him in this hellhole of a shack town perched on the side of a foothill west of Denver City.

Dunstan was bone tired; Betsy was on the sloping edge of exhaustion. In his determination to reach Denver, and end his quest for revenge against his wife's murderers by meting out justice to the last of her attackers, he had driven himself, and the girl, unrelentingly.

Admiration, and an emotion too close to love to be acknowledged, swelled inside Wade for the girl. Throughout the long, arduous ride from Montana, through numerous rainstorms and two snowstorms, Betsy had kept pace beside him, never uttering a word of complaint.

He and the girl had hit town late yesterday afternoon, their panting horses valiantly plodding through the two feet of snow already on the ground.

The blanket of white did little to soften the harsh ugliness of the unappealing town.

Fortunately, the only rooming house the squalid place had to offer turned out to be the only building in town that didn't look about ready to collapse. A small, hand-printed sign outside read simply ROOMS TO LET. APPLY, MRS. SWIGART.

The proprietress of the house was a miner's wife, a stout, strong-looking woman with a thick German accent and a brisk but friendly manner.

To Wade's surprised relief, the inside of the house was spotlessly clean, and the meal of tender chicken and plump dumplings in a rich and savory broth the woman served up to them was delicious as well as filling.

The beds in the rooms Mrs. Swigart allotted to them were firm but comfortable; the bedding was clean. Even so, Wade had not slept well.

Betsy, on the other hand, had dropped into bed after a quick washup and was dead to the world moments later. She was still sleeping when Wade left the rooming house just after noon. He had not returned to the house since then. And though it was now early in the evening, for all Wade knew, Betsy might still be asleep. He hoped she was; she had earned the rest. Life had not been easy on her, and it hadn't improved much with him.

She deserved better.

Dunstan had made a solemn vow that she would have the best Denver had to offer.

One obstacle stood in the way of Dunstan's making good his own vow. The obstacle's name was Robert Mason.

Bringing the glass to his lips, he narrowed his eyes on his prey, and lowered his right hand to the holstered Colt pistol tied to his thigh.

Soon, he promised himself, grimacing as the sip of whiskey laid a trail of fire down his throat. It was almost over, his unholy quest of destruction. Very soon now the bullets in the first two chambers in his Colt would find a home in the heart of Robert Mason.

Then he would be free to find a new life for Betsy, and seek his own ultimate freedom in death.

Soon, Mary, he repeated the promise, this time to his beloved wife. We'll be together soon.

But for the time being, he had to hang on to his patience and bide his time. Dunstan would not chance endangering bystanders by calling Mason out while he was inside the saloon.

Tired, bored, and sick of the taste of the rotgut whiskey he was now only making a show of sipping, Wade paid scant attention to the talk swirling around him until a taunting question was flung at

Mason from the grinning drunk seated at the table one over from Dunstan.

"Hey, Mason, how come you ain't at that party?"

"What party?" Mason snarled, scowling as he left off pawing the whore.

"The one bein' thrown down to that new private school by that teacher who runs it. You know the one I mean. That pretty lady who's been tearin' around the county, rescuin' women and homeless little girls."

Although his hunched body didn't react to the banter by as much as a flicker, Dunstan was suddenly wide awake, taut, straining to hear every word.

"Name's Darcy Flynn," Mason said, licking his lips. Even from the distance separating them, Dunstan could see the lecherous gleam that leapt into his eyes. "I mean to have myself a piece of that pretty lady someday."

Hooting laughter greeted Mason's assertion. "You sure do a lotta big talkin', Mason," one man gibed.

"And that's all it is, too," the man over from Dunstan ridiculed. "All a lotta hot air and no action."

Mason visibly bristled. "Ya think so, huh?" Shoving the whore aside, he swaggered across the room, coming to a halt just beyond Dunstan's chair. "Well, I'll show you who's a lotta hot air," he bragged. "I reckon I'll just mosey on down to that there school right now, get that uppity Darcy Flynn, and give her a humpin' she ain't never gonna forget."

Drunken shouts of encouragement egging him

on, Mason spit on the floor, wiped the back of his hand over his mouth, and hiking up his grimy pants, stormed out of the saloon. Dunstan followed after him a few moments later, unnoticed by the remaining customers, who were busy laying odds for and against Mason's chances of success.

Dunstan could easily have caught up with Mason, ending his quest right there in the slush-mired road. But his interest had been aroused by the remarks made by the taunting drunk about the pretty lady teacher who was rescuing homeless girls, and the private school she had recently opened.

His footsteps muffled by the deep snow, Dunstan trailed Mason from the saloon to the one livery stable in the town. Flipping the broad collar of his coat up in defense against the biting wind, he waited around the corner of the building until Mason led his horse out, mounted, and rode off down the street. Then he slipped into the stable, saddled Rascal, and tracked him at a comfortable distance.

Moments later, at an equal distance to the rear, a small, slight figure set a horse into step behind Dunstan.

Light and laughter filled the large common room. The scent of perfume mingled with the distinct odor of melting candle wax, overshadowing the smell of the newly laid hardwood floor. Music wafted on the air from the far corner of the room, where a piano player and two fiddlers were working up a sweat earning their pay.

Standing next to the refreshment table, fairly

sagging under the weight of an array of roasted meats and specialty dishes and an elaborately decorated three-tiered cake set in the center of the table, Darcy tapped her foot in time with the music, and smiled misty-eyed at the two couples gliding around the cleared floor.

The party was being held in celebration of the double ceremonies performed earlier that evening, uniting Jane and James Singleton and Molly and Clancy Dugan in holy wedlock.

The other residents of the newly established, and now accredited, school, stood about on the fringes of the dance floor, their expressions rapt as they watched the two glowing, obviously ecstatic couples.

Returning from the kitchen after having refilled a large cut-glass bowl with a fresh quantity of champagne punch, Katie set her heavy burden onto the table and grinned at Darcy.

"That imported champagne you had shipped in for special occasions sure is a rousing success at this party," she observed in dry tones. "Either that, or weddings tend to make this bunch mighty thirsty."

Darcy smiled. "Or their thirst might be attributed to their frenzied activity the last few days in preparing the house, the food, and Jane and Molly for today," she suggested. "You, Dora, everyone worked hard to make this special occasion a success." Her glance shifted to the two brides being swept around the dance floor by their beaming grooms. "Molly outdid herself with the wedding gowns she created for Jane and herself; they are perfectly lovely."

"Hmm." Katie nodded. "Especially considering how scared Molly was to make the first cut in that beautiful cream brocade material you ordered from Chicago."

"I had supreme confidence in Molly's ability," Darcy said, then added, "As I have in the individual and diverse abilities of every member of this house."

"Home. You have turned this house into a home, Darcy," Katie corrected her.

"Thank you," Darcy murmured around the sudden emotional tightness in her throat. "I have found a home here as well." Reaching out, she clasped the other woman's hand. "A home and, more importantly, good friends, like you."

It was true, Darcy mused, her gaze following Katie as she returned to the kitchen to refill an empty meat platter. Though she had formed friendships with all the members of her household, the strongest bond had been forged between Darcy and Katie. Which was strange, she acknowledged, in view of the fact that of all Colleen's "girls," Katie had been the only one chosen as a bed partner by Jonathan.

"I was seriously beginning to despair of ever witnessing this occasion," Jonathan commented in blatantly apparent amusement—and very probably to change the direction of her thoughts. "I think that Jane and James and Molly and Clancy have much to thank you for, my love."

Thank me! Darcy was so startled, she nearly forgot herself and exclaimed aloud. *But I did nothing.* Distracted by his claim, she did forget to keep time to the music; her right foot ceased its rhythmic tapping.

"Nothing?" Jonathan lifted that same errant brow into a mocking arch. "All you did was give Molly an excuse to fling herself into Clancy's arms in relief and happiness when he arrived at the house with young Sue." His expression went wry, his lips curved in a droll smile. "From the way Molly praised him, consequently encouraging him to reveal his feelings for her, one would have thought Clancy had rescued the girl from that mining town den of iniquity."

Well . . .

"As to Jane," he continued, speaking before she could finish her thought. "I doubt you could ever convince her you had nothing to do with earning complete respectability for this house-cum-institution, and a measure of same for the inhabitants herein, thereby allowing James to believe he could take Jane for his wife without fear of being ostracized by the entire population of Denver and its environs."

Perhaps, Darcy conceded. *Nevertheless, I feel certain that both James and Clancy would have declared themselves to Jane and Molly . . . eventually.*

"Perhaps," Jonathan said in gentle mimicry. "If Jane and Molly managed to live that long."

Darcy shrugged, and then she smiled as the musicians began playing a waltz. Her foot resumed tapping in time, and at the sight of the two couples circling the floor, a soft sigh of longing whispered past her guard.

Gliding forward, Jonathan turned to face her, smiled, and held out his arms.

"May I have this dance, Miss Flynn?" he asked in a tone of formality belied by the sparkle in his gray eyes.

But I can't, Darcy thought, yearning to join the smiling couples. She indicated the others in the room with a barely perceptible hand movement. *They will think I've lost my senses.* She bit her lip to contain a giggle. *Or that my senses have danced away.*

"Or since the only other *visible* men in the room already have partners, they might conclude that you decided to enjoy the waltz by yourself," he theorized. "Come, be as brave as you were when you went dashing off to rescue Sue," he entreated. "Waltz with me, my love."

The music lured Darcy; Jonathan lured her even more. Stepping forward, she raised her arms, held her right hand slightly above his broad, but substanceless, shoulder, and placed her left hand next to his waist, smiling up at him as he moved in step to the three-quarter time of the music.

Immediately, they—she—became the focus of every pair of eyes, the object of each surprised comment, the reason for every look of astonishment. Darcy saw, but didn't care. Seemingly dancing by herself, she whirled around the room, smiling at the man invisible to all eyes save her own.

"You are an excellent dancer, Mr. Stuart," she murmured through her smiling, but almost motionless lips. "So very light on your feet."

Without breaking . . . glide, Jonathan threw back his head and let his rich laughter pour forth.

Although her arms grew weary and felt weighted

by the time the music ended, the waltz was the most delightful Darcy had ever danced.

It was later, after the wedding party had ended, the newly married couples sent laughingly on their way to their secret wedding night hideaways, and all the others reluctantly drifted off to bed, tired from the bustle and excitement of the day, that Darcy's sense of delight ebbed, and she was assailed by a feeling of unfulfillment.

Though she loved Jonathan with every breath in her body, she was merely human, Darcy reflected, absently going about her usual bedtime rituals. She was young and healthy, with all the needs and desires natural to a woman.

And so she suffered moments of weakness when, while loving Jonathan, she wanted a normal marriage, like the ones she had witnessed that day. She wanted her life to evolve in a normal manner, growing old with her husband, and the children they had created together, by her side.

She wanted to feel her beloved in her arms when they made love . . . and when they waltzed.

"Tired, my love?" Jonathan's quiet voice drew her from her reverie, scattering her thoughts.

"What?" Darcy asked, distractedly fastening the buttons on the full, long-sleeved flannel nightgown she didn't remember having pulled over her head and nude body.

"I asked if you were tired." His smile was gentle, and faintly sad. "You are pensive tonight."

"Yes, I am tired," she said, turning away to slip into bed, and conceal her eyes, and thoughts, from him. For Darcy felt deeply ashamed of her feelings, for wanting more than the glimpse of paradise his love had given her.

"Then sleep, my precious love," he murmured. "I am here."

Jonathan was restless. Long after Darcy had fallen into a deep sleep, he floated around the room in his own unique manner of pacing.

A very humanlike ache tugged at his essence, and his intellect. Darcy had not turned away from him quickly enough to hide the emotional upheaval revealed in her eyes.

She loved him. Jonathan was as certain of Darcy's love as he was of the sun rising in the east. But he was equally certain that in her heart of hearts she longed for a more natural existence, a flesh-and-blood husband, children, a future as bright with promise as the one before Jane and James and Molly and Clancy. A future he, in his present state, could not offer her.

But his spirit guide had told him there was a man coming, a man through whom Jonathan might reexperience the joys and sorrows of earthly existence. And Jonathan had felt that strange sensation of destiny contracting inside him more strongly with each successive day.

Where is he? Jonathan silently demanded of his spirit guide.

He draws near.

Hope leaping inside him, Jonathan literally flew to the window to peer out at the snow-mantled scene. Not a sign of human movement marred the moon-washed whiteness.

When? he cried in anguished impatience.

Soon. Look out once more, south along the roadway.

Leaning forward until the upper half of his spiritual body protruded through the pane, Jonathan peered down the snow-crusted road to the south. In the distance he noted first one then, moments later, another dark form.

Which one? Jonathan asked, continuing to watch the progress of the figures as he drew back inside the window. *There are two of them.*

The one badly wounded but still breathing.

Jonathan frowned. Neither of the men appeared injured, let alone badly wounded. Suddenly his essence stilled, imbued with a certainty of impending violence.

I'm still not sure of how this process of spirit exchange works, he appealed to his guide. *Tell me what I must do.*

Commune with the higher self of the entity. The entity must be absolute in his determination to depart the earth plane, and willing to make the exchange.

And if the entity is not willing, or changes his mind?

All is choice.

But . . .

Jonathan's thoughts were disrupted by the harsh sound of a man's voice from the road below.

"Mason! Come away from the house and face justice for the murder of Mary Dunstan."

Recognizing the name of the man who had forced his way into the house months earlier, Jonathan zapped himself down to the front yard in time to see the man turn away from a long dining room window, which he had been attempting to pry open.

Another man, tall and solidlooking, was moving

toward Mason in slow, measured strides. The tall man's coat had been pushed back on the right side, revealing the holstered pistol tied to his long, muscular thigh. His arms hung loose at his side, right hand close to but not touching the weapon.

"Make your move, Mason."

Even as the tall man spoke, Jonathan saw Mason raise the gun he had held concealed behind him. The gun discharged. The tall man's body jerked, and yet in that instant, the pistol at his side appeared to leap into his hands. Two shots rang out from the pistol, and then both men crashed to the ground.

There was complete silence for a minute, then shouts were called from the house and the homes located down the road. A small, slight figure ran from behind a tree and dashed to the tall man sprawled in the snow. The figure's voice rose above the others in a shriek of sheer anguish.

"Marshal."

But Jonathan heard the terrified cry of only one person, the woman he was determined to live for.

"Jonathan!"

17

Darcy sat bolt upright in the bed, her eyes wide, her breathing harsh and ragged, her heart pounding as if it were trying to beat its way through her rib cage. Her body was shaking in frightened reaction to the gunshots that had awakened her, and the shouts now breaking the quiet of the night.

Her eyes probed the shadows of the room, frantically searching for another denser shadow—who was not there. She was alone, and scared.

"Jonathan, where are you?" Darcy despaired of the faint, plaintive sound of her own voice.

"I am here, my love." He appeared, as usual, out of thin air, looking as solid as the bedpost next to him. "There is nothing to fear."

"But I heard shots, shouting," Darcy said, pushing back the bed covers. "What has happened?"

"There's been a shooting," he explained, flicking a hand at the front window. "Outside, in the yard."

"In my yard!" Darcy cried, leaping from the bed.

"Darcy, listen to me, I . . ." Jonathan began, but she wasn't listening; she went running to the window.

The scene below both upset and annoyed her at one and the same time. The front yard was full of people, her own from the house, and those from neighboring houses. Several individuals were holding lamps aloft, illuminating the area. The two bodies lying in the snow were clearly defined.

"My God!" she said, shocked by the evidence of the recent violence.

"Darcy, you must listen." Jonathan was beside her, his voice taut with urgency. "I want you to go outside and have one of those men brought into the house."

"What?" Darcy whirled to face him, her eyes going wider still with disbelief. "Why?"

"It's crucial to both of us that he be brought inside, into this room," he said in tones of mounting urgency. "Please, trust me. Go outside, order the man brought into the house, and into this room. Please, do as I ask."

Darcy hesitated, confused by the strangeness of his request, his manner. But his gray eyes pierced her, urging her to obey and, sighing, she relented.

"But there are two," she said, moving to the bed for her wrapper and slippers. "Which man do you want me to have brought inside?"

"The one still breathing," Jonathan instructed, repeating his guide's answer of a short time before.

Darcy shook her head, but hastened from the room. "I don't understand," she muttered, moving quickly along the hallway to the stairs. "Of what possible importance could this stranger be to you?"

"To us," Jonathan murmured, gliding by her

side as she descended the stairs and crossed the foyer to the open doorway. "You will understand . . . in time."

Baffled as to his motives, but trusting him above all others, Darcy suppressed the questions clamoring in her mind and strode across the deep veranda to call out to a recognizable figure bathed in the glow from a lamp held above her head.

"Katie, is either one of them alive?"

"One of them is," Katie called back over her shoulder. "The big one there, near to the tree." She jerked her head in the direction of the dark shape sprawled in the snow.

There was a smaller form huddled over the man, obviously a female from the unmistakable sound of feminine sobbing. Daisy, the orphan who had run away from a dismal life in the orphanage, hovered over the sobbing girl, murmuring indistinguishable words of encouragement and comfort.

Who was the girl? Darcy wondered, staring at the slight form. Who were these men? And why in heaven's name had they chosen *her* property on which to stage their shoot-out?

"Now, Darcy." Jonathan's razor-edged voice sliced through her confusion-knotted thoughts. "Tell them to bring him into the house. Quickly, my love. He must not die before I can—" He stopped abruptly, then repeated, "Now, Darcy!"

Darcy no longer paused to ponder, but reacted to the note of command in Jonathan's voice.

"Katie, have the big man brought inside," she called, her raised voice reflecting Jonathan's urgency.

"What?" Katie whipped around to gape at her.

"Please, don't question me now," Darcy said. "Just ask the men to carry him into the house."

Katie stared at her a moment longer, then with a fatalistic shrug, she trudged toward the milling group of male neighbors, her trailing nightclothes leaving a broad swath through the moonlight-sparkled snow.

"Oh, and Katie!" Darcy raised her voice another notch. "Send Clancy for"—she paused, remembering that Clancy wasn't there, and why—"send someone for a doctor."

Katie's surprise at Darcy's order to have the wounded man brought into the house changed to stunned disbelief when, as the neighborhood men carried their burden into the foyer, Darcy bid them follow her up the stairs and into her bedroom.

"Lay him down here, please," Darcy said, pulling the covers to the far end of the bed.

"Darcy, that's your bed," Katie stated the obvious, frowning her disapproval as she watched the men shift the injured man onto the mattress. "He's wet, and bloody, and—"

"I can see that," Darcy interrupted the other woman with sharp impatience. "But where else can I put him? All the rooms are now full," she improvised, not about to tell her audience that having the man moved into her room, her bed, had been the suggestion—no, command—of her resident wraith.

After settling the tall man, the neighborhood men stood shuffling their feet, looking awkward and uncomfortable, until Dora lured them into the hallway and down the stairs with the promise of a reward of hot coffee and large slices of left-over wedding cake.

Thanking the men for the third time, Darcy at last closed the door and turned to face Katie, who had moved to the side of the bed, fingers at work unbuttoning the man's shirt to get at the wound in his chest.

"It looks to be close to his heart, too damned close," Katie muttered, easing the blood-soaked material away from his skin. "You could have moved Sue in with one of the older girls," she went on in the same muttered tone, as if the two statements were not unrelated.

"We must stem the flow of blood," Darcy said, striding to the chest of drawers where her supply of bath towels was stored. "And why ask the girls to share a bed?" she asked in response to Katie's second statement. "I can move the chaise lounge into my sitting room and sleep there," she explained, pulling thick white towels from the top dresser drawer.

"Well, I still don't understand, but you're the boss," Katie said, reaching for a towel as Darcy came to stand beside her. A frown scored her brow as she gently applied the towel to the ugly wound on the man's chest. "What in the hell is all that racket about out in the hallway?" she demanded, forgetting herself and cursing for the second time in mere minutes.

"I have no idea," Darcy replied, placing the pile of towels close to hand. "But I'll find out."

Her expression rife with disapproval, Darcy hurried to the door, pulled it open, and stepped into the hallway, wincing at the sound of a young girl's keening outcries, and appalling language.

"Goddamn you, lady!" the struggling girl screamed at the buxom Daisy, who had her held fast in her strong grip. "I gotta get in there, damn your hide to hell!" she snarled, tears streaming down her small, pretty face. "I gotta see him, can't you understand? I gotta see him for myself, make sure he ain't dead!"

"Silence." Darcy's stern, austere voice was an exact echo of Miss Reinholt's at her severest; it garnered the exact same results.

The girl immediately ceased her struggles. Her mouth formed a startled, soundless *oh,* and she stared at Darcy from enormous, shock-darkened eyes.

"That's better," Darcy said, in a softened, even tone. "Who are you, child?"

The girl eyed Darcy warily and wet her lips. "N-name's Betsy," she said in a rush after the brief hesitation. "And I gotta see him, please," she begged, between choking sobs. "I gotta make sure he's really alive!"

"He is . . . but who is he? Is he your father or a relative?" she asked, giving the girl a gentle smile. "What is his name? Is he from around here? Does he have family we should notify?"

Betsy shook her head and cast a longing look at the bedroom door. "His name's Dunstan. Wade Dunstan. And he's not my pa. My pa's dead, so's my ma. Mr. Dunstan . . . well, he's been kinda takin' care of me. He's a United States Marshal from New Mexico. Never mentioned any family."

She swiped the back of her hand across her wet cheek. "Please, ma'am, can I see him?"

Darcy felt sympathy for the girl, for the very genuine concern she had for the wounded man, but there were questions she had to have answered.

"In a moment, I promise," she assured the distraught girl. "But first, can you tell me who that other man is—was?" Darcy asked, shuddering.

"Called himself Mason," Betsy replied, reluctantly shifting her gaze from the door to Darcy. "But Mr. Dunstan said the name was an alias. All the marshal would tell me was that Mason, or whoever he was, and three other men had murdered a woman back in New Mexico. That's why the marshal was after them." Her eyes took on a glow of satisfaction. "Caught 'em too. Mason was the last of the four."

"I see." Darcy swallowed and drew a deep breath. "Then I'll have to leave Mr. Mason to the local authorities." Blocking all consideration of the dead man, and his horrible deed, from her mind, she raised her eyes and smiled at the woman holding the girl. "You can let Betsy go now, Daisy."

Daisy complied, then stepped around the girl to offer her a friendly smile. "I didn't hurt you, did I?"

"No, ma'am, you didn't," Betsy said, returning Daisy's offer with a tentative smile of her own. "I . . . I'm sorry I cussed at you the way I did."

Daisy's smile spoke volumes Betsy was beyond comprehending. "That's all right, Betsy. I understand. You see, I'm an orphan too." She slanted a speaking glance at Darcy. "And Miss Flynn's been taking care of me."

"But you're big!" Betsy exclaimed. "I mean, you're a woman, all grown up."

"Ah, yes, but you see, Betsy, even all-grown-up women need to be taken care of at times."

Betsy frowned.

Darcy deemed it time to intervene. "Come along, Betsy, I'll take you in now."

Betsy uttered a low groan at the sight of Wade Dunstan's ashen face, and cried aloud as she glimpsed the blood-soaked towel Katie pressed against the wound on his chest.

"And whom have we here?" Katie asked, sounding remarkably like Darcy. "Male or female?" She wrinkled her nose in distaste at the girl's disreputable boy's clothing.

"Her name is Betsy, and she has been traveling with him," Darcy told Katie, inclining her head to the man on the bed. "His name is Wade Dunstan. He's a federal marshal."

During their exchange, Betsy stared at the gray-tinged face of the wounded man, her slight body shaking like a small tree in a windstorm. "Is . . . is he gonna live?" she asked in a fearful, quaking voice.

"I don't know, but it don't look good," Katie answered with blunt honesty. "He has lost an awful lot of blood."

"He can't die!" Betsy cried, dropping to her knees beside the bed. "Marshal, please, please don't die!"

At the sound of her broken cry, Wade Dunstan opened his eyes a narrow crack. "You be good, kid," he said in a reedy, barely there voice. "Mind your manners, you hear?"

"Marshal, you can't die." Betsy could hardly speak around the sobs racking her small body. "I . . . I love you, Marshal, and I ain't gonna let you die on me!"

Darcy felt her own eyes sting with a rush of tears, and saw Katie blink against a welling moisture.

Wade Dunstan exhaled a shallow, weary sounding sigh. "You'll do all right without me, kid," he murmured, his voice dwindling to an almost inaudible whisper. "You . . . you find that lady who rescues girls . . . that Miss Flynn lady. She'll . . ." His voice failed; his eyes closed; his breathing was nearly nonexistent.

"Marshal?" Betsy's pitiable cry, her rasping breaths, sent Darcy's and Katie's tears cascading down their faces.

"Come, Betsy," Darcy murmured, placing a trembling hand on the girl's shoulder. "He must rest, and so must you.

"I can't leave him," Betsy wailed. "I gotta—" She broke off, sobbing, just as the bedroom door was opened.

"The doctor's here," Daisy announced briskly, showing the man into the room, her controlled expression melting as she caught sight of the weeping girl.

The doctor, a thin, overworked-looking man of about fifty, introduced himself as Jeffrey Denton, then leveled a compassionate but determined stare at the girl.

"Get her out of here," he ordered, stepping back to clear a path to the doorway.

Betsy fought every inch of the way, sobbing and pleading to be allowed to stay. All of Darcy's and Daisy's combined strength was required to remove the girl from the room. Once they had her in the hallway, Darcy called out for assistance. Twelve females, ranging in age from Sue's eleven to Dora's forty-odd, reacted to the call, running to Darcy's aid from every section of the large house.

Satisfied that the overwrought girl was in capable, sympathic hands, Darcy returned to her bedroom to be of whatever use she could be to the doctor.

"I've done everything I could for him," Jeffrey Denton said nearly an hour later, sighing heavily as he straightened up from his unconscious patient. "The rest, his life, is now in God's hands."

"It always was," Jonathan murmured close to Darcy, and for her ears alone. "But the Creator also bestowed free will, and the decision is Wade Dunstan's."

Blasphemy! Darcy thought, startled by Jonathan's sudden reappearance, and shocked by his assertion.

"No, my love. Choice. There is always choice."

But . . . but . . . Darcy's tired mind groped for a response, but came up blank. Too much had happened in too short a period of time. Assisting the doctor in his gory task of removing the bullet from Wade Dunstan's shoulder, and mopping up as he closed the wound, had drained her body and her mind.

She was exhausted, and the day was not yet half over. Her mental wheels stuck in the mire of weariness, Darcy dragged her attention back to the doctor's brisk voice as he gave instructions to her and Katie as to the method of care they were to employ for the patient.

"And pray," he said in conclusion, walking to the door. "It is still the strongest medicine."

"I'll see the doctor to the door," Katie offered when Darcy moved to usher him from the room. She grimaced as she glanced down at her blood-spattered skirt. "I'll be back as soon as I've washed, changed, and had a few words with Betsy."

Darcy thanked the doctor, smiled at Katie, then turned back to stare bleakly at the ashen-faced man in her bed. Wade Dunstan was not a handsome man. His features were too rugged, too sharply chiseled to be termed handsome. But his broad forehead, straight nose, high cheekbones, masculine mouth, and firm, square jaw combined into an image of strength and character. The type of strength and character that would not shirk the burden of taking on a young orphan.

Recalling the girl brought her plight to mind. So intent had Darcy been with the task at hand, she had almost forgotten the girl, Betsy, and her terror of losing Wade Dunstan.

Katie would talk to the girl, Darcy knew. She knew as well that Daisy, and most likely all the other women in the house, would offer comfort and consolation.

The marshal was still unconscious. For now, there was nothing more Darcy could do for him. Shoulders drooping, she crossed the room and sank wearily onto the chaise lounge, feeling scared, alone, and lonely.

"Jonathan?"

"I am here, my love." He materialized at the foot of the chaise, a gentle smile for her curving his lips.

"I'm afraid, Jonathan, and I feel so helpless," Darcy said, biting her lip to stifle a sob. "The doctor was not encouraging." She raised tear-washed hazel eyes to his. "The marshal is going to die, isn't he?"

"Yes." Jonathan's reply was flat, unequivocal. "The entity who is now Wade Dunstan is firm in his determination to quit this mortal plane."

Darcy's tear-drenched eyes flew wide in surprise. "But . . . how do you know this? How can you speak with such assurance?" she demanded, unsure herself that she really wanted to hear his answer. He gave it just the same.

"I have communicated with the entity. The choice has been made. He is going to depart this earth."

Darcy didn't understand, couldn't fathom how Jonathan's claim of having communicated with what he referred to as the entity of Wade Dunstan could be possible, but she didn't question or doubt the veracity of his claim either.

Her mind shying away from further spiritual discussion, Darcy suddenly recalled the girl.

"Poor Betsy," she said with heartfelt sympathy. "She will be inconsolable if Wade Dunstan dies."

"Not if she doesn't know he has died."

Darcy blinked. "Doesn't know?" she repeated in tones of amazed disbelief. "She is here in the house. How could she possibly not know?"

"If he appears to still be alive." Jonathan's voice held an odd undercurrent of anticipation.

"Appears to still be . . ." Darcy's voice failed her; so did her mental process. Staring at him in slack-jawed incredulity, she attempted to speak, managed only a dry squeak, swallowed, then made another, successful attempt. "Jonathan, what are you saying? How can he appear to still be alive?"

"Darcy, please, listen carefully to what I'm about to say." Jonathan's voice had regained the urgency of that morning. "Do you remember me telling you that there was a way possible for me to live again, through another?"

"Ye-yes, I remember you mentioning it, b-but . . ." Darcy couldn't continue. The very idea of some sort of an exchange of souls in a single body conjured thoughts of possession, despite Jonathan's assurance to the contrary, his claim that the exchange could occur only on the prear-ranged and mutual agreement of the souls in-volved. A shaft of undiluted fear spearing through her, Darcy was reduced to slowly shaking her head in denial of such an unholy concept.

"My love, my love," Jonathan murmured. "Don't surrender to fear of the unknown. For there is truly nothing to fear. Can you, in all truth, believe that I would willingly countenance evil in-tent?"

"No," Darcy answered at once, and with com-plete honesty. "I know you would not." Banishing her fear, she drew a deep, self-composing breath before venturing a question. "If you can, explain this phenomenon to me."

"I'll do my best," he said in a deep tone of appreciation of her trust. "My spirit guide has told me that all systems are open. Who are we to know or question the gifts of love so generously showered upon us? The entity now perceived as Wade Dunstan is satisfied that his work on this earth plane is completed. His choice is a mortal death." He paused, passing a hand along his image to indicate himself. "The entity you see before you, known to you as Jonathan Stuart, now knows there is still much work for him to finish, and a love stronger than death. His choice is life. An exchange will be made." A smile tugged at the corners of his mouth. "An exchange not unlike moving from one house into another."

"When . . ." Darcy paused once more to wet her parched lips. "When will it happen?"

"You will know," Jonathan said, repeating the promise given to him by his guide. "Lie back now, my love. Rest. You have earned it this day."

Darcy didn't want to sleep—she wanted to continue their discussion—but sheer weariness stole over her, weighing her eyelids, blanketing her mind. Settling comfortably on the cushioned chaise, she drifted off into a soothing state halfway between sleep and wakefulness.

She had no sense of how long she had been floating in that in-between realm when a jarring sound jerked her into the world of harsh reality. The sound had come from the man in her bed. Jumping up, Darcy ran to his side.

Wade Dunstan's face had an odd greenish-gray tinge. The sound Darcy had heard had been the rasping gasps he expelled in his struggle for breath.

Darcy started to turn away, to run to the door

and call for help, when the marshal gave up the struggle. A strange, beatific smile feathered over his pale lips. She heard a terrible rattling sound from his throat. Then he went still.

Darcy stared at the man in disbelief for an instant, her mind running wild with denial. Wade Dunstan could not be dead! Jonathan had assured her an agreement had been made. Unable to accept the truth of her sight, Darcy bent to place one hand over his heart, the other along the side of his throat. She could feel not the weakest of beats from his heart, not the faintest of pulsations in his throat.

He was dead.

No! Darcy screamed in silent protest. This was not the way it was supposed to be. Jonathan was supposed to have assumed Wade Dunstan's body, and life!

What had gone wrong?

"Jonathan?" she cried, fighting the sharp teeth of panic nipping at the edges of her mind.

There was no answer, no sudden appearance of the solid-looking figure of her beloved.

There was nothing, nothing but the rough sound of her rapid breaths . . . the absence of breath from the man on the bed.

With a terrifying certainty growing inside her that she had lost her love and her patient, Darcy closed her eyes and sank to her knees beside the bed in the exact same spot Betsy had occupied hours ago.

Weeping softly, feeling abandoned, bereft, Darcy was unaware at first of the flutter against her fingers pressed to his neck and chest. When the flutter strengthened to a rhythmic thump, she was so startled, her eyes flew wide and she reared back, pulling her hands away from his cool skin.

Not knowing what to think, almost afraid to think, Darcy stared at his still body until, slowly, his chest expanded, very slightly, unevenly, then, with each successive breath, the movement of his chest regulated to an even rate.

Wade Dunstan was alive!

But where was Jonathan?

Torn by conflicting emotions of relief for her patient and despair for her love, Darcy cried out in desolation.

"Jonathan."

At the mournful sound of her voice, Wade Dunstan's eyes flickered, then opened. Darcy stared into gray eyes now clear and alert, and caught her breath when his masculine lips curved into a weak but definite smile.

"I am here, my love." Though the voice was different, deeper, the cadence, intonation were joyously familiar.

"Jonathan?" Darcy whispered, longing yet afraid to believe. Tears poured like life-giving rain from her eyes. "Darling, is it really you?"

"Yes, my love." His voice was wispy, but certain. "I am with you now. I will always be with you."

His eyes drifted shut, but his smile remained. His chest expanded, each breath growing steadily stronger.

The crisis, and the agony of physical separation, was over, for both of them.

Epilogue

Light, laughter, and music wafted into the warm June night air through the opened windows of the common room. Inside the room a party was being held in celebration of Darcy's arrival in Denver one year ago that day, and in thanksgiving for the full recovery from the life-threatening wound suffered more than six months before by the former United States Marshal . . . turned newly installed minister of a nearby church.

The rousing music came to a lively end, followed by a burst of appreciative applause. Then the strains of a waltz soared above the chatter of animated conversation.

"May I have this dance, my love?"

Darcy raised her eyes to the elegantly attired, tall, whipcord-lean man standing before her. Staring into the rough-hewn face of Wade Dunstan, she perceived the sparkling eyes, teasing smile, and rakishly arched eyebrow characteristic of Jonathan Stuart.

"Are you light on your feet, Mr. Dunstan?" Darcy asked in a laughing voice.

"Though I can no longer float around the

floor," he rejoined, laughing with her, "I will do my best, Mrs. Dunstan."

Thrilling to the feel of his strength, the flow of life warming his hands at her waist and against her palm, Darcy gave herself into his care as he swept her onto the floor.

At that same time, another couple waltzed abreast of them, looking more enthusiastic than graceful. Clancy, his ruddy face aglow with happy anticipation of the birth of the child his Molly carried proudly inside her body, carefully held Betsy's dainty figure in his arms.

The girl was the picture of a charming young lady, radiant in the muslin summer frock Molly had so lovingly made for her on the new treadle sewing machine Darcy recently had shipped to Denver by rail from back East.

"Hey, Marshal, you like my new dress?" Betsy called over the music as she and Clancy danced by, grinning unrepentantly for her continued use of his former title.

"It's real pretty, kid," he responded, grinning back at her. "And so are you."

Betsy laughed with delight, and tossed her head coquettishly as the couple danced away.

"She loves you," Darcy murmured, her gaze following the awkward progress of the pair.

"I know," he said, his glance following hers. "I love her too."

"But which one of you loves her?" Darcy asked, her hazel eyes bright with a teasing light. "The marshal or the minister?"

"Why, we both do, my love," he replied, spinning her around in time to the music. "As we both love you."

His touch, his nearness as he whirled her around the floor, set Darcy's mind swirling with delicious memories of the beautiful nights they had shared since his recovery.

During the daylight hours, when there were always ears within hearing, Darcy was careful to call him Wade. But at night, when the house was at last silent, she called him . . .

"Jonathan! You'll hurt yourself!"

Weeks had passed since Jonathan had spoken to her through Wade's lips. His wound was not yet completely healed, and Darcy feared he might cause himself harm.

"No, I won't," he said, drawing her down onto the bed beside him. "I can't wait any longer. I want to hold you in my arms, feel your heart beating next to mine. I want to caress your body with my hands, and my mouth. I want to kiss you, taste your desire on your mouth. And then I want to join with you, be inside you, feel your body enclosing mine."

Willingly seduced by the resistance-melting sound of his passion-roughened voice, Darcy discarded her nightgown, set her glorious mane of auburn hair free to flow around them, and surrendered herself into his hands.

Jonathan's hands made a delightful prison. Where before, Darcy had felt only the heat of his spirit tongue, she now experienced the sensual pleasure of his physical tongue, and moaned in response to it plunging into her mouth, trailing a shiver-inducing fire down her neck, curling around the tip of her breast, and then suckling her until she cried out and grasped his hair to hold him to her.

Her senses retreating before the advance of her inflamed desire, Darcy returned each and every one of Jonathan's loving caresses, learning the contours of his angular body with the touch of her hands and mouth.

"Oh, Jonathan, I love you," she cried, blessing the wound on his chest with a healing kiss.

"And I you, my precious love," he said, drawing her up to sip the blessing from her lips.

She was on fire, a shimmering flame burning only for him, ever for him. When she could no longer bear the sensual tension coiling tighter, and tighter inside her, she grasped his hips, urging him into the cradle of her thighs.

Murmuring sweet words of his undying love, Jonathan carefully, gently pierced the barrier of her maidenhood. The shock of pain stiffened her muscles in a reflexive move against the intrusion of his body into hers.

His touch light, Jonathan soothed her, stroking her taut muscles until the strain eased. Then, slowly, he began to move. For a moment, Darcy remained still, waiting for another piercing pain. But instead of the pain, the tension began coiling again, spiraling upward, sparking to life a flame of wild desire. Arching her body high, she moved with him, now at one with him, craving his driving thrusts toward completion.

When it came, Darcy did not experience the same breathtaking glimpse of paradise she had felt with her shadow lover. But the shattering ecstasy she shared with the physical Jonathan was more thrilling, more deeply satisfying, simply because it was real, of this earth.

"What thoughts have put that dreamy smile on your tempting mouth, my love?"

Darcy blinked, then blushed, then laughed.

"Thoughts of you, my darling," she confessed, leaning into him to whisper close to his ear. "Memories of the first time we made love to each other . . . real, physical love."

Jonathan's eyes acquired a recognizable gleam, and his eyebrow rose in a familiar arch. "Careful, my love," he warned in murmured teasing. "Or I might just waltz you out of this room, up the stairs, and into our bed to engage in a different, infinitely more stimulating dance."

"Tonight, after the party is over and our guests have all sought their rest," Darcy whispered, "I shall hold you to your enticing warning, my darling."

"You can depend upon it, my love," Jonathan vowed.

It was a warning joyously fulfilled.

Please turn the page for
an exciting sneak peek
of Joan Hohl's newest
contemporary romance

I DO

coming from Zebra Books
in December 2001!

1

"In the name of the Father, the Son, and the Holy Spirit. Amen."

The solemnly intoned benediction seemed to hang like a pall on the chill March air long seconds after the pastor closed his prayer book. A muffled sob shattered the silence, and, as if the cry had been a signal, the large crowd around the grave site began to move in a slow, unsure manner.

Some distance off to one side, in a small, sparse stand of trees, a tall man stood, unobserved by the group of mourners. Hands thrust inside the deep pockets of a hip-length sheepskin jacket, broad shoulders hunched, wide collar flipped up against the cold, damp air, all that was visible of his head and face was a shock of sun-gold hair and a pair of amber eyes, narrowed and partially concealed by long, thick, dark brown lashes. At the moment, the eyes were riveted on the flower-draped brass casket suspended over the open grave.

The figure remained still as a statue, but the eyes, cold and unemotional, shifted to the source of the low sobs. A small, fair-haired woman, dressed entirely in black, stood unsteadily, supported on both sides by two tall, slender, fair-haired young men who wore the same face. The cold eyes flashed for an instant with cynicism, gone as fast as it came, then moved on to rest on the face of a younger woman, also dressed in black, standing close to one of the young men. There was an oddly protective attitude in her stance, although she was much smaller than the man. The amber eyes grew stormy as they studied the small, pale, wistfully lovely face, the soft, pure lines set in fierce determination. The lids dropped, and the eyes again became clear and cold and moved on to briefly scan the crowd before once again coming to rest on the coffin, gleaming dully in the gray, overcast morning light.

"I loved you, you old bastard."

The softly muttered words bounced off the warm fleece of the collar; then the man turned sharply and strode through the trees to the road some yards away and a sleek black BMW parked to the side.

Anne rested her head against the plush upholstery of the limousine, eyes closed. She was tired and the day wasn't half over. There would be a lot of people coming back to the house and she'd have to act as hostess, as her mother obviously wasn't up to it. The soft weeping coming from the seat in front of her gave evidence of that. Not for the first time Anne wished she'd known her father, for she surely must have inherited his character. For although except for hair color she resembled her small, fragile mother, beyond the surface features there was very little comparison. Her mother was gentle natured but had always been high-

strung and of delicate health, whereas Anne had
enormous stamina and strength for such a small
woman. About the only thing she and her mother
shared by way of emotions was the gentle nature.
Anne was a pushover for any hard luck or sob
story and had been taken in by and involved with
so many of her friends' problems she had finally
had to harden her heart in self-defense.

Taking advantage of the drive back to the house
to relax, Anne's mind was going over what still
had to be gotten through that day when a disturbing thought pushed its way forward: he didn't
even come to his father's funeral. Her head moved
restlessly; her soft lips tightened bitterly. For days
now, ever since her stepfather's death, she had
managed to push away all thoughts of her stepbrother, but even so she had felt sure he would
be at the funeral. Of course it had been ten years,
but still, he had been notified and the least he
could do . . . She felt the car turn into the driveway and, opening her eyes, sat up straight, pushing
the disquieting thoughts away.

During the next two hours Anne was kept too
busy to do any deep thinking, but still her eyes
went to the door each time the housekeeper
opened it to admit yet another friend offering
condolences.

When finally the door was closed after the last
well-wisher, Anne sighed deeply before squaring
her shoulders and walking to the door of the library. With her hand on the knob she paused, her
gaze moving slowly around the large, old-fash-
ioned foyer. The woodwork was dark, gleaming in
the light of the chandelier that hung from the

middle of the ceiling. The furnishings could only be described as heavy and ornate. Anne didn't really care too much for the house, yet it had been the only home she'd ever known, as Judson Cammeron, Sr. had been the only father she'd ever known. Sighing again, she turned the knob and entered the room.

Mr. Slonne, the family attorney, sat dwarfed behind her stepfather's massive oak desk, hands folded on the blotter in front of him. He was speaking quietly to her mother, who was sitting in a chair alongside the desk. As Anne gently closed the door he glanced up and asked, "Everyone gone?"

Smiling faintly, Anne nodded and moved to the chair placed at the other side of the desk. As she sat down, her eyes scanned her mother's face.

"How are you feeling now, Mother?"

Margaret Cammeron smiled wanly at her daughter, her eyes misty. "Better, dear." Her tremulous voice had a lost, childlike note. "I don't know how I'd have managed to get through this without you and your brothers." Her breath caught and her hand reached out for, and was grasped by, that of her son who leaped from his chair and came to stand beside hers.

"Well, you don't have to get through anything without us, ever." Anne spoke bracingly, her eyes going to first one, then another, set of matching blue eyes, in the faces of her identical twin half brothers.

Like a small mother hen, Anne was proud of her younger brothers. Usually carefree and unhampered by responsibility, due to too little discipline and too much indulgence, their conduct the last few days had been faultless. At twenty-one and in their last year of college, Troy and Todd Cammeron had never done a full day's serious work. They had inherited their mother's sweet nature and their father's quick temper, but little of his iron will and tenacity. They were good looking and well liked and too busy having a good time to worry about the future. Their father was rich and they had known they would go to work in his business when they left school. Meanwhile they had been busy with girls and cars and girls and fun and girls. Their father's sudden death had shocked them, as it had everyone, but they had rallied well in support of their mother. Although only four years their senior, Anne also admitted she had had as much of a hand, if not more, in their spoiling as anyone.

Mr. Slonne glanced at his watch then cleared his throat discreetly. "I think we had better begin, Mrs. Cammeron. The time stated was two o'clock and as it is now two-fifteen I—"

He stopped, startled, as the library door was thrust open and Anne felt the breath catch in her throat as her stepbrother walked briskly into the room. He paused, his eyes making a circuit of the room, then proceeding to her mother.

"Sorry I'm late, Margaret, I stopped for something to eat and the service was lousy."

Anne shivered at his tone. So unfeeling, so cold, could this hard-eyed man be her stepbrother?

Margaret raised astonished eyes to his face, murmuring jerkily, "That—that's all right, Jud. But you—you should have come home to eat."

His smile was a mere twist of the lips before his head lifted to turn from one then the other twin, standing on either side of her chair.

"Troy, Todd, still the same bookends, I see."

Their faces wore the same strained expressions, but both stretched out hands to grasp the one he had extended. He nodded to the lawyer, murmured, "Mr. Slonne," then turned to Anne. She felt a small flutter in her chest as he walked to the chair next to hers.

"Anne."

His tone was low, but so coolly impersonal that Anne again felt a shiver go through her. Was it possible for a man to change so much in ten years? Apparently it was, for the proof of it was sitting next to her.

He had left home a charming, laughing, teasing young man and had walked through that door a few minutes ago with the lazy confidence of a proud, tawny lion. And tawny was the only way to describe him. The fair hair of ten years ago had darkened to a sun gold, and his skin was a burnished bronze. His features hadn't changed, of course, but had matured, sharpened. The broad forehead now held several creases as did the corners of his eyes. The long nose that had been perfectly straight now sported a bump, evidence of a break surgically corrected. The once firm jawline now looked as if it had been cut from granite. The well-shaped mouth now seemed to be permanently cast in a mocking slant. And the once laughing amber eyes arched over by sun-bleached brows now held the mysterious, wary glow of the jungle cat. Incredibly he seemed to have grown a few inches and gained about thirty pounds and he looked big and powerful and very, very dangerous.

With a feeling of real grief Anne felt a small light go out inside for the death of the laughing, teasing Jud Cammeron she'd known ten years before.

Mr. Slonne lifted the papers that had been lying on the desk and with a sharp movement Jud lifted his hand.

"If you'll be patient just a few more minutes, Mrs. Davis is bringing me something to drink." Then he turned to Margaret. "I hope you don't mind."

Her still lovely face flushed, Margaret whispered, "N—no, of course not."

At that moment the library door opened and the housekeeper, her face set in rigid lines of disapproval, entered the room carrying a tray bearing a coffeepot, cups, sugar bowl, and creamer. Mrs. Davis had been with the Cammerons only six years and she obviously looked on this new arrival as an interloper. Placing the tray, none too gently, on a small table beside Jud's chair, she turned on her heel and marched out of the room. Hearing him laugh softly, Anne thought in amazement, *He's enjoying her discomfort. No, he's enjoying the discomfort of all of us.* And for the third time she felt a shiver run through her body.

Mr. Slonne waited patiently while jud filled his cup and added cream. Then he began reading. The atmosphere in the room grew chill then cold as he read on. Anne, her hands gripping the arms of her chair, couldn't believe her ears. Her mother's face was white with shock. The twins wore like expressions of incredulity. Jud sat calmly sipping his coffee, his eyes cold and flat as a stone and his face a mask. When the lawyer's voice finally ground to a halt, the room was in absolute silence. After a few long, nerve-racking minutes Jud's unemotional voice broke the silence.

"Well, then, it seems, in effect, he's left it all to me."

"Precisely."

Mr. Slonne's clipped corroboration brought the rest of them out of their trance.

"I—I don't understand," Margaret wailed.

Mr. Slonne hastened to reassure her. "There is no need for concern, Mrs. Cammeron, you've been well provided for. Indeed you've all been well provided for. It is just that Mr. Cammeron, young Mr. Cammeron, will have control of the purse strings, so to speak. In effect, he will be taking over where your husband left off."

"You mean I'll have to ask Jud for everything?" she cried.

Before Mr. Slonne could answer, Jud rapped, "Did you have to ask the old man for everything?"

Margaret winced at the term "old man," then answered wildly. "But you've been away for ten years. Not once have you written or called. It was as if you'd died. He never mentioned your name after you left this house. Why should he do this?"

Jud's eyes went slowly from face to face, reading the same question in all but Mr. Slonne's. Then with cool deliberation he said, "Maybe because the business that made him so wealthy was started mainly with Carmichael money. My mother's father's money. Maybe because he was afraid there was no one here who could handle it. And just maybe because he trusted me. Even after ten years."

He paused as if expecting a protest, and when there was none he continued. "Don't concern yourself, Margaret. You're to go on as you always have. I will question no expenditures except exceedingly large ones. This house is as much your home as it ever was. I have no intention of interfering with its running."

"You are going to live here?" Dismayed astonishment tinged Margaret's tone and one not quite white eyebrow arched sardonically.

"Of course. At least for the next few months. As you said, I've been away for a long time. I'll have to familiarize myself with the company, its management. Perhaps make a few changes."

Anne didn't like the ominous sound of his tone or the significance of his last words. Incautiously she snapped, "What changes?"

She realized her mistake as he turned slowly to face her. He didn't bother to answer her, he didn't have to. His eyebrows arched exceedingly high, the mocking slant of his hard mouth said it all loud and clear: *Who the hell are you to question me?* Anne felt her cheeks grow warm, heard him laugh softly when her eyes shied away from his intent amber stare.

"Now, then." The abrupt change in his tone startled Anne so much she actually flinched. "Mr. Slonne, thank you for your time and your assistance. You will be hearing from me soon." The lawyer was ushered politely, but firmly, out of the room. Margaret was next. In tones soothing but unyielding, Jud saw her to the door with the opinion that she should rest for at least an hour or so.

When Jud turned back to face Anne and her brothers, she felt her palms grow moist, her heart skip a beat. In no way did this man resemble the Jud she remembered. The Jud she had known ten years ago had had laughing eyes and a teasing voice. This man had neither. His eyes were alert and wary, and his voice, so far, was abrupt and sarcastic. This man was a stranger with a hard, dangerous look that spoke of ruthlessness.

"Now, you three," Jud said coolly. "I think we had better have a small conclave, set down the ground rules, as it were."

Troy was the first one to speak. "What do you mean ground rules? And who the hell are you to lay down rules anyway?"

"I should think the answer to that would be obvious, even to you, Troy." Completely unruffled, Jud moved around the desk, lazily lowering himself into his father's chair.

"Sit down," he snapped. "This may take longer then I thought."

"I prefer to stand."

"So do I," Todd added.

The twins then began to speak almost simultaneously. Beginning to feel shaky with the premonition of what was coming, Anne was only too happy to sink into the chair she had so recently vacated. Jud pinned her there with a cold stare.

"I'll get to you shortly."

He turned the stare to the twins and his voice took on the bite of a January midnight. "I will tell

you exactly who I am. As our father saw fit to leave
me in control, from now on I'm the boss. And
there are going to be a lot of changes made, starting with you two earning your keep."

"What do you mean?"

"In what way?"

He silenced them with a sharp, slicing move of
his hand.

"From today on every free day you have, except
Sundays, will be spent at the mill learning the tex-
tile business from the ground up, starting with the
upcoming Easter vacation."

"But we have plans made to go to Lauderdale
at Easter," Troy exclaimed angrily.

"*Had* plans," Jud stated flatly. "There will be no
romping on the sands for you two this year."

"We're over twenty-one," Todd sneered. "You
can't make us do anything."

"Can't I?"

Anne felt her mouth go dry at the silky soft
tone. Her eyes shifted to the twins' faces as Jud
continued.

"Perhaps not. But I can stop your allowances. I
can neglect to pay your school fees for the final
term. I can demand board payment for living in
this house—my house."

White-faced, Troy cried, "We still have our income from the business."

"Wrong," Jud said coldly. "You heard the terms
of the old man's will. Unless I choose to sign a
release, every penny of that income goes into a
trust fund until you are twenty-five. I'm the only
one who can draw on that fund for your mainte-
nance. Now, unless you want to be cut off without

a penny for the next four years, when I say jump,
the only question I want from either of you is:
How high?"

Anne closed her eyes to shut out the glazed expression of shocked disbelief on her brothers'
faces. With a tingling shiver she heard Jud coolly
dismiss them with the advice they attend their
mother; then her eyes flew open at his crisp, "Now
you."

"You can't frighten me, Jud. You have no control over me whatsoever. I have simply to pack my
things and walk out of this house to be away from
your—control."

Anne felt an angry flush of color flare in her
face as he studied her with amused insolence, his
eyes seeming to strip her of every stitch of clothing
she was wearing.

"That's exactly right," he finally replied silkily.
"But you won't. The old man was no fool. His
plan was beautifully simple. He knew full well the
sons of his second marriage were incapable of taking over, while at the same time he wanted to in-
sure their future, so he split up forty-five percent
of the company stock between them but left me
in control of the actual capital. At the same time
he knew I could handle the business and the twins,
and that I would. But he wanted a check rein on
me, too, so he only left me forty-five percent. That
leaves you, right in the middle, with the other ten
percent."

"To do with as I please," she inserted warningly.

"But of course," he countered smoothly. "But
as I said, the old man was no fool. He was reasonably sure you would not surrender your share to

me, thus giving me full control. On the other hand, he could also feel reasonably sure you would not throw in with the twins, as you are as aware as he was that they would probably run the company right into the ground. Does it give you a feeling of power, Anne?"

"You can't be sure I won't sell or give my share to Troy and Todd." Very angry now, she lashed out at him blindly. Everything he'd said was true, and she hated his cool smugness.

"Right again," he mocked. "But, like the old man, I am reasonably certain, and being so, I'll call the shots. And I'll give you one warning: if you decide you can't hack it, and to hurt me you sign over to the twins, I'll ruin them—and I can easily."

Wetting her lips she stared at him in disbelief. He meant it.

"But you'd be destroying your own interests as well."

Mocking smile deepening, he shrugged carelessly. "I'll admit that I want it, but I don't need it to survive. The twins do. And don't, for one moment, deceive yourself into thinking I won't do it. I will."

She believed him. He wasn't just bluffing or trying to scare her, though he did. He meant it. Confused, frightened for her brothers, she cried, "Why are you taking this position? Do you hate us all so much?"

"Hate? The twins?" Again the brows rose in exaggerated surprise. "You forget, the twins are my brothers, too. I'll be the making of them."

The fact did not escape her that he referred to

Troy and Todd only. Shocked by a pain she had thought long dead, she argued. "You're being too hard on them."

"Hard?" He gave a short bark of laughter, shaking his head. "You call it hard to expect them to learn a business they have almost a half interest in? Good grief, they are twenty-one years old and have never done a full day's work. Do you know how old I was when I went to work for my father?"

Subdued by his sudden anger, Anne shook her head dumbly.

"I was fourteen. Fourteen." His tone hardened on the repeated word. "And how old were you? Don't answer, I know. You've had almost sole care of those two ever since you were six. You've cared for, protected, and played general guard dog to them from the time they could say your name. How old were you when you went to work in the old man's office?"

"Eighteen."

"Eighteen," he repeated softly. "No carefree college days for Anne."

"I wasn't his daughter," she protested. "I never expected—"

"No, you weren't his daughter," he interrupted. "You were, for all intents and purposes, his slave."

"He was very good to me." She almost screamed at him.

"Why the hell shouldn't he have been?" he shouted. "You never made a move he disapproved of."

Anne drew deep breaths, forcing herself to calm down. This was proving nothing. Her voice more steady, she said quietly, "I won't argue anymore about this, Jud. If there is nothing else you want to discuss I'll go up to Moth—"

"There is," he cut in firmly. "If you have any papers or anything else pertaining to the office here at home, I'd like you to get them together. My secretary will be in the office tomorrow and it will be easier for her if—"

Now it was Anne's turn to interrupt. Her voice hollow with shock, she cried, "Your secretary? But that's my office."

Even though his voice was bland, it chilled her.

"I don't need you in that office, Anne; that's what I pay my secretary for. So if there's anything here, collect it before tomorrow. Now if you'll excuse me, I have some phone calls to make."

Turning quickly, Anne left the room. She heard him dialing as she closed the door. Then she stood staring at her trembling hands. That easily, that coolly, she had been dismissed, not only from the room but from the office as well. Fighting tears, she ran upstairs to her bedroom. What was she supposed to do now?

2

Anne paced the deep rose carpet in her bedroom, Jud's words still ringing in her ears. If she wasn't to go to the office and he didn't want her to move out of the house, what was she to do? Get another job? Work for a rival company? That didn't make much sense. Maybe he meant her to stay at home, run the house, live the kind of life her mother did. Women's clubs and bridge games and shopping week in, week out. Anne shivered. She would go out of her mind. Maybe if the twins were still small enough to keep her running, but not now. She was too used to the office. Tears trickling down her face, she riled silently. Didn't he realize she knew almost as much about the managerial end of the business as his father had? She could be of help to him while he was familiarizing himself with it. Why had he turned her out? Did he hate her that much?

In frustration she flung herself onto the bed and stared at the ceiling. He had changed so drastically. Uninvited and unwelcome, a picture of him as he was the last time she saw him formed in her mind. How young she had been then. Young and naive and so very much in love. Anne's face burned at the memory of how very gullible she had been at fifteen.

It had been Jud's twenty-fifth birthday and Anne had waited with growing impatience for him to come home to dinner. She felt her spirits drop when her stepfather came home alone, and when he told her mother that Jud would not be home for dinner as he had a date, her spirits sank completely.

The hours had seemed to drag endlessly as Anne, unable to sleep, sat in her room, ears strained for the sound of his car on the driveway. On the table beside her small bedroom chair lay a tiny birthday present, its fancy bow almost twice the size of the package. At intervals Anne touched the bow gently, lovingly. She had saved so long to buy this gift, had been so eager to give it to him. Eager and also a little nervous. It was not quite a year since she had first seen the brush-finished gold cuff links and she had known at once she wanted to give them to him. At first she had thought of giving them to him at Christmas but she had not been able to save enough money. So she had taken the money she had and had talked to the store manager. He in turn had removed the links from the display window, put her name on them, and had set them aside for her. She had made the last payment on them the previous week. Now, staring at the small, wrapped box, she saw the matte surface of the gold ovals, could see the initials engraved on them. J.C.C., Judson Carmichael Cammeron. How she loved him. And how she prayed he'd like her offering.

The slam of the car door startled Anne out of a daze. The front door being closed brought her fully aware. She heard him come up the stairs, pass her door, and close his own door farther down the hall. What should she do? It was past two-thirty. Would he be angry if she went to his room now? Should she wait until morning?

Anne hesitated long minutes. Then she thought fiercely, *No, it won't be the same. By morning his birthday will be truly over.* Without giving herself time to change her mind, she slipped out of her room and along the thickly carpeted hall on noiseless bare feet. She tapped on his door softly then held her breath. It seemed to take a very long time for him to open the door, but when he did she knew why at once. He had obviously just come out of the shower, as his hair was damp and he was wearing nothing except a midcalf-length belted terry cloth robe. At the sight of him Anne felt her resolve weaken, but before she could utter an apology or whisper good night, he caught her hand and said with concern, "Anne! What is it? Is something wrong?"

Her voice pleading for understanding, Anne shook her head quickly and answered softly, "No, nothing. I'm—I'm sorry to disturb you. I'm silly. I wanted to give you your birthday present and I couldn't wait till morning."

Jud sighed, but his voice was gentle. "You're right; you are silly." He paused, then chided, "Well, where is this present you couldn't wait to give me?"

Flushing, Anne slid her hand into the pocket of the cotton housecoat she'd slipped the gift into before leaving her room. As she withdrew the gift, he gave a light tug on the hand he was still holding and murmured ruefully, "You had better come in. We don't want to wake the household for the event of giving and receiving one gift."

She stepped inside and he reached around her to close the door before taking the small package from the palm of her hand. Silently he removed the wrapping and silently he flipped the case open and stared a very long time at the cuff links. When he raised his eyes to hers they were serious, questioning. Fear gripped her and she blurted breathlessly, "Don't you like them, Jud?"

"Like them? Of course I like them, they're beautiful. But, chicken, they must have cost a bundle. Why?"

More nervous than before, Anne plucked at the button on her robe.

"I—I saw them in the window and—and I wanted to buy them for you."

"When was this?" he asked softly.

"Almost—not quite a year ago."

"And you've been saving all this time?" His voice was even softer now and Anne shivered. His tone—something—was making her feel funny.

"Are you angry with me, Jud?"

"Angry? With you? Oh, honey, I could never be really angry at you."

"I'm glad," she whispered. "I wanted to give them to you tonight so badly. I could have cried when you didn't come home for dinner."

His beautiful amber eyes seemed to flicker, grow shadowed, and he carefully laid the jeweler's box on the night table by his bed, then brought his hand to her face. Again a tiny shiver went through her as his fingers lightly touched her skin. Now his voice was barely above a murmur. "And do I get a birthday kiss, too?"

"Yes." A mere whisper broke from a suddenly tight throat.

His blond head descended and then she felt his lips touch hers lightly and tenderly. The pressure on her lips increased and then he groaned softly and pulled his head away with a muttered growl. "You had better get out of here, Anne."

She felt stricken, shattered, and as he turned away she cried, without thinking, "Jud, please, I love you. What have I done wrong?"

He swung back, his eyes filled with pain.

"Wrong? Oh, chicken, you've done nothing wrong. Don't you see? Can't you tell? I want to kiss you properly and you're so young. Too young. I think you'd better get out of here before I hurt you."

His eyes burned into hers, and with a feeling of fierce elation she couldn't begin to understand running through her, she pleaded, "Oh, Jud, please don't make me go. Tell me, show me what to do, please."

He moved closer to her, his eyes searching hers as if looking for answers. Again his hand touched her face lightly, then his forefinger brushed, almost roughly, across her lips. Her lips parted fractionally in automatic reaction and leaning closer he whispered, "Like that, honey." Again his finger brushed her mouth, this time the lower lip only, and she could hardly hear his murmured, "Part your lips for me, Anne," before his lips were against hers. She obeyed him and felt a shock of mingled fear and joy rip through her as his mouth crushed hers. Never could she have imagined the riot of sensations that stormed her senses.

When his mouth left hers, she gave a low "no" in protest, and grasping her arm, he whispered, "Come."

He led her to the side of the bed, sat her down, then sat down beside her. Cupping her head in his hands he stared broodingly into her face a long time before saying quietly, "Sweetheart, if you're at all frightened, tell me now while I can still send you back to your room."

Her eyes clear, she faced him without fear. "I could never be afraid of you, Jud. How could I be? I told you. I love you."

"Yes, you told me," he groaned. Then he was on his feet, moving away from her. "But, honey, I'm not talking about brother-sister love. You know the facts of life?"

She looked up indignantly at the sharp question. "Yes, of course I do."

His tone lost none of its sharpness. "Then you know what I want?"

Unable to voice the answer, Anne lowered her eyes, nodded her head.

"Honey, look at me."

Some of the edge had left his tone and in relief Anne looked up.

"Ever since the day you first came to this house, I loved you. Like a brother with a small sister, I loved you, wanted to protect you. A little over a year ago, some months after your fourteenth birthday, I began to feel different." Anne felt a pain twist at her heart and she would have cried out but he held up his hand to explain. "Suddenly one day I realized I did not love you as a brother loves a sister. I was in love with you, the way a man loves a woman." His eyes closed but not before Anne saw the pain in them.

"Jud." She made to get up and go to him.

"No." It was an order. Anne stayed where she was. His eyes were again open. His voice racked with torment, he went on. "I don't know how. I don't know why. But, dear God, Anne, I love you and you are too young. Get out of here, chicken. Go back to your room while I can still let you go."

"No."

"Anne."

"No, Jud," she repeated firmly then more softly, "Jud, please. I don't want to go. I want to stay with you."

In three strides he was back beside her, his hands again cradling her head. "You are a small, beautiful fool. And I will very likely burn in hell, but, honey, I need you so, want you so."

This time when his mouth touched hers she needed no prompting. Eager to experience again that wild riot of sensations, her lips parted beneath his searching, hungry mouth. His hand dropped to her shoulders then moved down and over her back, drawing her slight, soft body against his large, hard one.

Slowly, reluctantly, his lips released hers, moved over her face and she felt her breath quicken as he dropped featherlight kisses across her cheeks, on her eyelids, and along the edge of her ear. Breathing stopped completely for a moment when his teeth nipped gently on her lobe and he whispered urgently, "Anne, I want you to touch me. Put your hands on my chest, inside the robe."

Her hands had been lying tightly clasped on her lap and at his words she relaxed them, brought them slowly up. Slowly, shyly, she parted the lapels of his robe, then placed her palms against his hair-roughened skin. Enjoying the feel of him, she grew braver and slid her hands across the broad expanse of his chest. He shuddered, then moaned deep in his throat when her fingertip brushed his nipple. Made still braver by his reaction to her touch, she whispered. "Do you like that, Jud?"

"Like it?" he said huskily. "Lord, sweetheart, I love the feel of your hands on me. I just hope you enjoy the feel of my touch half as much." His hands moved to the buttons of her robe, unfastening them quickly. His lips close to hers, he murmured, "I don't think we need all this material between us."

He slipped the robe off then gathered her close against him, his mouth driving her to the edge of delirium as he explored the hollow at the base of her throat. Anne stiffened with a gasp when his hand moved caressingly over her breasts, his touch seeming to scorch her through the thin cotton of her short nightie, but the heady excitement his gently teasing fingers aroused soon drowned all resistance. His mouth sought hers over and over again, becoming more urgently demanding with each successive kiss and Anne felt desire leap and grow deep inside.

She felt a momentary chill when his arms, his mouth, released her and he leaned away from her.

Dimly she was aware of his movement as he shrugged out of his robe and tossed it aside. The flame inside her leaped higher when he pulled her close against his nakedness. Afire with a need she didn't fully understand, inhibitions melting rapidly in that flame, she slid her hands along his body, loving the feel of his smooth warm skin. When she ran her fingers up and over his rigid, arched spine, he shivered and groaned against her mouth. "I could kiss you forever but, Anne, baby, it's no longer enough. Raise your arms."

She obeyed at once and sat meekly as he tugged her nightie up and over her head. When she was about to drop her arms, he caught her wrists in one of his hands and pulled them high over her head then forced her down against the bed. Stretched out below him, she felt her cheeks go pink as his eyes went slowly, burningly, over her body. Her color deepened when his hand followed the route his eyes had mapped out and her eyes closed with embarrassment when, without conscious thought, her body moved sensuously under his fingers.

"Open your eyes, Anne," he ordered softly, and when she did she found herself staring into warm liquid amber.

"Don't ever be embarrassed or ashamed with me. From tonight on, you are mine. You belong to me. No, we belong to each other, for I am surely yours. There's no reason for you to be shy with me. You are beautiful and I love every inch of you. Do you understand?"

Unable to speak around the emotion blocking her throat, Anne nodded. He kissed her hard then whispered, "Tell me again that you love me, Anne."

"I love you, Jud, more than anything or anyone else on this earth."

Anne heard his breath catch and then his head lowered and his mouth followed the path of his eyes and hands, branding her with his ownership. They were both breathing heavily, almost painfully, when his hard body moved over hers and between short, fierce kisses, he vowed, "I love you, Anne. I'll always love you."

Neither one of them heard the door open and they both went rigid when Jud's father said coldly, "Get away from her, Jud."

Jud hesitated a second then through clenched teeth spat out, "Get the hell out of here, Dad."

"I told you to get away from her and I mean it. Now, move."

Judson Cammeron had not raised his voice, but there was an icy, angry command in his tone. Overwhelmed with disappointment and shame, Anne moaned softly, "Jud, please."

Jud remained still, every muscle in his body tense with anger; then he moved, slowly, pulling his robe over her body as he went.

Shaking with reaction, Anne lay listening to the silence crackle angrily between father and son. Her stepfather finally broke the silence. "Haven't you had enough with all the girls you've had in the last year? Must you bring your appetite home? Use your stepsister? Good God, man, she is little more than a child."

Jud started tightly, "Dad, you—" His father cut him off. "I'm taking Anne to her room, but I'll be back." He tucked the robe around her shaking body, then lifted her in his arms. At the door he paused, his voice thick with disgust. "Get some clothes on."

He carried her to her room, laid her on the bed, then turned his back to her, saying, "Put on a nightgown and get into bed. I'll be back. I'm going to get you something to help you sleep."

Tears running down her face, she leaped off the bed the minute he closed the door. With jerky movements she pulled a clean nightie over her head, crawled back into bed, turned her face into her pillow, and sobbed brokenly.

By the time he returned she was shaking so badly he had to help her sit up and hold the glass for her while she chokingly swallowed the two pills he handed her.

"Don't cry so, Anne, you'll make yourself ill. I don't blame you in this, you're too young to understand."

"Mother?" Anne sobbed.

"She's asleep and I give you my word she, or anyone else, will not hear of this."

He left her and slowly, as the pills, whatever they were, took effect and she grew drowsy, the sobs subsided.

It had been late when Anne woke the next morning. A beautiful Saturday morning that didn't fit at all with her depressed state. Feeling hurt, uncertain, very young, Anne showered and dressed, afraid to think about Jud and what had happened. She felt ashamed that her stepfather had found them the way they were, but she felt no guilt. She loved Jud and he said he loved her and their lovemaking, aborted though it had been, was a natural outpouring of that love.

Things might be uncomfortable for a while, but somehow she felt sure Jud would make it right. On that thought she had squared her shoulders and gone downstairs.

The twins were nowhere around, but her mother and stepfather were having midmorning coffee in the living room. Anne started into the room, then stopped, a finger of fear stabbing her heart at their expressions. Her stepfather's face was set, stony. Her mother looked upset, near tears. Fearfully Anne asked, "What happened? Is something wrong?"

Judson opened his mouth, but before he could speak her mother cried, "Oh, Anne, it's Jud. Sometime during the night he packed his bags and left. He left no word of where he was going or when he'd be back, nothing."

Feeling her knees buckle, Anne dropped into a chair.

"But—"

The sight of her stepfather's eyes dried the words on her lips, for although his face was set, his eyes were filled with disappointment and despair. When he spoke, his voice was cold and flat.

"Margaret, I don't want his name mentioned in this house ever again, do you understand?"

"Judson!" her mother's voice mirrored her astonishment.

"I mean it," he went on in the same flat tone. "Talk to the twins; make them understand. Not ever again. Anne, do you understand?"

Anne had nodded her head bleakly, not understanding at all.

* * *

Anne, coming back to the present, stirred restlessly on the bed, eyes closed against the tears and
pain that engulfed her. She had thought she had
left the pain behind a long time ago. At first she
had waited hopefully for a phone call or a letter.
But as the weeks became months the hope died,
only the pain went on. As one year slipped into
two, then three, the pain dulled, flaring at intervals as word of him began to reach them.

He had come into a sizable inheritance from
his mother's estate the same day he left and he
had used it well. Jud had always had a flair for the
use of fabrics in clothes and he used that flair by
opening an exclusive menswear shop. Somewhere
he had run across two budding but avant-garde
designers and he hired them. They had obviously
worked well together, for by the time Anne and
his father heard of it, he had expanded to four
stores in key cities. The first contact between Jud
and his father had been made through Jud's assistant four years before.

Anne would never forget the look on Judson
Cammeron's face the day he had called her into
his office and silently handed her a letter. It had
been a request for an interview to discuss the possibility of the production of a particular fabric and
it had been signed by a John Franks, assistant to
Judson Cammeron of Cammeron Clothiers. The
only word that could describe her stepfather's expression was stunned.

Maintaining a rigid control she had asked quietly, "Will you see this John Franks?"

He had hesitated, then replied heavily, "We may
as well, Anne. If we don't, they'll only go to the

competition. Besides which, I'm curious to know what he has in mind for this fabric." He, of course, being Jud.

The meeting was held, a deal was struck, and they had been supplying Jud with special fabrics off and on ever since. But never at any time had personal contact been made between father and son. And at no time did Jud's name pass his father's lips although Anne knew by his attitude that he was pleased by even this small contact.

At last report Jud's stores numbered eight and he was reputed to be becoming a very rich man. The word that had filtered down to them was that there were some very wealthy men who bought almost exclusively from Jud and that their numbers were growing by the week.

And now, Anne thought, he would have it all. The company that produced the fabric, the designers who whipped up the original clothes, and the stores where they were sold. *Not all,* Anne corrected herself, *not if I can help it.* She had no right to any part of the company, but Troy and Todd did, and somehow she had to make sure they got it.

Suddenly Anne realized that her train of thought in the last few minutes had alleviated, to a degree, her pain and shock. The tears were gone, replaced by determination. She had taken care of the twins since they were toddlers. Her protective, mother's instinct was to the fore, replacing the hurt, humiliated feeling of that long ago fifteen-year-old girl.

Her lips set in a determined line, Anne slid off the bed and walked to the window. The light was gone from the day that had never brightened above gray. Anne's room was on the side of the house and below, some distance beyond, the bright lights above the doors of the triple garage lit the surrounding area in an artificial glare. Eyes bleak as the weather, Anne studied the dark tracery of bare, black tree limbs. The stark branches in that eerie light had the effect of many arms raised in supplication to the heavens.

Restlessly she turned from the harsh etching, her eyes moving slowly over the muted pinks of the room bathed in the soft glow of the bedside lamp. She had felt a measure of security in this room the last few years, had thought her shattered emotions healed, her heart becoming free once more. Now she felt scared, vulnerable, not unlike that tree outside with limbs lifted as if in yearning. She knew a longing deep inside that had to be quickly squashed.

Moving with purpose, she slowly undressed. She could show no sign of weakness with Jud, for if she did, she was sure he'd trample her as completely as would a wild, fear-crazed mob. She had allowed, no, invited, his trampling before. She wasn't sure she could survive it a second time.

Anne's head came up in defiance and her spine went taut with determination. She may have allowed him to hurt her, but she would not let him hurt her family. The thought that they were his family, too, was dismissed out of hand. He had disclaimed all rights to any of them ten years ago. The clock could not be turned back.